Child's Play

DANIELLE STEEL

Child's Play

A Novel

Delacorte Press

New York

Published in the United States by Delacorte Press, an imprint of Random House, a division of Penguin Random House LLC, New York.

DELACORTE PRESS and the HOUSE colophon are registered trademarks of Penguin Random House LLC.

Hardback ISBN 978-0-399-17950-1
Ebook ISBN 978-0-399-17951-8

Printed in the United States of America on acid-free paper

randomhousebooks.com

2 4 6 8 9 7 5 3 1

First Edition

Book design by Virginia Norey

To my wonderful so much loved children,
Beatrix, Trevor, Todd, Nick,
Samantha, Victoria, Vanessa,
Maxx, and Zara.

May you make wise decisions,
choose loving, caring partners
who treat you well,
keep you safe and protect you,
make you smile,
and share your dreams,

And to all of us, as parents,
who are constantly surprised
by our children!!

Thank you for the lessons you teach me!

I love you so very much!
Mom/d.s.

. . . A foolish man which built his house upon the sand: And the rain descended, and the floods came, and the winds blew, and beat upon that house: and it fell and great was the fall of it.

. . . A wise man, which built his house upon a rock: And the rain descended, and the floods came, and the winds blew and beat upon that house; and it fell not: for it was founded upon a rock.

MATTHEW 7:26–27, 24–25

Child's Play

Chapter 1

It was one of the first really warm days in early June, as Kate Morgan looked at the meticulously neat stacks of files on her desk. She liked everything to be precise around her, and an orderly life. She had lived through the unexpected shocks that can happen when her husband died nineteen years before, and she'd had to make order from chaos. Her children, Tamara, Anthony, and Claire, had been thirteen, ten, and seven at the time. She herself had been thirty-five, and had never expected to be widowed at that age.

Her husband, Tom Morgan, had been a beloved congressman. They'd met when she was in college and he was in law school, and married when she graduated. His dream had been to go into politics, hers to go to law school, but she had staunchly stood beside him instead, as the perfect political wife, raising their three children. He had died in a helicopter accident in a storm, while visiting a disaster area in Upstate New York after a flood. The news coverage about him had made him sound like a modern day saint.

Friendly, open, accessible, he had been popular ever since his first election. Kate and the children had been devastated, and she had struggled to put meaning back into their lives without him. He had been a wonderful father, and a good and loving husband for most of their marriage. Now, nineteen years later, the children still revered him, and Kate had seen to it that their memories of their father were untarnished.

The insurance money he had left for them had made them comfortable though not rich by any means, and had given Kate options she hadn't considered before. A year after Tom's death, she had started law school at Columbia University in New York. It had been a struggle managing school and taking care of the children, but she'd hired a housekeeper and also had her mother to help her. At thirty-six, she was the oldest student in her class, and had graduated with honors at thirty-nine.

She had worked at Berrigan Feldman and McCarthy for the past fifteen years, since she'd passed the bar, and was a senior partner now. Her specialty was corporate law, and she was a talented litigator, handling some of the firm's most important lawsuits.

Kate had three trials scheduled in the next few months, if they didn't settle first. She was a tough negotiator and a strong person, though a devoted mother and gentle in her private life. Becoming an attorney had added a whole new dimension to her life. She loved her work, and her children had adjusted to her schedule as her career grew exponentially. They were as proud of her as she was of them. She worked hard and was a strong role model for them. Now that they were grown up, she had more time and worked even harder. It had been a juggling act when they were younger, helping them with homework every night, and getting them to their sports games and school performances, but she did it. She expected excellence from them, and set the bar high for her children and herself. The results had been impressive, three solid, stable, well-balanced kids, all good students who had moved on to jobs they loved. She'd never had a serious problem with any of them, which Kate assumed was the norm, although she occasionally conceded she'd been lucky.

She had encouraged her children to pursue careers that were meaningful to them. They had survived their father's death with no visible signs of damage, no drug or alcohol problems, no failing grades, no problems with the law. Neither of the girls had ever gotten pregnant. Kate was the envy of her friends. As adults, all three were nice human beings with social consciences, and had graduated from good schools and colleges. Her own successful career had supplemented Tom's insurance handsomely. She loved spending time with her children, and was grateful for their time together now, despite busy lives and demanding jobs.

None of her children were married, although Anthony had gotten engaged six months before. Kate thought his fiancée was perfect for him. Anthony was twenty-nine, Amanda twenty-eight. Her father was an investment banker who lived in Bronxville, and had done extremely well. Amanda had gone to a respectable college, and had left school for a job as an assistant editor at *Vogue*. She worked for the beauty editor, and was a striking looking girl, with blond hair and blue eyes, like Kate herself. Both women were tall. Amanda could have been a model, and she had made her debut ten years before at the cotillion in New York. Her parents were socially prominent and very nice people. Kate loved the idea of Anthony being married to a girl like Amanda, and the life they would lead together.

Anthony had gone to MIT, and was almost a computer genius. He was also a graphic designer and designed videogames for the largest videogame company in the world. He was handsome, lovable, and talented, but sometimes socially awkward, and she knew that with Amanda, he would have respectable friends in good social circles, not just the geeks he worked with. Amanda would broaden his horizons beyond his computer screen, which tended to mesmerize him until he forgot everything else.

She took him to parties, and they wound up on Page Six of the *New York Post* occasionally, which pleased Kate. She was sure Amanda would be a terrific wife. She had no great ambitions at *Vogue,* but she enjoyed her job. She was more interested in marriage than her career.

For the past six months, she and her mother had focused on every detail of the wedding. She had bought her wedding dress the week they got engaged, which Anthony's sisters thought was silly, but Kate thought was sweet. They had met at a mutual friend's wedding in Martha's Vineyard the summer before, and got engaged at Christmas. Their wedding was scheduled for December, which was only six months away now.

Kate left her office in perfect order, taking long graceful strides toward the elevator. She looked a dozen years younger than her fifty-four years, with long blond hair she wore pulled back. Her body was fit and athletic. A trainer came to work out with her three times a week. She was smiling in anticipation as she walked to the French restaurant ten minutes from her office on Park Avenue and East Fifty-fourth Street, to meet her youngest daughter, Claire. She looked just like her father, with dark hair and dark eyes. She was smaller than her mother, with a casual sexiness she was unaware of. She had graduated from NYU law school a year before, and worked for a rival firm as an associate corporate attorney, following in her mother's footsteps.

At twenty-six, Claire was on an excellent career path, which pleased her mother, and she frequently asked Kate for advice. She was waiting outside the restaurant in a short black skirt and high heels, with her dark hair piled on top of her head. Kate beamed when she saw her. Claire's office was nearby, and Kate loved having lunch with her. She was bouncy and fun and young, and irrepressibly romantic. She had gone through a string of short-term boyfriends before, during, and after law school. Her relationships never lasted long, but they were intense and burned themselves out quickly, and then she would move to another one. She was never alone for long. There was no shortage of men in her life, unlike her older sister, Tammy, a senior vice president of marketing at Chanel, who never had time to date. She said relationships were something she'd think about later. Her rise in the company had been rapid, at the expense of her personal life, which she neglected, somewhat like her mother. Claire managed to do both, work hard and date, and men could never resist her.

Kate kissed her and they walked into the restaurant, and heads turned when they entered. Claire had the looks that attracted men to her, and had even as a teenager, and Kate was a beautiful woman. The maître d' was pleased to see them both and gave them their favorite corner table.

"You look happy," Kate commented as soon as they sat down, and Claire grinned as she nodded.

"They gave me three new cases to do discovery on. Really interesting ones." She never revealed anything confidential to her mother, but loved talking shop with her, and getting insights into the laws and precedents that affected the cases she was working on.

"That should keep you out of trouble," Kate teased her. They both ordered lobster salad for lunch, and the conversation moved quickly as they chatted. "Have you seen your brother lately?" Kate asked her, as they finished their salads and ordered coffee.

"Ugh, I never see him anymore. He barely answers my texts. I facetimed him last weekend, and he was in Bronxville at Amanda's parents'. He's always with her. I think he likes their pool. It feels like he's been kidnapped by aliens. He used to be fun to hang out with. Now he never has time for anyone but Amanda."

"They're engaged. It's pretty normal for them to spend a lot of time together," Kate said calmly. She knew Claire's views on the subject diametrically opposed her own.

"All she talks about is the wedding. The dress, the shoes, the bridesmaids' dresses, the flowers. She's going to bore him blind in a year. He deserves better, Mom, and you know it."

"She's perfect for him," Kate insisted, as she always did when the subject came up between them. "She comes from a good family. She has nice parents. She has a good education."

"Which she's wasting, picking out lipsticks for someone to write about in *Vogue*. She's going to drive Anthony crazy. Don't be such a snob, Mom. No one cares that she made her 'debut.' After this it'll be all about babies, and she'll be even more boring. Anthony's not ready for kids. I don't think he's ever even seen one, except on a videogame. Amanda pushed him into getting engaged."

Kate looked serious when she answered. "He loves her, Claire, even if it doesn't make sense to you."

"Does he? He looks like a deer in the headlights every time I see them together, and she never lets me see him alone. He's my brother for God's sake. We used to have fun together, and now he's becoming as boring as she is. It's pathetic."

"They'll think about other things once they're married. Right now the wedding is the priority," Kate said firmly.

"Yeah, *her* priority, not his. Why don't you want more for him, someone smarter or more interesting or exciting?"

"She'll ground him. He needs that. Otherwise he'll be lost in his virtual world forever. She's the best thing that ever happened to him."

"I can't believe you really think that. If I had a job like hers, you'd kill me."

"She's not you," Kate said simply.

"Grandma agrees with me too," Claire said, as though that were the definitive word on the subject. Kate's mother had been the second most important person in her children's lives, and a strong voice in their midst. She was usually the only one Kate listened to, but not this time. Margaret Chapman, Kate's mother, was seventy-six years old, vibrant and alive, and had retired three years before as a psychologist and marriage and family therapist. Kate and her mother were not just mother and daughter, but had always been best friends too.

"You're both wrong on this, trust me," Kate said without hesitation about her son's fiancée. "If he married a geek like him, they'd never figure out how to cook dinner or where the kitchen is and they'd starve."

"And Amanda can cook? Please. She makes him take her out every night."

"It's good for him. He'd stay in his office till two A.M. if she didn't. She complements him." Kate was definite about it, and had been thrilled with the match since the beginning.

"I can't stand her," Claire said, looking glum, and then a smile crept onto her face again, as her mother looked at her intently, happy to change the subject. It was an argument neither of them was going to win.

"Why is it that I get the feeling that you're happy about more than just three new cases you've been assigned?" Claire had that all too familiar look she got when she was infatuated with someone. Kate knew her children well. "New man?" Claire was usually fairly open with her mother. She had no secrets, or couldn't keep them for long when she did. She was the romantic in the family.

"Hmm . . . maybe," she said vaguely as the waiter set the café filtre down in front of them, and Claire smiled dreamily at her mother, with a total shift of gears. "I met someone, Mom. He's incredible. I've never known anyone like him." Kate didn't remind her of the hundreds of times she had said that before, but Claire could see it in her eyes. "No, seriously, I mean it. He's an adult, Mom. He's a man." She generally fell in love with irresponsible young boys.

And however appealing at the outset, they didn't hold her interest for long.

"That's a point in his favor. How did you meet him?" she asked, praying it wasn't online. Kate had a strong aversion to online dating and had expressed it often. She thought it an ideal way to meet sociopaths and liars, and considered it very high risk.

"I met him at work," Claire said cryptically.

"Is he a young associate like you?" which Kate assumed. There were lots of attractive young men starting out at most law firms, so this might not be such a bad thing. Claire shook her head in answer and Kate raised an eyebrow. "A partner?" That could be awkward, particularly a senior partner chasing a young girl, and worse yet if he was married. Kate hoped he wasn't. Claire shook her head again. "Okay, I can't stand the suspense, a paralegal? A janitor? A messenger?" she teased her.

"He's a client," Claire said with a dreamy look and her mother frowned.

"Wow, that could be *very* awkward. Does the partner you work for know?" Claire shook her head.

"They brought me in to take notes at a settlement conference. And after everyone left, he talked to me for a few minutes. As soon as he looked at me, I knew this was it." Kate almost groaned as she listened. They'd been here before. But with a client of the firm, Claire could jeopardize her job. She had to tell them at least. Kate felt she owed them full disclosure to be above board about it.

"When did this happen?" Kate looked stunned.

"Two months ago. We've been seeing each other almost every day since."

"Is he married?" She'd never done that before.

"Of course not. He hasn't had time to get married. He works all the time. Mom, I know this sounds crazy, but I know he's the one. He says the same thing. It was like destiny the minute we met." Kate wanted to cry at how naïve her daughter was.

"You can't say that after two months, it's too soon. Besides, you're too young." Although she knew that reason never impressed her daughter, once she was involved with someone.

"You were married and had two kids at my age," Claire said, dismissing her mother's comment.

"That was different. People married younger then, and your father and I dated for a lot longer than two months before we knew it was right. And more important, you ought to tell the firm. They can't stop you from seeing him, but they should know. You can't work on his legal matters anymore."

"It's not an issue. They settled the case."

"You should still tell them, so it doesn't come out later. Sweetheart, you have to be careful. You can't fall head over heels for every client."

"I haven't. Just him." She looked like a child as she said it. Claire was more immature than her older brother and sister, and somewhat spoiled since she was the baby. Everyone let her get away with it. She sometimes pouted for weeks to get what she wanted.

"What's his name?" Kate asked, still looking worried. Claire made it sound serious. She always did, and it was to her.

"Reed Bailey." Her mother was silent for a moment. She knew the name. Everyone did. He was one of the most successful young venture capitalists in New York. He had worked for an important firm in Silicon Valley, and came back to New York to start a firm of his own, which was a booming success. She wondered if he was just toying with Claire. It seemed unlikely that at somewhere close to forty, he would be as smitten as she was, although she was a beautiful girl. Kate knew nothing about his personal reputation, only his success in business. On paper certainly, he was an impressive guy. But Reed Bailey being "the one" in Claire's life seemed unlikely to her. He could have any woman he wanted, not just a young associate he picked up at a law firm.

"How old *is* he?"

"Thirty-nine. He's never been married. He's dying to settle down and have kids. He just hasn't had time or found the right woman." Kate knew that was the oldest excuse in the world for men who hadn't married.

"And you're not ready to have kids." Claire was still a kid herself, in many ways. "You're playing in the big leagues with him. He's way down the road from where you are now at your age."

"I know that, Mom. But we're crazy about each other. I know this is it. He says he can see me as the mother of his children, someday. He's never said that to anyone before." She was off and running at full speed.

"Can you calm this down for a while? If it's real, it'll hold until you know each other better. Neither of you should be making these statements or decisions right now. It's all chemistry. You're a beautiful young woman. You're intelligent, and fun to be with. You need to take your time. You both do. Forever is a long time, Claire. If it's right, it will wait."

"We don't want to wait, Mom. He asked me to move in with

him." Kate's heart sank at the words. It was all much too soon. Nothing good ever came from rushing.

"Be smart about this. Stay with him, go out with him, get to know him. Don't give up your apartment or move in with him. You've felt this way before," she reminded her, and Claire looked offended.

"No, I haven't. This is different. You don't understand."

"Yes, I do. But you have to be sensible. It feels perfect right now, but you really don't know him. Give it a little time."

"He's the one, Mom. I *know*." Kate wanted to shake her, but she couldn't. All she could do was pray that Claire would slow down. But she was playing with a grown-up this time, and Kate had no way of knowing if this was a game to Reed Bailey, or real. The only thing she did know was that Claire had fallen for him, head over heels, and she did not want advice from her mother. She never did. Kate just didn't want her to get hurt in the process. And what he was saying to her was heady stuff. She was drunk on his words, and in love with love.

"Let's talk about it again, soon. Try to slow it down and get to know him better. I have a three o'clock meeting and I can't be late." They left the table after Kate paid, and the lobster she had eaten was tied in a knot in her stomach. It was so hard to reason with Claire when she got like this. She was the most stubborn of all of her children. Kate just had to count on fate intervening as it had before, and stay in close touch with Claire on it. She was eager to talk to her own mother about it now. They were having dinner that night.

She kissed Claire goodbye and went back to her office. She almost collided with two pedestrians, she was so distracted thinking about Claire's confessions. She'd never gotten in any trouble or badly hurt with her romances before, but Reed Bailey was a powerful man, and Kate had no idea what his motives were. She found it unlikely that after two months, he thought Claire was "the one" too. She was scowling by the time she got back to her office. One of her partners walked in before their meeting in the conference room.

"Bad news on the case?" He looked worried and Kate shook her head.

"No. Sorry. Something else. I just had lunch with my daughter."

"That'll do it every time." Adam Berrigan laughed. "Mine just dropped out of college. She wants to move to Florence to become an artist." None of Kate's children had ever done anything like that. They'd always been sensible, and in the end, Claire always was too.

She picked up the file from her desk, and followed Adam to the meeting with their client, a hostile adversary and his attorney. It was going to be a long afternoon. Her worries about Claire and Reed Bailey would have to wait. Their romance was probably just a shooting star in the sky, and would disappear just as quickly. She might think he was "the one" for now, but Kate was sure he would last no longer than the others. All her romances till now had been short, and sometimes not so sweet.

Chapter 2

The weather was still so warm when Kate left the office at seven that she walked the twenty blocks to her mother's apartment on Park Avenue and got there right on time at seven-thirty. Margaret was waiting for her in the large room she used as a studio for the oil painting she had been doing as a hobby for fifty years, and now could spend more time on. She put serious effort and work into it, and still took classes at the Art Students League to perfect her technique. She had talent and had won awards in some of the shows she had entered. Her work was very powerful, and she loved doing it. If she hadn't discovered her passion and ability for psychology, she probably would have been a professional artist, and a good one. She was standing with a glass of white wine in her hand studying her latest canvas, when Kate let herself in with her key, found her mother, and gave her a hug.

"That's a nice one, Mom," Kate said. Her mother's work had a haunting quality to it, and an interesting tension. She painted every day now. And when she was willing to part with her paintings, a gallery downtown sold her work. Margaret painted for the love of it, not the money. She had worked hard, invested her money sensibly, and her late husband had left her more than comfortable. She could enjoy the fruits of their work now.

"Thank you. I've had a strange urge to do something more contemporary. I've never done that before, but I think I'm ready for something different." Margaret smiled at her daughter. Their looks were very similar, except that Margaret had had red hair instead of blond. It had faded to a pale strawberry blond now. Like Kate, she had youthful looks and a well-toned athletic body. She went to yoga twice a week. She didn't look her age, and her thoughts were often more modern and flexible than her daughter's. She read voraciously, and was always open to new ideas.

Kate had definite ideas about how things should be done. She was a hard taskmaster with herself, and sometimes with others. A perfectionist. Her mother was comfortable letting things flow more gently. Margaret's willingness to consider other options and explore different concepts kept her especially close and in tune with her grandchildren. She had been there as a sounding board and a safety net as they were growing up without a father. Margaret brought balance to all their lives, and her training as a psychologist and therapist had been helpful to them all after Tom's death. Kate had leaned on her heavily then too, not sure how she would survive it in the first extremely painful months. It was Margaret who had encouraged her to go to law school. She had always wanted to, and with Tom gone, and some help with the kids, Kate had the chance. It had been the best advice anyone had ever given her.

"How are things at the office?" Margaret asked, smiling at her daughter, as she perched on a high stool in paint splattered jeans and an old shirt that Kate could tell from the initials had been her father's. It was battered and well-worn now, unlike the pristine state it must have been in when her father wore it. Her father had been a banker, the head of one of New York's oldest banks. In contrast to his wife's modern outlook on life, he had been very old school, an old-fashioned gentleman, in love with his wife until his last breath. Theirs had been a happy, stable home, an example Kate had tried to follow with her own kids.

Margaret had saved a stack of his elegant shirts when her husband died. She loved wearing them when she painted. Kate's father had passed away ten years before, nine years after Tom had. They were both widows now, which was another common bond.

Kate's parents had had a remarkable marriage, and her mother's love for her husband had continued long after he was gone. It was he who had encouraged her to get her PhD in psychology after Kate started school, and later to establish her own practice, which had been a rewarding career for her for more than forty years.

Margaret had never looked at another man and always said she didn't want to, although she was still very attractive. Kate had had her share of romances after Tom died, though none of them were ever serious. She kept the men she dated separate from her children. None of the men had ever tempted Kate enough to want to marry them. She had never given her heart since Tom, and didn't want to be married again. She enjoyed male companionship, but she had learned how painful it was when it ended, and the acute agony of losing someone she loved. She had no desire to get too deeply involved. She and her mother had discussed it at length. Margaret understood why she felt the way she did, but was sorry Kate had chosen not to risk her heart again.

For the past six years, Kate had dated a senator from Massachusetts. He was fifty-nine years old, divorced, with a bitter ex-wife and four grown children. He wasn't interested in marriage either. He would have liked to see more of Kate, but they were both busy. He came up from Washington to see her once or twice a month, which she said was enough for her. They went out to dinner, to the theater or ballet, and spent quiet evenings together at her apartment. He was a familiar figure in her building now, the other tenants recognized him and smiled at him discreetly in the elevator, but no one made a fuss about it. Her mother felt sorry for her. She would have liked to see Kate fall in love again, or have real passion in her life, but Kate liked the arrangement she and Bart had, even though her mother thought it inadequate. Kate was satisfied with it just as it was. They were currently planning to spend two weeks at Shelter Island that summer, in a house he rented every year. Margaret thought they should go to Italy or Spain or somewhere more romantic. Kate didn't want passion at this point. She'd been burned by it before. The men she went out with were always less exciting than Tom had been. He'd been thrilling for her but she didn't want that again. A nice tame relationship based on companionship, like the one with Bart, suited her perfectly. Kate always stayed at a safe distance from the men she went out with.

"We're crazy busy with mergers and acquisitions, and a couple of big lawsuits." Kate filled her in about work. "We've got a nasty one heating up right now." Her eyes lit up as she described it, and took a sip of the wine she had poured for herself. "It looks like I'll finally get back to court again. I don't think my client is going to settle. We're ready for a good fight. I suspect we'll win, so I'm not pushing him to settle." Margaret smiled.

"Who knew you'd turn out to be a killer in the courtroom," Margaret said, looking amused, as they wandered into the kitchen. The housekeeper had left them a roast chicken, vegetables, and a salad, and had set the table for them.

"I had lunch with Claire today," Kate said with a sigh, as they helped themselves to the simple meal, which was all either of them wanted. "She's in love again, this time with a client. I told her that's not a smart thing to do. She seems to have caught a big fish with this one. He's a well-known venture capitalist and a huge deal on Wall Street. She says he's 'the one,' and he wants her to be the mother of his children." She glanced at Margaret. Kate trusted her mother's instincts and reactions, most of the time anyway. "Should I be worried?"

"No, I don't think so. She dropped by on Sunday, and told me all about it. She always sounds like that in the beginning, and then she loses interest, although I'm not sure she will this time. He sounds very seductive and very exciting. And he's way more sophisticated than any of the boys she's gone out with." They both knew that was a double-edged sword, and fraught with risk.

"Now I am worried." Kate put down her fork and looked at her mother.

"I don't think she's interested in marriage and won't be for a long time. She says she doesn't believe in it. She'll change her mind about that, of course. At least I hope so. Maybe she'll get her heart broken this time, if he gets tired of her first, and if she does, she'll survive it. It doesn't sound like it's heading in that direction, for now anyway. He sees her every night. He sounds infatuated."

"She wants to move in with him. She's only known him for two months. That's not reasonable. I don't care if she sleeps with him every night, I don't want her to give up her apartment. She needs her own place in case this falls apart like all the others. And two months is nothing. She needs a year, at least, to get to know him." Everything Kate said made sense.

"I told her that too. She won't listen to either of us, and that's not such a bad thing. You can't expect her to do the right thing all the time. You know what I think? You set the bar too high for your children. They never screw up, no one ever got in trouble in school, they all have great jobs. They're as driven as you are, and you expect them to be perfect. That's not healthy. One of them is going to do something you don't like one of these days. You'd better brace yourself for it, and better now than when they're forty, and married with two kids. Maybe Claire needs to throw her heart over the wall for this guy, and take some risks, instead of ending it in three months and moving on to the next one."

"I just don't want my children to get hurt," Kate said, looking unhappy. It was an old refrain between them, and a subject she and her mother disagreed on. There weren't many. As an only child, her parents had had high hopes for her too, especially her father. Her mother had been more lenient and expected less of her. But her childhood had been a happy one.

"No, you don't want them to make mistakes. That's different. They have to. They can't be perfect all the time. If they don't make mistakes now, when they're young, when are they going to make them? I worry about Tammy. She works too hard to even date, let alone have a serious relationship. At least Claire is trying to figure out what she wants, by process of elimination. And I agree with Claire about Amanda, by the way. She *is* a mistake for Anthony. I think you like her for all the wrong reasons. She's going to shrink Anthony's world to nothing. All she cares about is getting married and having babies. Anthony deserves more than that. I've never known you to be a snob before. I think you're more in love with her than he is. He doesn't give a damn about her parents' social connections, or her having been a debutante. How can you want so little for him? She bores me to extinction. Just listening to her describe her job or talk about the wedding puts me to sleep," Margaret said and Kate looked unhappy.

"You and Claire are so mean about her. She'll be a good wife and a good mother," Kate said stubbornly.

"Is that all you want for him? He went to MIT for Heaven's sake. Have you watched his videogames? They're brilliant." Margaret was proud of her grandson, and all her grandchildren.

"Not lately. I haven't had time. If he marries a nerd like he is, he'll never be able to function in the real world. He'd rather create games than talk to people. That's not good for him either."

"Why does he have to get married? He's twenty-nine years old. What's the hurry?"

"I didn't propose to her," Kate said, looking irritated. She'd already had the same conversation with Claire about Amanda over lunch, and several other times since they got engaged. "He did. He obviously thinks she suits him too."

"She forced him into it with an ultimatum. She wasn't going to keep dating him unless he made a commitment, so he got engaged."

"Why is that my fault?" Kate asked her.

"Because he knows how much you approve of her, and he wants to please you. He'd never have thought of marrying her on his own, and he's looked bored and miserable ever since he proposed. Don't let your social ambitions for your kids run away with you, Kate. I don't think he should marry her. He'll be miserable in six months."

"It's too late. She's already bought her wedding dress."

"So what? She can return it, I broke two engagements before I married your father. Practice rounds. And in all honesty, I don't know if he'd have the guts to call it off. He's such a sweet kid. He never wants to hurt anybody. He'd rather sacrifice himself and marry the wrong girl than disappoint her, or you."

"She's *not* the wrong girl," Kate insisted vehemently. "She may be wrong for you and Claire, but she's not wrong for him. Trust me on this one." But so far, no one was convinced.

Tammy said that whatever made her brother happy was fine with her, and had stayed out of the heated arguments. She never liked getting in the middle of family disagreements, and preferred keeping her opinions to herself, unlike Claire and her mother and grandmother who never hesitated to share their views on any subject. It made for some very lively family dinners. Anthony was more like his older sister, hated confrontation, and preferred disappearing into his virtual world.

"I just think there's going to be trouble if he goes through with it," Margaret insisted. "Maybe not immediately, but later. It's not up to me to interfere, but I think you ought to give it some serious thought, and maybe have a talk with him. This isn't just about now, it's about his future happiness. Young people forget that."

"Who would you rather have him marry? Some bimbo, or a computer geek like him? Why would that be an improvement?"

"It might be a lot more fun for him. A computer nerd like him would speak the same language, and a bimbo would be a hell of a lot more exciting than Amanda."

"Beware of what you wish for. He's never gone out with bimbos. He wouldn't know what to do with some jazzy girl. And he can't marry a girl like that."

"He doesn't need to," his grandmother said blithely. "Why does he need to settle down with a girl like Amanda, and wind up in Bronxville like her parents? He's in his twenties, not his seventies. I'm seventy-six and I wouldn't want to live there."

"He loves her," Kate said simply.

"He probably does, but that doesn't mean he has to marry her. I'm just not comfortable about the whole thing."

"I know you're not, and neither is Claire, but we're not marrying her, he is," she said, exasperated with her mother.

"That's the whole point. He needs more spice in his life at his age, and the bridal catalogue from Bergdorf is the last thing he needs."

"They're going to put on a beautiful wedding. They've already ordered the tent, *with* chandeliers," Kate said, impressed by the lavish wedding they were planning.

"Good, then let them find some nice boy from Greenwich to marry her in it. Your son deserves better, that's all I'm saying to you. Stop expecting them to do what you think is perfect for them. Let them figure it out. They're never going to make the same choices you did. It's not fair to them if they do, to please you."

"Stop trying to rabble rouse, Mother," Kate growled at her. "They're very traditional kids."

"Maybe they're not as traditional as you think, or want them to be. You can't expect them to live in the perfect little cookie-cutter mold you laid out for them. Sometimes you expect too much of them," Margaret said more gently. "They can't be perfect all the time. You've imposed that on yourself. Don't do that to them, Kate. Let them make some mistakes. It'll be better for them in the end." Kate didn't answer for a minute, wishing her mother didn't make so much sense.

"I'm not trying to tell them what to do," Kate said weakly.

"Maybe not, but you've always told them what they shouldn't do."

Kate knew that was true. She believed that you had to set the bar high. They were all successful in their chosen fields, no one had made any terrible mistakes, and Kate liked it that way.

They talked about it for a while longer, then about Kate's work, and after she left, Kate thought about what her mother had said. They didn't always agree with each other, but the things her mother said always had value. She had extraordinary insight into people, and she was rarely wrong about her grandchildren. They trusted her advice more than their mother's. The generational jump and the way she expressed herself made what she said more palatable to them. Kate was more judgmental, which made her comments harder to take.

She let herself into her silent apartment when she got home, and thought about them. They were each so different. She had had to be both mother and father to them, and the older they got, the harder it was. She had begun to realize, more and more since they'd grown up, that children really did need a father, and sometimes one parent, even an adoring mother, just wasn't enough.

When Kate left her mother's apartment after dinner that night, Claire and Reed had already made love twice in his Tribeca apartment since she'd arrived at eight o'clock. The first time was on the floor of the entrance hall. They made it no farther than that. He pinned her up against the wall and undressed her, and they slid breathlessly to the floor, starving for each other.

They made it to a chair in the living room after that, a big comfortable chair which engulfed them, and it was another hour before they made it to his bedroom, with a view of the Hudson River. They couldn't get enough of each other, in bed, in the shower. They were insatiable, in a frenzy of passion whenever they were together. Claire had never known anything like it. Reed was an expert lover, and they made promises to each other that Claire's mother and grandmother would have known they could never keep. But the words tumbled out of them with the same abandon as Claire's screams. And then afterward, she would settle into his arms for a tender lull until they had to have each other again. No one could keep up the frenzied pace forever. They were like Jack and Jill tumbling down the hill unable to stop their free fall of passion, helter-skelter at full speed, and not wanting to. It felt great to both of them. It was love and sex at its most intoxicating, and when he told her again that night that he wanted her to move in with him, she didn't doubt the wisdom of it for a moment, forgot her mother's words at lunch, and agreed immediately. She would have done anything for him.

Anthony and Amanda had spent a quiet evening, while she brought him up to date on the latest details of the wedding. She and her mother had it all under control. Amanda was their only child, and her parents wanted her to have the wedding of their dreams. They genuinely liked Anthony. He was undeniably a brilliant boy, and even if a little shy and awkward at times, they could see how loving he was with her. He was a good person, with solid values, and her father was impressed that he had gone to MIT, and graduated magna cum laude.

Amanda had another fitting for the dress coming up in a week, since she had lost some weight. She had been swimming in her parents' pool every weekend, and her body was long and lean. Her boss at *Vogue* had special ordered the shoes for her at Manolo Blahnik with cameo blue soles, for "something borrowed, something blue." Her parents were going to fly roses in from Ecuador, and lily of the valley from France in December. The heated tent was being custom made by the leasing company to their specifications, with crystal sides and parquet floors, and their wedding coordinator had found three matched antique Austrian chandeliers to hang in it. Anthony would have fainted if he'd known the price. It was going to be the wedding of the century and *Vogue* was going to cover it for their March issue since they had a three-month lead time. Her wedding gown was white velvet trimmed in white mink, with a white mink cape over it, which Anthony also didn't know. She wanted him to be surprised when she appeared looking like a Russian princess.

The night before the wedding, they were planning to have a skating rink installed and to give a skating party, so Kate didn't have to host a rehearsal dinner. The skating party was going to be a surprise for Anthony, with snow machines to cover the grounds with snow, and ice sculptures of prancing horses larger than life size, as part of the decor. She had told him about everything else. He knew most of the important details. They had a cake tasting scheduled in July, and one for the wedding meal booked in September. Amanda's father was ordering the wines, since he was something of a connoisseur and had a remarkable cellar of great vintages of the most famous French wines. Anthony knew very little about wine but Amanda told him the vintages were worth a fortune.

Anthony was stunningly handsome, with his father's dark hair and eyes, like Claire. Amanda was a beautiful blonde with almost translucent porcelain skin. There was no doubt they would have beautiful children. Amanda couldn't wait to get pregnant. They had agreed to start trying right after the wedding. She hoped to be pregnant by spring. He wasn't in a hurry for a baby, but she was, and she said this was the right age to start a family. They wanted to have children while they were young, which was safer. She had everything planned, and it was easier for Anthony to just go along with it. It was like drifting down a river, while she told him her plans for them. She could envision everything about their future. He had never thought that far ahead before. He figured that once they were married, she'd relax and be more casual about everything. There would be nothing left to worry about. She'd have everything she wanted. It was simpler letting her plan it all, since it made her happy. It felt like one giant video to him.

She was an easy woman to please, unlike other girls he'd gone out with. They got along famously and never argued, mostly because he gave in. There was no fire in their relationship, and no challenge. It was peaceful and effortless for him, with Amanda and her parents running everything.

Amanda never objected to the time he needed to develop his videogames, which she knew was important to him. He stayed late at the office frequently, and lost track of time. It only bothered her if they had a dinner to go to and he forgot about it, and had turned off his phone so he could concentrate. He had missed a few events that way, but each time he promised he wouldn't do it again.

Their conversations were mostly about the wedding now, and before that they had been about her job. She was planning to give it up before the wedding. The last month or two before their big day would require her full attention. It seemed a little excessive to him, how time consuming it could be to organize a wedding, but he knew she didn't like her job, and he made enough money to support them. He had agreed to move into her apartment. Her father owned it and didn't want them to pay rent. Anthony's apartment was too small for both of them, and he didn't have enough closets for Amanda's wardrobe.

Her apartment was in SoHo, which she loved. The only thing

missing from Amanda's life was a husband and children, which was all she'd ever dreamed of. He knew she'd be a wonderful mother because she wanted kids so much. And once they had a child, they were going to look for a house out of the city, maybe near her parents. She had it all mapped out. He wanted to have more say about their future, but he figured they would work that out after they were married.

Getting married had been her idea. He was comfortable with the arrangement they had, but she had told him she wanted a commitment from him, or she didn't want to see him anymore. It made him realize that he didn't want to give her up. He assumed that marriage would be like dating, but in one apartment, and eventually with kids. He liked her parents, and his mother thought Amanda was perfect for him. He liked making Kate happy. She had been a fantastic mother in his opinion, and had been both a mother and father to them. She had always encouraged him to follow his dreams. Amanda was part of them now. As long as she gave him the time he needed to develop his games, he was happy. He dreamed of having his own videogame company one day. Her father thought he could find investors for him. All the pieces of the puzzle fit perfectly.

It annoyed him that Claire was critical of Amanda and didn't think she was intellectual enough. Anthony was part of the creative board of the company he worked for, and got enough stimulation there. He didn't need to come home at night and talk to Amanda about work. He didn't expect her to understand technical issues.

Plans for the wedding had taken over their life since the engagement, but in December that would be all over, and they could settle back into ordinary life, go to the movies, see their friends, go sailing in the summer. They were going skiing in Europe for their honeymoon. He wanted to spend more time doing sports with her, but they'd been too busy lately. He wanted to get back to that too, although she warned him that they would have to postpone anything strenuous if she got pregnant.

He wanted to make love to her that night after she told him about the latest details of the wedding, but she was asleep by the time he got out of the shower. There was a stack of bridal magazines on the floor next to her side of the bed, and two new books she'd found about table settings for weddings. They were her bibles now. He wondered if other women spent as much time planning their weddings. He couldn't imagine Claire or Tammy doing that, but Amanda was different. She was more of a girl than either of them. His sisters didn't dream about babies either. They were both more focused on their work, like their mother. He had talked to his grandmother about it, and she had advised him to be sure that he and Amanda had common interests and the same goals, which he thought they did.

Their common goal was their future, hiking, skiing, and doing all the sports they loved together, building his videogame business one day when he was ready, and having kids whenever it happened. That was enough view of the future for him. The rest was details. Amanda was good at those, so he was leaving them to her. For now, they just had to get through the wedding. It was boring for him, but he knew how much it meant to her. If he had to listen to her talk about it for the next six months, he didn't care. He could put up with it for now. He loved her, and it was worth it in the end. He still couldn't believe that in six months they'd be married. He smiled at her, as she lay sleeping next to him. He liked knowing that they would be together forever. She was a beautiful girl and they loved each other. What more could he want?

Chapter 3

As he often did on short notice, Bart called Kate mid-week and told her he had time to spend the weekend with her, if she had time for him, and wasn't locked down working on a case she was preparing for court or deposition. They hadn't seen each other in six weeks. He'd been traveling a lot, and had been in the Middle East on an information gathering mission for a Senate subcommittee. He was on two important committees. Kate loved hearing about what he was doing. It kept things interesting whenever they met, and he was always intrigued by her work too.

The six years they had been dating had flown by, and had gone smoothly, once he understood the ground rules. At first he'd thought she was the kind of woman he would want to marry, if he ever ventured on the choppy seas of marriage again. He'd been divorced for ten years by then, and was still engaged in constant battles with his ex-wife, and frequently with two of his daughters on her behalf. Their marriage had always been stormy, and had finally ended with an embarrassingly public affair on his part with a twenty-three-year-old congressional assistant. In the end, the divorce was a relief for him, even if expensive.

He had liked the fact that Kate had grown children when they met. They were from twenty to twenty-six then, so she'd be free. It took him months to realize that she was married to her work and her children, and had managed well on her own for so long that she had little interest in marriage and no great emotional need for a relationship that was too close and might interfere with her freedom, work, or kids. Once he understood that it made her even more appealing to him. She didn't want anything from him, just to spend time together when it was convenient for both of them, take occasional trips together, enjoy intelligent conversation, and a peaceful weekend now and then when they could both relax. Despite her cool, sometimes standoffish independent style, she met his own emotional needs surprisingly well, more than he had expected. She was a kind, warm, caring person, she just didn't want to be someone's wife again and she didn't need a man to survive. She was doing fine on her own. Better than fine. Extremely well in fact.

Their relationship was based on an even trade of intellectual exchange and fun. Two smart people who enjoyed each other's company, with neither of them strangling the other. He hadn't dated anyone else in the past two or three years. Kate was enough for him, and no one else quite measured up to her in his eyes. She never asked him about it, and he was sure she had no other involvements either. She was discreet, had integrity, and believed in playing fair, unlike his ex-wife, who still wanted money from him.

Six years after they'd started, Kate was still more involved with her children than he was with his. He never had been. He readily admitted that he hadn't been the father he should have been when his kids were young. He hadn't been there for them as Kate had been for hers. He had relied on his wife for that. He had been building his political career then, and his marriage had gotten stressful early on. He'd had numerous infidelities when he was on the road for campaigns. His constant absences took a toll on his relationship with his kids, two sons and two daughters, all of whom clearly remembered the important times he hadn't been there for them or their mother, and they never missed a chance to remind him of it. As he always said to Kate, you can't un-ring a bell. It was too late now. All four had married and had young children of their own. Two lived in Boston, one in L.A., and the fourth one in Hong Kong. He invited them skiing for a weekend occasionally, but he didn't see them often, unlike Kate whose three children lived in New York. She saw them regularly.

He had met Kate's mother a few times, liked her enormously, and thought she was a remarkable woman, candid, intelligent, who had impressive insights into people. She was a lively, interesting woman and he had enjoyed their infrequent contacts. He liked Kate's children too though he rarely saw them. When she and Bart were together, she focused on him, and he liked that too. He thought she had been luckier than he was with his children, which he also knew wasn't an accident. She had spent a great deal of time with her kids, and was devoted to them, in spite of her career. He thought she was even a little too involved with them now at their ages, and that she continued to expect too much from them, though they had never let her down. One of his sons had struggled with drugs when he was younger, two were divorced, and his youngest daughter suffered from depression. But he felt it was too late for him to take an active role in their lives now. The die was cast, and they were closer to their mother than to him. Kate encouraged him to spend more time with them, but the opportunities to do so now were rare, and he was never at ease with them. He preferred spending time with her.

She was pleased that he was coming to New York for the weekend. They had no special plans, and they both loved spring in New York. In winter, they often hibernated in her apartment, and wouldn't go out for two or three days. This time, they were going to walk in the park, relax at home, and would have time to catch up on each other's activities. They texted and spoke several times a week, checked in with each other on FaceTime, which they both enjoyed. It helped maintain the link between them, even though they were busy in their own lives.

She made him a martini just the way he liked it, as soon as he came through the door. She was wearing jeans and a white sweater, little Chanel ballet flats, and looked almost as young as her daughters. Bart loved her looks, and it *always* excited him to see her. Their sexual rapport was great. He liked everything about her. He was a tall, handsome man, with a very masculine craggy face, graying hair, lively blue eyes, and a cleft chin. She thought he looked like one of the old-time movie stars, Gregory Peck or Gary Cooper. There was something very sexy about him, and he smiled gratefully as he took the martini, and stretched out his long legs, as they sat down in her living room. He knew generally what she'd been doing lately, but not the details, and she filled him in.

"Claire has a new romance," she said after they'd covered the latest political news of the week.

"That's not an unusual occurrence for her, is it?" he teased her, with mischief and a warm look in his eyes. He knew of her kids' activities and foibles better than he knew them. He was aware of how pleased she was about Anthony's impending marriage, Tammy's latest promotion in the hierarchy at Chanel, Claire's job as a fledgling lawyer, and her tendency to change boyfriends every few weeks.

"She's involved with a big fish this time, a client of the law firm where she works," she said, with a fleeting look of disapproval. "Reed Bailey," she said and knew Bart would recognize the name immediately, as most people would.

"Wow, that *is* a big one. Not serious, I assume, for either of them. He must be the flavor of the month."

"She says he's 'the one,' and he's supposedly claiming he can see her as the mother of his future children."

"That's the oldest line in the world," Bart said with a grin as he took another sip of his martini. She knew exactly the way he liked them, dirty, with lots of olives, and mostly gin. "I think I used it myself a few times. Unfortunately, Belinda took me seriously." Kate gave him a scolding look and he laughed.

"Anyway, she thinks it's serious. I hope not. She's too young to get married or settle down. She needs to focus on her career."

"That's what you want for her. Is that what she wants?" He knew how hard Kate drove herself, and her children in some ways. She had always expected them to do well, and they had. They didn't seem to question the values she had taught them and modeled for them, or the lofty goals she set for them, spoken or implied. He was impressed by them, and the fact that none of them had ever rebelled, or gone sideways on her. Their professional lives were a straight line toward success. She expected the same from them in their personal lives too.

"Claire says she wants to get ahead quickly," she answered his question. "She's at a great firm. They're known to foster women's law careers, and she could make partner in a few years, if she works hard."

"Your kids always work hard. How old is Bailey?"

"Thirty-nine, thirteen years older than she is."

"He's probably just having some fun with her. She's a very pretty girl." He smiled at her. "Like her mother," he said, stretching an arm toward her, and holding her hand for a minute as she smiled back at him. She was happy to see him. It had been too long this time. "Are you worried about her?"

"I'm not sure. Maybe. She seems completely besotted with him, and insists he is too. I told her she should tell the firm she's dating him, to keep things clean, and so they don't assign her to the work they do for him. I'm not sure she will though. She has a mind of her own, and thinks my ideas are antiquated."

"I know that speech. I used to get it all the time from mine. I don't offer them advice anymore." His children were slightly older than Kate's, enough so to not want to be counseled by a father they felt had fallen short for them. "They have to learn by their own mistakes, though it's painful to watch sometimes. I've gotten used to it. It's the only way they learn not to make the same mistakes again."

"That's a very male perspective," she said, taking a sip of the wine she had poured for herself before they sat down. "I just don't want them to get hurt."

"You can't stop it, and you shouldn't try. It's the way of the world. Did you listen to your parents?"

"Actually, most of the time I did. Though not always. Why can't they benefit from our experience?"

"It's not the nature of the human race. All you can do is hope they heard you early on, and that the information you want them to have is in there somewhere for them to draw on when they need it. If not, they fall off the cliff, and eventually pick themselves up again, bruised and battered like the rest of us. Do you regret your mistakes?"

"Usually," she said. Kate was honest with herself, and had her share of regrets. "I want things to be easier for them."

"We all do. It doesn't work that way."

She sighed, thinking about it, wondering again if Claire's love affair with Reed Bailey was real or a passing fling. Only time would tell. She doubted that it would be any different from the others, but she didn't want an experienced man toying with her daughter and breaking her heart, which could easily happen. A man of his enormous success wasn't likely to be serious about a twenty-six-year-old girl, nor should he be, in her opinion. And Claire wasn't ready for it. She'd never been involved with anyone like him. Tammy might have been old enough to handle it, but not Claire.

"You can't worry about them all the time, Kate. They're not ours forever to coddle and protect. At this point, they belong to themselves." She nodded, listening to him, but not fully convinced.

"I know you're right, but I hate it. It makes me feel obsolete." He gently pulled her toward him then and kissed her, and reminded her of why she liked spending time with him.

"You're not obsolete with me," he said in a whisper, and a few minutes later, they set down their drinks and walked to her bedroom. He liked spending weekends with her there. The apartment was like Kate herself, neat, orderly, everything was where it was meant to be, warm enough but not stifling. It was a place where he could let down his hair and be himself, have all his needs met, and was then free to leave again. Their relationship suited them both perfectly. There was no drama between them, no demands, no expectations, no commitment either, beyond what they each wanted to give. It suited him better than he had ever expected it to.

They had a great time in bed, and eventually made their way to the kitchen, where there was a light dinner she had picked up waiting for them in the fridge. They shared it at the kitchen table, where he told her the latest entertaining stories about what was going on at the Senate. She never told anyone else. He trusted her totally.

They watched a movie in bed, and fell asleep before it ended, as they almost always did. They both had demanding weeks as a rule, and by the weekend, were more exhausted than they realized. They went for a walk in the park after breakfast the next morning, had lunch at a delicatessen on the way back, and got back to her apartment and made love again. It was a perfect weekend. They had dinner at a discreet restaurant they liked, and they both had work to do on Sunday morning, and sat together in comfortable silence doing what they had to do, side by side. Then they read *The Wall Street Journal* and *The New York Times,* worked on the crossword puzzle together and almost finished it. In some ways they were an ideal couple, and agreed that they were because they weren't one. For different reasons, or maybe in fact similar ones, they were both leery of marriage, and had no desire to change the relationship they had that worked so well for both of them.

Tammy brought her grandmother a box of croissants and pains au chocolat on Sunday morning, as she often did, and came uptown to do it. She always called first, and Margaret loved the fact that one or the other of her grandchildren often dropped by during the weekend.

She saw less of Anthony now that he spent most weekends in Bronxville with Amanda's parents, and wondered if it would stay that way once they were married. Claire had been busy lately with a new job and a new man, but still managed to come by. Tammy came almost every Sunday morning, which gave Margaret a chance to catch up with her.

Tammy always seemed the deepest and most solitary of her three grandchildren. She was single-mindedly focused on her career to the exclusion of all else, with impressive results, and a major position at her age, in the dog-eat-dog milieu of luxury, fashion, and beauty.

Margaret worried about her. She always had the sense that Tammy was holding back, but she usually relaxed after they'd spent some time together. There was a guarded quality to her, which Margaret sensed came from the fierce competition where she worked. She had had to fight hard to get where she was, and was willing to sacrifice everything personal for her work. She traveled a lot in her job, which Margaret knew could be lonely too. She worried that she'd be one of those women who gave up having a relationship for her job, and would wake up one day at forty-two wondering where her life had gone. She had no dating life at thirty-two, although she had her mother's striking blond beauty. She had never had a serious relationship, and always said she had time for that "later." But her grandmother knew that "later" came faster than someone Tammy's age could imagine, and she didn't want that to happen to her.

Tammy was much less willing to talk about her personal life than her brother or sister, and Margaret was careful to respect that and didn't pry, although she and Kate discussed it frequently. Kate worried about her too, and was concerned that her own reluctance to marry again had sent the wrong message to Tammy so that all she cared about was work. Kate said that choice was fine for her, but not a woman Tammy's age.

She sat happily at her grandmother's kitchen table. She'd come all the way up from Tribeca to deliver the pastry. She was a thoughtful person, and adored her grandmother.

"What are you doing today?" Margaret asked, always fascinated by how different Kate's children were from each other. The romantic, Claire, the dreamer, computer geek, and artist, Anthony, and Tammy, the deep thinker and the most ambitious.

"I thought I'd run around the reservoir before I go back downtown. I brought home some work, and I'm flying to Cleveland to-morrow, to solve some problems there, and I'm going to Paris on Thursday, to make an appearance at the introduction of our new beauty products. We want to get the press on board, and I want to be sure it all goes smoothly. I have to go back in a few weeks for the haute couture show." It was a fun business to be in, but Margaret knew how demanding and competitive it was.

"That's a lot of traveling. You don't mind being on the road so much?"

"I love it. There's so much happening in the company, and in the luxury business now. It's never boring. And now is the time for me to do it. I couldn't move around this much if I were married and had kids. Eventually, the women with children can't keep up, or their kids run amok or their marriages fall apart. It gives me a real advantage." That was one way to look at it, but Margaret always wondered if her granddaughter realized what she was giving up for her job. She was always beautifully dressed, very chic, and a perfect ambassador for the company.

"Be careful you don't give everything to your job. You can't wrap your arms around that in your old age," she warned her gently.

"I know, Grandma." Tammy smiled at her. She asked about the painting her grandmother was working on, and told her she should go to Paris for the art shows. Margaret loved to travel, but didn't enjoy it alone, and her friends were traveling less than they used to. "You could come with me sometime when I go," Tammy suggested with a warm smile, and Margaret was touched. Tammy was always thoughtful.

"You don't need to drag me around," Margaret said, pouring them each another coffee. It was a quiet, sunny Sunday morning and was going to be a beautiful day.

"It's not dragging you. The last time we took a trip together, you wore me out, and I could hardly keep up." They'd gone to London two years before, for the opening of a lavish new Chanel store. Tammy had taken two days off at the end of the trip so they could go to museums together, and do some shopping. "You're hell on wheels in a museum, Grandma." Margaret smiled at the compliment, and knew it was somewhat true. She had always had a lot of energy, and that had changed very little. She was almost as busy and active now that she'd retired as she had been when she was working.

"Maybe I'll come with you one of these days," she said with a hopeful look. "I have this crazy idea that I want to go back to India someday, but that's a big trip. I loved it when your grandfather and I went, but that was fifteen years ago. The poverty was appalling, but the colors and the light, the textiles, and the people were amazing."

"If we ever do a show there, I'll go with you. We did a Paris–New Delhi collection two years ago, but I couldn't make it. We were launching a new perfume then, and I was up to my ears in that."

"Am I allowed to say you work too hard?"

"No," Tammy said with a grin.

"I figured. Have you seen your brother lately?"

"No, he's working on a new videogame, I think, and busy with wedding plans."

"Your sister and I are worried about him. I can't see him with Amanda for the long haul. What do you think?"

"I think it's up to him," she said diplomatically. "You can't tell what works for people. He seems happy with her." It was a typical answer for her, Tammy didn't like getting sucked into family gossip, or passing judgment on the others. She had a strictly live and let live attitude about all of them.

"What do you think about her?"

"I'm not marrying her. It works for him, or he wouldn't be marrying her. And she seems to be crazy about him."

"She's crazy about the wedding and the idea of marriage. I can't think of two more different people."

"Sometimes that works." Tammy smiled at her grandmother. They talked about the refugee situation and the violence in Europe for a while, and how it was affecting the economy in France, and ultimately the luxury business, and then Tammy hugged her and left for her run around the reservoir.

Margaret was pensive after she left. She always felt as though she knew nothing more about the private side of Tammy's life than she'd known before. As gentle and kind as she was, and attentive to her grandmother, she kept her deepest thoughts to herself, and didn't share them with anyone. It made Margaret sad for her. She needed more than new products at Chanel and haute couture shows to focus her attention on. She needed someone to care about, as much as she did her work. She had achieved the impressive goals that her mother aspired to for her, but it wasn't enough, and Margaret wondered if Tammy would ever let someone in behind her walls. There was no sign of it yet.

She had been at Chanel for ten years now, with a two year hiatus to go to business school at Wharton, which had projected her forward at an even more rapid rate. Her career was on the fast track, but she seemed to have no personal life at all.

As she ran around the reservoir, Tammy wondered why she never opened up to her grandmother. She was the least judgmental and most open-minded of her entire family, but Tammy liked keeping her private life to herself. It was so much simpler that way. And she didn't want advice from any of them. She knew what she wanted, and she had most of it. The rest would come one day. In the meantime, she had an orderly life that worked perfectly for her.

When Bart left Kate's apartment on Sunday night, he kissed her. They had no set plans to meet again, but hoped it would be in the next few weeks. The weekend had been just what they both wanted, a peaceful time, some meals together, great sex, and they had gone to the movies on Sunday afternoon, eaten popcorn, and held hands. It was like being kids again, without kids, which was a great relief to him, and good for her too. From what he could tell, she had stopped talking about Claire's new romance, and didn't think about her other children once during the weekend.

"I'll try to get back in a week or two," he promised, as he kissed her again and then waved when he got in the elevator with an elderly woman with a French poodle who smiled when she recognized him. He smiled back. It had been the perfect weekend with Kate. It always was. He could count on her for a good time, and an oasis of peace in their busy lives. He followed the woman with the poodle out of the building, and hurried to the car and driver waiting for him at the curb. The rat race he loved was about to begin again.

He couldn't wait to get back to Washington, but he smiled thinking of Kate as the car drove away. While she hung his silk dressing gown in her closet, until the next time, Kate was smiling too.

Chapter 4

Anthony got up at five on Monday morning as he did every day, and left for the gym at five-thirty. He was careful not to wake Amanda. He ran there in the early morning darkness and got there in twenty minutes. The run was a good warm-up for his workout. It cleared his head and always made him feel ready to face the day.

Once at the gym, he got on the treadmill, followed by a bike he put on the highest setting, going uphill. He was soaking wet by the time he finished and headed for the steam room. It was nearly seven A.M. by then. After he showered at the gym, he dressed for work, in jeans and a T-shirt, feeling great. He stopped at the juice bar for a protein shake. He loved his morning routine. It challenged him, and calmed him, and made him excited about his work again. He could hardly wait to start the day. He had tried to get Amanda to join him, but she preferred ballet class twice a week as her only form of exercise. She wasn't keen on gyms, or the heavy workout he needed.

"That looks evil at this hour of the day," a husky voice next to him said. His drink was mostly broccoli and kale, with lime juice, and it was a wicked shade of green. "Your workout looked rugged," the woman said as he turned to see who was speaking. She was the most exotic-looking creature he'd ever seen, with faintly Asian eyes, and warm, pale café au lait skin. She looked Spanish or Mexican, or Indian, he couldn't figure out which, and her body was so toned, she looked like she lived at the gym. She was drinking carrot juice. The jet black hair she released from an elastic was wet as it tumbled down her back in loose curls. She had full lips and delicate features and huge eyes. She smiled at him.

"It gets my day off to a good start," he said, not sure what to say. She was almost as tall as he was, and her exercise clothes were persimmon colored and soaking wet. He could see the shape of her nipples through them, and tried not to look.

"Do you box?" she asked, perching on the stool next to him, and he shook his head.

"You should try it. It's a great workout, if you don't get a black eye or hit in the gut and wind up flat on your ass. The boxing coach here is pretty good. I had to stay home from work for a week with a black eye once, so I'm careful now. It teaches you to be fast on your feet, pay attention, and stay focused." He was mesmerized by her, and wanted to continue the conversation so she wouldn't leave.

"What kind of work do you do?" He was curious about her.

"I model bathing suits and underwear. I'm an actress but the modeling pays my rent, and I go to Hunter College at night. I'm still trying to get my BA degree. I'll probably be a hundred when I do." She smiled at him again, a row of dazzling white perfect teeth in the pale brown face. It was easy to believe she was an underwear model. Her body was incredible. He was six-three, and figured her for just under six feet, but her features were delicate and exquisite, her body perfectly toned and a little too thin, probably for the modeling.

"Where are you from?" He was intrigued by her, watching as she finished her juice. He had almost finished his but wanted to linger so he could talk to her.

"San Juan. My father is Puerto Rican. My mother is half Chinese." It explained her exotic looks. "They got divorced and I came here as a kid with my mom. I grew up in Spanish Harlem," she said it with pride as though it were a good place to live, which seemed unlikely to him. He nodded, not knowing what else to say, and she walked away. "Have a nice day." He was grateful she didn't look back over her shoulder as he stared at her. He couldn't take his eyes off her.

"You too," he called after her, feeling stupid. She had knocked the wind out of him even more than his grueling workout. He left a few minutes later, and took the subway to work. He knew Amanda would just be getting up by then, and heading for the shower. She had a beautiful body, but nothing like the girl from San Juan. There was something cocky about her that he liked too. She seemed undaunted by anything, and looked like she could take care of herself in any situation. He thought about her all day and tried not to. The tilt of her head, the dazzling smile, the outline of her nipples in the coral T-shirt, the sound of her voice.

He looked for her the next day, and was disappointed not to see her. Chiding himself for what he was doing, he stopped at the boxing ring two days later and saw her, with protective headgear on and boxing gloves, sparring with one of the coaches. She was lightning fast on her feet, and graceful, her long legs kicking out at the trainer. Anthony stood mesmerized again, watching her for a few minutes. She glanced his way when she was finished, and smiled at him.

"Come to check it out?" she asked as she walked over to him. Her movements were fluid and sexy. She had a catlike grace about her.

"You're good," he said admiringly.

"I was a scrapper as a kid. I just refined it here," she said laughing, followed him to the bikes, and got on one next to him. They didn't talk for a few minutes, intent on what they were doing. He liked being near her. She was curious about him too. "What do you do?" she asked him.

"I design videogames."

"Is it fun?"

"I love it. You gave me an idea for a new game today, watching you box. A girls' boxing game." He wanted to make the girl look like her, but wasn't sure he could capture her beauty with a computer. She was incredible looking, like a perfectly trained tigress ready to strike. It made him want to wrestle with her. He stopped at the juice bar with her afterward. They ordered their drinks and said nothing as they finished them, and then he headed for the men's locker room, with a wave to her.

"See you tomorrow?" she called out to him, and he nodded and waved again as he disappeared, then wondered what he was doing as he stood in the shower. He was in love with Amanda, they were engaged, but he wanted to see the girl from San Juan again. How was that possible? What could he say? Everything he felt was entirely visceral. He was feeling a pull to her like nothing he'd ever felt before, and got a hard-on every time he thought of her, which made him feel even guiltier.

He watched her box again the next day, and wanted to get in the ring with her, just to hold her, and feel the power of her limbs. There was something so sleek and strong about her. It drew him to her like a magnet, and when they rode the bikes together, he glanced at her, and tried to sound casual.

"Do you want to have a drink sometime?" he asked, forgetting Amanda for a minute. She was part of another world.

"Sure, why not?" she answered, and they went on pedaling in silence, while he wondered if he should tell her he was engaged. He didn't want to. They agreed to meet the next day at a bar on Third Avenue. He had no idea what he was doing, but he knew he couldn't stop himself.

Her name was Alicia Gomez, and she was all he could think about that night, while Amanda told him the latest details of the wedding plans. She had found the perfect party favor, heart-shaped frames to put a picture of them at each place. He felt faintly sick when she said it. The frames were from Tiffany and they'd have to pick the photograph to go in them. Her voice blended into a blur, as he was torn between guilt and desire for Alicia.

He lay awake half the night, and didn't see Alicia at the gym the next day. She had said she had an early shoot, and when he walked into the bar on Third Avenue at six o'clock she was there, waiting for him. She smiled as soon as she saw him. She was wearing very little makeup, a skintight short black dress and high heels, and was as tall as he was when she stood up. He looked pained as he approached. What he felt for her was torture, it was physical and deep in his gut. He didn't understand it. How could he love one woman and want this one so much?

"I can't stop thinking about you," he said as they sat at a table beyond the bar and ordered white wine.

"That's good," she said, looking pleased by what he'd said. "You need to start working with a boxing coach. It will relax you. I do yoga twice a week," she said, as their wine came, and she took a sip while he watched her, feeling as though he was losing his mind. He could feel his life unraveling as he looked at her, and he couldn't stop it. "It's okay, Anthony, it's just a drink," she said in a soothing tone, and he felt as though she could read his mind and see the anguish there. "Are you seeing someone?" she asked and he nodded. It was the perfect opportunity to tell her he was engaged, but he couldn't. If he did, she might not see him again and he couldn't bear that.

"Yes, I am," was all he said. He didn't tell her he was up to his neck in wedding plans which bored him to tears. She shrugged at his answer, and didn't seem to care. She figured if the relationship was important he would tell her and he didn't. She was thirty years old, smart, and understood perfectly when he told her how he built his videogames. She asked all the right questions.

They both had two glasses of wine, and took a cab to her place downtown, in the West Village. They didn't talk on the way. His mind was whirling. He had never cheated on Amanda. He followed Alicia into her apartment, and as soon as the door closed, he peeled off the black dress that molded her incredible body, and had the best sex he'd ever had in his life. As he lay next to her afterward, he knew that he wanted more of her. She laughed and teased him back to life. Then they stood in the shower and made love again. It took every ounce of willpower to leave her at ten o'clock and go home. He wanted to run back to Alicia the minute he left her apartment. He *needed* her.

Amanda was worried, and looked up the minute he got in. She'd been sitting on the bed reading a stack of bride magazines, searching for the bridesmaid dresses she hadn't found yet. Her entire mind had been given up to the wedding. He couldn't even remember what they used to talk about before. He looked at her and a shiver ran down his spine. He knew that Alicia Gomez owned his soul. Wanting her this badly was torture and he knew he was in trouble, but nothing in the world could make him stop it.

"Where were you?" Amanda asked him, going back to the magazine she had in her hand, to mark the page with the bridesmaid dress she had liked. It was royal blue velvet and had a regal look to it that would go well with her dress, without grabbing too much attention. She had eleven bridesmaids and a maid of honor, and her father had promised to pay for their dresses if the one Amanda picked was too expensive. Some of the girls she'd asked from work couldn't afford the kind of gown she wanted.

"We had a meeting that went late," Anthony said vaguely, turning his back to her as he took his shoes off and squeezed his eyes shut. He was lying to her. But what choice did he have? An hour before he'd been making love to Alicia, and now he couldn't touch the woman he was going to marry. How could he? Alicia had wrung him dry. What if he tried to make love to Amanda and couldn't get it up? The thought was terrifying.

"You don't look good. Are you okay? You look pale," Amanda commented as she put the magazine down and stared at him as he turned around.

"I have a headache from the meeting. I'm fine. I didn't have time for lunch today."

"There's some salad in the refrigerator. I didn't eat dinner." She didn't offer to get the salad for him, and he didn't want it anyway. He wanted Alicia. Now. In their bed at home. He felt like he was going crazy, and only Alicia could make him sane again. He liked who he was when he was with her, strong and confident, as though they were equals, physically and mentally. He didn't have to pretend to care about the wedding he didn't give a damn about.

He went to take a shower although he had just taken one with Alicia. He felt like he needed another one before he got into bed with Amanda, to wash away his guilt.

He looked apologetic when he came to bed. They hadn't made love in several days, and he started to say something awkward to her, and she looked relieved.

"It's fine. I got my period today. I'm sorry I've been so wrapped up in the wedding. I just want to get everything right and then we can coast until December."

"Hmm . . . right . . . yes . . . coast. I know you'll make it fabulous." He kissed her cheek, switched off the light on his side of the bed, and turned his back to her, wondering what he was going to do now. He was not going to throw his whole future out the window and break Amanda's heart for a woman he barely knew, but how was he going to walk away from Alicia? He couldn't. He lay there with his eyes closed, and Amanda walked into the other room to talk to a friend on the phone. He was still awake but pretending to be asleep when she came back an hour later. He finally fell asleep at four-thirty, and woke up at five-thirty to leave for the gym. He felt like a thief, leaving Amanda's apartment, and ran faster than ever to the gym. Alicia was waiting for him.

"You look like shit," she said when she saw him. "Are you sick?"

"No, I couldn't sleep last night." He smiled at her. "I missed you."

"Nice," she said, pleased with his answer.

They started on the bikes, and he had an appointment with the boxing coach at six-thirty. Alicia stood by and watched his first lesson, and it was so exciting that Anthony forgot his sleepless night and concentrated on what the coach was telling him. Anthony was fast on his feet, had good reflexes and a natural aptitude for boxing, and Alicia smiled approval when he finished and they headed for the juice bar together. They shared the Green Eyed Monster while she gave him boxing tips.

"You'll be good if you work on it. Don't be afraid to hit him. He can defend himself. It took me a while to really swing at him too. He's decked me a bunch of times."

"You must have been a terror as a kid." He grinned at her. "I'm glad I didn't know you then."

"I'm tougher now," she said, "and don't you forget it." She leaned over and kissed him.

"Can I see you tonight?" he whispered to her.

"I can't. I have school," she said primly. "You don't want to be boxing with a dummy, do you? After this semester, I need eight more credits to get my degree. I'm an English lit major. I can always teach if the modeling dries up. It's something to fall back on."

"You're no dummy," he said. She understood everything technical he said to her, more than some of the people he worked with. He knew that getting an education as a girl in Spanish Harlem couldn't have been easy. He admired her for it.

"I just beat the shit out of any of the guys who gave me trouble," she said, grinning, putting up her fists. She was an incredible combination of smart and brave, ballsy and determined, and stunningly sensual and feminine at the same time. He had never met anyone like her. He wondered what his mother and sisters would think of her, or if they'd even give her a chance. He would have liked to introduce her to his grandmother, but there was no way he could. He was supposed to be spending his time with Amanda, not some girl he'd met at the gym. There was no way he could explain this situation to them, or even to himself most of the time, except that he admired her and liked her, and was falling in love with her. And he was going to marry Amanda in six months.

Anthony felt like he was on an express train and wanted to jump off, but the train was moving too quickly and he couldn't. Alicia didn't know he was engaged to someone else, or anything about Amanda. He hadn't had the guts to tell her, and wasn't sure he ever would. She would know he was a cheat and a liar then. How would she ever respect him after that? There was no way she could, and he wouldn't blame her for it.

For the next several weeks, they went to her apartment every night when he finished work. He even left work early a few times.

He waited for her outside Hunter College when she had class, and took the subway downtown with her. They cooked dinner at her apartment, when they bothered to eat, and he got home late every night, and told Amanda he was working on a new game. He completely forgot a dinner party he was supposed to attend with her, and said he had to work that weekend, so she went to her parents' for the weekend without him, and he stayed with Alicia. Miraculously, Amanda never found out.

He turned off his cellphone when he was with Alicia, and told Amanda it was a new policy at work. His life had become a combination of Heaven and Hell. Guilt was his constant companion, and so was desire. Passion was the driving force in their lives, and when they weren't making love or at the gym, they were laughing together. He couldn't remember the last time he and Amanda had laughed, and now their over-the-top gargantuan wedding had begun to seem ludicrous to him, except that too was his life. His real life, the one everyone expected of him. He couldn't leave Alicia now. He loved her too much. But what if it was just a wild fling that would burn itself out, and his life with Amanda was the path he was supposed to be on? Anthony had never been so happy and miserable in his life, or so confused, all at once, and he had no one to talk to about it. He couldn't admit this to anyone.

By the time he and Alicia had been dating for a month, he had lost ten pounds and looked gaunt. Amanda complimented him on it and said he looked great. His workouts were really paying off. He said it was because he was boxing now too. He loved it, and sparred with Alicia occasionally, although she was better and faster than he, and she had a mean right hook. She loved pinning him down, and then they would both laugh hysterically. She jumped rope faster than anyone he'd ever seen, and was one of the brightest women he'd ever met. But the specter of Amanda was always with him when he slept with Alicia. He tried to forget her, but he couldn't, and he knew this couldn't go on forever. Sooner or later he'd get caught, and he knew how wrong it was. Anthony didn't want to hurt either of them, and he knew he didn't want to lose Alicia. He couldn't. Every day he promised himself he'd deal with it, and he didn't. He gave himself one more day with Alicia as a gift. He was using every excuse he could think of not to have sex with Amanda, and only made love with her when he couldn't avoid it. She seemed like a different person now. But he had changed, she hadn't. Amanda was the same as she had always been, and for now she didn't turn him on. Alicia lit him on fire.

"Is something bothering you?" Alicia asked him one night. She was more perceptive than Amanda. He had been staring into space with a look of despair.

"Just some problems at work. Nothing important." She nodded and didn't press him further. They had never gone to his apartment. He hadn't been there in months, since he'd moved in with Amanda, and he was afraid she could show up there. He told Alicia it was depressing, and he liked hers better, and she was fine with that. She believed everything he told her, she knew he was the kind of guy who would tell the truth. She had no reason to suspect otherwise. He had told her in the beginning that he'd been seeing someone when they met, but he'd never mentioned it again, so she assumed it was over. He was spending all his time with her, and staying with her on weekends. He had no time to see someone else now. Amanda was in Bronxville with her parents three days a week, on *Vogue's* summer schedule. Anthony hadn't been to Bronxville with her in a month, while claiming to be developing a new game, which he said was an intense process.

He lay in bed holding Alicia, wondering how long he could live like this. He knew he owed it to both women to clean it up. Their days were numbered and he didn't know how Alicia would react. Tears slid down his cheeks as he thought about it. She slept in his arms and he held her tight. He never wanted to let her go, but if he lived up to his obligations to Amanda, he would have to. Leaving Alicia was going to be the hardest thing he had ever done. Thinking about it made him cry harder. He could no longer imagine the rest of his life without her. But he was going to have to face that some-day. Soon.

The phone rang next to Kate's bed at eleven o'clock one night in July, while she was looking over some depositions. Her heart al-ways skipped a beat when her phone rang at that hour. With three children out in the world, she was always afraid that something would happen to one of them. She picked it up and answered with an anxious hello. It was Claire, and she didn't sound as though any-thing terrible had happened. She sounded happy and in good spir-its, and had told her mother only two days before that things were great with Reed. They'd been dating for three months now, and she still hadn't told the firm, and didn't see why she should. She dis-agreed with her mother.

"Are you okay?" It was Kate's standard opening question.

"Of course," she said blithely. "Can I come and see you tomorrow after work? Will you be home?"

"Yes, I think so. I don't have any plans. Why?" She hoped Claire wasn't coming to tell her that she and Reed were getting engaged. It was much too soon for that.

"I just want to come by for a visit." She never did that, and Kate was instantly suspicious.

"Nothing's wrong?" Maybe she was getting fired and Claire wanted to tell her in person. She hoped not. Kate couldn't guess what it was.

"Everything's fine."

"Okay. Do you want to stay for dinner? I'll pick something up on the way home."

"No, it's fine. We're going to the Hamptons for the weekend. We'll leave after I see you."

"All right, see you then." Kate had a feeling of trepidation. Something was up, but Claire didn't sound upset, so she hoped it was nothing too bad. But it gnawed at her, and she had trouble falling asleep. Whatever it was, she'd have to wait until the following day to hear it. Claire obviously wanted her advice about something. She finally drifted off to sleep, after realizing that she hadn't heard from Anthony in a long time. She promised herself she would call him over the weekend. She wondered when one stopped worrying about one's children. At what age did they really take flight and take off? Whatever age it was, it hadn't happened yet, and she still worried about all of them most of the time.

When she woke up in the morning, she remembered her appointment with Claire that night after work, and she still couldn't guess what it was about. Maybe she had decided to break up with Reed after all. His time had come. But they were going away for the weekend, so that didn't add up. Kate put the depositions she'd been looking at the night before back in her briefcase and headed for the shower. Whatever Claire had to say, it could wait until that night. Her workday had begun.

Chapter 5

Claire showed up at Kate's apartment at six-thirty, five minutes after Kate got home. It had been a long, stressful day, full of
irritating surprises, difficult clients, and a minor argument with the
managing partner of the firm. She took a cab home so she wouldn't
be late for Claire, and felt rumpled and tired when she kicked off
her shoes, put away her briefcase, and the doorbell rang. The doorman had let Claire come up without announcing her, since he knew
her so well.

Claire was wearing white denim shorts and a pink T-shirt and
sandals to go to the Hamptons, and she dropped her purse near the
front door. It was a big Balenciaga tote.

"How was your day, Mom?" she asked casually.

"Honestly, lousy. I had arguments with everyone. I'm going to fire
a client who's lying to me and I can't defend him, and don't want to.
And the air-conditioning was broken in my office. I've been sitting
in a steam bath all day." The outside temperature had reached a

hundred at noon. "How was yours?" She smiled at her daughter, took off her lawyerly suit jacket, and tossed it on a chair, as Claire sat down on the couch and looked at her.

"My day was okay," Claire said, as Kate sat down across from her, trying to guess what would come next. She figured she was either going to break up with Reed, or having problems at work. "There's something I want to tell you," Claire said, without further preamble. "I'm pregnant." The words hung in the air as Kate wondered if she had heard correctly. She couldn't have. That had never happened before to either of her girls, nor with any girl Anthony had gone out with. It wasn't possible. But the look on Claire's face said it was true. Kate felt like she couldn't breathe for a minute. Then she took a breath to speak.

"Are you going to have an abortion?" She could hardly get the words out. She had her own views on the subject, but it was obviously the first question in a situation like this. She made no move toward Claire. She was too shocked to do anything except sit there and stare at her daughter in disbelief.

"Of course not. It's Reed's baby. We love each other." She made it seem obvious and normal. She didn't seem frightened or upset, nor in the least apologetic. Claire looked even more shocked than her mother that Kate would even ask the abortion question. She acted as though she was married and this was the result of careful planning. For an instant, Kate wondered if it was.

"How pregnant are you?" she asked in a hoarse voice.

"About six weeks." She said it almost proudly, which was a jolt to Kate. But at least it wasn't too late to do something respectable about it, if she was going that route. It wasn't what Kate wanted for her, but the questions had to be asked now. She wanted to know Claire's plans. "I'm having the baby, Mom," Claire said, to make it clear to her mother. Kate could feel her stomach turn over and a chill run down her spine. In her whole life, it had never occurred to her that she'd be living a scene like this with one of her girls. It was like bad reality TV.

"What does Reed say about all this? Does he know yet?"

"Of course," Claire said, looking deeply offended. "We did the test together. He's ecstatic."

Wonderful. "Could it be a false positive? Home tests aren't always reliable," Kate said, clutching at straws.

"I had a blood test too, to confirm it. Reed said the same thing, and we wanted to be sure. I'm definitely pregnant." She said it like it was a victory, not a tragedy or defeat. Claire smiled and Kate was fighting back tears.

"Are you going to get married?" Kate said, and Claire looked her mother in the eye and shook her head.

"We talked about it. Reed wants to, but I'm not ready. I love him with all my heart, but I don't feel ready for marriage and all it entails." Kate looked as though someone had slapped her.

"Wait a minute. You don't feel ready for marriage, but you're ready for a child? Do you know how crazy that is? You can undo a marriage if you make a mistake. You can't undo a child. A child is forever, for the rest of your life, and you'll be tied to Reed, whether you're married to him or not, if you have a child together. If you're not ready for the commitment of marriage, how can you possibly be ready for the responsibility of a child? Explain that to me."

"Marriage doesn't mean to me what it does to you, Mom. It's not this big voodoo, have-to, all-important goal in life. It's fine if it's what you want. But I don't. What I feel for Reed is much more important to me and our baby. That's all I care about. I don't need to be married to him. That's so yesterday, Mom. This is now. No one gets married anymore." She looked cocky as she said it, which made Kate angry.

"Oh yes, some people do. The usual order is marriage, then babies, not the reverse, or babies and no marriage. That's insane, or not very respectable at least. And have you thought of your career? You work for a very conservative Old Guard law firm. They can't fire you for having a child out of wedlock in today's world, or you could sue them. But they can certainly pass you over for partner for the rest of your time there, or for a very long time."

"If they do, then I'll switch to another firm. They don't own me. There are plenty of more modern law firms who wouldn't consider it a problem." Kate knew that was true, but she hated what Claire was saying and wanted to do. Her children had grown up with traditional values, and now Claire wanted to be avant-garde and be an unwed mother. The thought of it broke Kate's heart. What part of her upbringing had she not understood, and why was she rejecting the most basic morality that Kate believed in profoundly, and expected her children to embrace too?

"So you're not getting married?" she said in disbelief.

"That's right." Claire looked belligerent as she said it. She knew her mother's views on the subject and didn't care.

"And you feel ready to be a mother at twenty-six? A *single* mother?"

"I'll be twenty-seven when the baby's born. It's due in March."

"You have enough time to get married now, and cover it up," Kate said desperately, "and have it look respectable."

"I don't need to get married. It already is respectable. Reed and I love each other and I won't be a single mom. He'll be with me. He said he'll marry me anytime I want if I change my mind in a few years. I've always said I didn't want to get married till I was over thirty."

"Was having an illegitimate child at twenty-seven part of that plan?" Kate said angrily. She was furious with her and wanted to shake her. She hardly recognized the brash young woman facing her, totally oblivious to all propriety and the traditions she'd grown up with.

"There's nothing illegitimate about this baby, Mom. I'm having the child of the man I love."

"Whom you've known for three months. You don't even know each other. And he says now that he'll marry you whenever you want but he may feel differently about it later. I don't think there's anything cool or trendy about having a baby out of wedlock. I think it's disgraceful and irresponsible. If you got pregnant and want to keep it, at least have the decency to get married. I'll give you a wedding."

"I don't want a wedding. I have everything I want, a man I love and his baby."

"I can't believe you're saying this to me, as blithe as can be. You have no idea what you're taking on."

"Yes, I do. I watched you with us. You did it alone. If I have to, so can I."

"I was *married* to your father when all of you were born."

"That was thirty-three years ago. It doesn't matter anymore. Hardly anyone gets married to have a kid. And I'm not going to hide it now like it was some crime we committed. We're thrilled. I'm sorry if you're not, Mom, and you think it's such a disgrace. That's sad for you. You're having a grandchild. You should be happy."

"Not in these circumstances. How could I be? You're doing something that goes against everything I believe in and you were brought up with. I've never pushed any of you to get married, but if you're having a baby, I think you should. It's the least you can do, out of decency and self-respect, and for the child."

"We owe it to the child to be good parents. No one will care if we're married. And yes, you did push us into marriage, by the way. What do you think you're doing to Anthony? Encouraging him to marry that airhead because her parents are a big deal socially and have a big house."

"That's not why I want him to marry her. I think she'll ground him and be a terrific wife."

"Well, I think you're wrong on that score. I think she'll be a lousy wife and a huge bore and dead weight for him. And I don't want to be a wife right now, just a mother." Claire's cellphone buzzed and a text came in. She glanced at it and stood up. "It's Reed. He's downstairs. He went to put gas in the car and he's back. I have to go. There's going to be a lot of traffic. It's Friday night." She had been there for exactly thirty-five minutes, just long enough to tell her mother that she was pregnant, wanted to have the child out of wedlock, had no intention of getting married, and leave. In Kate's mind, it was like Hiroshima. She felt as though Claire had dropped a bomb on her. But there was nothing left to say. Claire had made it clear that her plans weren't open for discussion or negotiation. She had come here to announce them, not compromise. She had no intention of doing anything differently from what she wanted and it was up to her mother to adjust to it. Kate didn't even have the luxury of being happy about a grandchild. The whole thing felt like a tragedy to her. "I'm giving up my apartment and moving in with Reed. I was going to anyway before we found out about the baby. At least he's happy about it, even if you're not." Claire managed to look both angry and disappointed. She expected her mother to be supportive and thrilled. But how could she with the way Claire was going about it? Kate wouldn't have been happy if Claire was getting married this quickly, but a baby and not married was too much for her to swallow all at once, and to expect her to be delighted on top of it was completely unreasonable.

"I need time to digest this," Kate said in a grim voice and stood up too. "You're expecting a lot if you want me to be happy about this the way you want to do it."

"Marriage is an archaic tradition, Mom. No one sensible does it anymore."

"Well, some do, I'm just sorry you don't want to be one of them. It may be archaic, but it's the right thing to do."

"In your opinion, not mine." Claire started to walk to the door, as Kate followed her. She tried to put her arms around Claire to hug her, but she pushed her away. "Don't bother. I know what you think of me. I'm the family disgrace now. You love all of us as long as we do exactly what you want, get a great education, find a terrific job, work our asses off, and do everything 'properly,' your way. You may be able to con Anthony into that, but not me. I know what I'm doing is right for me. I'm sorry you don't think so."

"I'm not banishing you. You're not being fair. This is a hell of a shock for me," Kate said quietly.

"This isn't about you," Claire said coldly. "It's about me and Reed and our baby. And if you can't get on board, and don't want to be part of it, that's up to you." She was being incredibly nasty and immature about it, and every word she said cut through Kate like a sword. It was the first serious problem she had ever had with one of her children, and it was a big one. Kate wondered if the wounds between them would ever heal. She couldn't even think about the baby, she was so hurt and shocked by her own daughter.

"I love you. I'm sorry this is hard for both of us," Kate said in a sad voice. She felt as though she had just lost her youngest child, but she couldn't be dishonest with her. Claire had spoken her truth, and Kate had a right to speak hers, but apparently Claire didn't think so. She wanted her mother to tell her it was great news and go along with everything Claire was doing, and she couldn't. She had to at least speak up and try to reason with her. And even if Kate was angry, even furious, she loved Claire and wanted to make that clear to her.

"It's not hard for me," she said as she opened the front door. "I have Reed. I don't need you if you don't want to be part of it."

"I didn't say that. What I said is that I think you should get married and do this respectably."

"By *your* standards."

"And I didn't say I didn't want to be part of it. This is a hell of a shock you've just dished out while Reed was putting gas in the car. I need to sit with this for a while and think about it."

Claire started to walk out and turned back to her mother then. "Oh yeah, and Reed says he wants to meet you."

"I want to meet him too," Kate said quietly. "I'll let you know when I'm ready." Claire was being a brat about a very adult situation, and Kate didn't feel ready to meet Reed yet. She was deeply hurt by everything Claire had said and the way she had handled it.

"I'll call you," Claire said, and slammed the door behind her. Kate stood staring at it, and burst into tears.

She cried for an hour and was awake all night. She called Claire on her cell to tell her she loved her, but Claire didn't pick up. She texted her the message and got no response. There had been skirmishes with her children while they were growing up, over parties they couldn't go to, or minor restrictions for homework they hadn't done, but there had never been anything like this, with Claire rejecting their family values, aggressively insulting her mother, and doing something that would affect her life forever, and the child's. A baby and no marriage was huge, with a man she'd known for three months, and who might or might not stick around. At least he had offered to marry her, and Claire had refused, but much of what she'd said to her mother was cruel.

Kate sat nursing her wounds all weekend. She didn't want to talk to anyone, and didn't hear from Claire. Bart called her from Washington, but she didn't pick up and texted back that she had the flu.

She wasn't ready to tell him about it. They had a good time together, but Kate's soul felt raw, and she didn't want to share it with him. Her children and her relationship with them had always seemed so perfect compared to his. He always talked about what a good mother she was, and now her youngest was having a baby out of wedlock. She felt deep shame over it, and she couldn't tell him, or anyone.

She went for a walk on Sunday morning, and without thinking, she ended up at her mother's building, and called from downstairs.

"I'm sorry to show up without calling first," Kate said, sounding distressed. "Are you up?"

"I was reading the paper. Is something wrong?" She was worried. It was so unlike Kate not to call first and just show up.

"Nothing dangerous. Everyone's fine." Kate was quick to respond. After Tom's fatal accident years before, they were both sensitive to what could happen. This was serious, but not tragic, even if Kate felt like it was.

"Come on up," Margaret said, relieved. Kate walked past the doorman with a wintry smile, and Margaret opened the door to her daughter and saw that she looked ravaged. "Did something happen to Bart?" It was all she could think of unless Kate had been lying to her about the children being all right.

"No, and the kids are fine. They're all alive anyway." She walked into the kitchen and sat down, and Margaret followed her with an anxious expression. Kate looked at her mother mournfully. "Claire is pregnant. She's having the baby, and not getting married. She doesn't think marriage is 'necessary' anymore, it's an archaic tradition, according to her. She doesn't feel 'ready' for marriage, not for several years anyway, but she does feel ready for a child. According to her, they're ecstatic. He offered to marry her, and she refused." Margaret sat down across from her daughter at the kitchen table and looked at her intently.

"When did you find all this out?" Margaret looked as unhappy as her daughter.

"Friday night. I haven't stopped crying since. She hates me because I'm not happy about it. Maybe this is my punishment for setting the bar too high for them, as you always say. I never knew she had such an aversion to marriage. She's known Reed Bailey for three months. This is insane."

"Did she tell you how it happened?" Margaret said thoughtfully.

"The usual way, I assume," Kate said with a wry smile.

"I meant was it an accident, or did she plan this?"

"I was so shocked it never occurred to me to ask, and I don't think she'd tell me the truth anyway. I wouldn't be surprised if it was a decision on both their parts, since he told her he wanted her to be the mother of his children. I didn't think he meant this soon."

"She always gets carried away," Margaret said with a sigh, "although this is definitely extreme." Then she narrowed her eyes as she gazed at Kate. "It's not the end of the world though. Don't let it destroy you."

"It feels like it. It's so wrong."

"By our standards, not hers," Margaret said, sounding like a therapist again.

"She's not even embarrassed or remorseful. She was incredibly hostile with me. I'm so disappointed in her, Mom. And I know it sounds stupid, but it's embarrassing." She had a million emotions about it, and was proud of none of them, nor of her daughter, for the first time in her life. Claire was rejecting everything her family believed in, and the values she'd grown up with.

"The embarrassment is irrelevant. You'll get over it. My real concern is if she's ready to mother a child, and if this man is someone she can count on, or if she's just a passing fancy to him. We don't know him, and neither does she."

"She says he wants to meet me, but I'm not up to it." Kate felt as though her whole world had caved in. For the first time, one of her children had done something terrible and foolish that would impact her life forever. She was brokenhearted for Claire, who didn't understand what she'd done, and in some circles, her reputation would be ruined forever. The world wasn't as modern as she thought, not among the people they knew.

"You should meet him," Margaret said firmly, "and see what he says. Your judgment is a lot better than hers."

"Tom would die if he were still alive."

"Well, he's not. So you'll have to figure this out yourself." She paused for a minute then and looked at Kate. "Do they know about you? Have you ever told them?"

"No, that's irrelevant. They don't need to know."

"It's not irrelevant. It's about you. They're old enough to know and it will humanize you in their eyes. It's part of your history. You should share it with them."

"It's not going to change anything."

"You should have told them years ago," Margaret said firmly and Kate disagreed. She spent another hour with her mother, and then walked back to her apartment, feeling a little better but not much. She called Bart back, and he was shocked when he heard her.

"You sound awful. You must be really sick." He couldn't tell the difference between tears and the flu, and she had refused to do FaceTime with him. He told her to stay warm and get well soon. She still had no intention of telling him, but sooner or later, everyone would know. There was no hiding an illegitimate child. And Claire had no intention of keeping it a secret so Kate would have to get used to it. She wondered when Claire would tell her brother and sister and what they would say.

Claire called her that night, not to apologize for any of the things she'd said to her mother, but because she said Reed was insisting he wanted to see her. He had told Claire that no matter how angry she was at her mother, he wanted to meet her and at least let her know that he was an honorable man and wanted to marry her.

"She'll just try to force us to get married, and I don't want to, just because it's what she wants," Claire said to Reed. "I want to get married when we're ready to and want to, not for her, or because we 'have to.' She's expected us to be perfect at everything all our lives, I'm sick of it. I don't want to be perfect anymore. I want to do what's right for me, and for you," she added as an afterthought.

"It might be nice for the baby too if we did," he said gently, but she looked like a petulant child as she shook her head.

"Two of my friends have had babies without being married, and the sky didn't fall in," she insisted, and he didn't press the point.

He was happy either way, as long as he had Claire and their child. Things had happened quickly, but he really loved her, and wanted her family to know it too.

Kate reluctantly agreed to meet them the next day at her apartment after work. It felt like a déjà vu of Friday, when Claire walked in scowling, but this time Reed was with her, and he looked kind and apologetic from the moment he came through the door.

"I'm sorry this has happened so quickly, and that we've dumped it on you like this," Reed said, and sounded sincere. He was pleasant looking, with wavy brown hair and warm brown eyes, and appeared slightly older than he was. He seemed proper and respectful in khaki pants, a freshly pressed white shirt, and well-polished shoes. He appeared to be an adult and a gentleman, and he was very sympathetic with Kate. "I can imagine how upsetting this is for you. I would love to marry Claire, when she's ready to. I want to assure you that my intentions are honorable, and I intend to take good care of her. I love her very much." He smiled at Claire and then at her mother, as tears filled Kate's eyes. He was saying the right things, but the situation still shocked her. It was everything she had hoped never to face with one of her daughters, and didn't think she would. But at least he seemed like a decent man, and he loved Claire and wanted the baby. He explained that both of his parents had died when he was young, they had been older when he was born, and very conservative, and would have been shocked by the situation too, just as Kate was. He had grown up in New York and she could tell that he was well brought up, polite, and well educated. He wasn't a rebel like Claire had suddenly become, and he seemed like a responsible adult.

"Thank you," Kate said, fumbling for words. "I'm still stunned by the whole thing, and how adamant Claire is about not getting married. I never knew she felt that way." This was the rebellion her mother had warned her of for years, because she set the bar so high for them. But with a baby on the way, now was the time for Claire to be reasonable and mature, not act like an angry teenager. It was a little late for that.

"We'll get there eventually," Reed said soothingly. They didn't stay long. Kate offered him wine, but he declined, and he hugged Kate before they left, and thanked her for being so understanding, which she wasn't. He had done all he could to put oil on troubled waters, and she respected him for it. Claire was the problem more than Reed.

Kate called her mother after they left and told her about it.

"I think she got lucky. He sounds like a nice man." Something else had occurred to Kate when she saw them together. "He's very fatherly with her. She was only seven when Tom died. Maybe Reed is the father she didn't have. I get the feeling he'd prefer being married now too. Maybe he can talk her into it."

"Eventually, it won't matter if they're married, if he's a good man and a good father and doesn't run out on her. Let's hope he sticks around. And being married isn't a guarantee he'll stay either," as they both knew.

"It sounds like he will." Kate was slightly relieved after meeting him. She was glad he had insisted, but she still had the shock about the baby, her disappointment in her daughter, and the embarrassment factor to deal with. It was a lot. She decided that her mother had been right about something else. She texted Claire that night and asked her to come back to the apartment the next evening, alone this time, and she assured her it wouldn't take long.

Claire looked hostile and suspicious as soon as she arrived, and somewhat mystified about why Kate wanted her there, but at least she had come.

"If you got me here to try and convince me to get married, it won't work, and I'll leave now."

"Actually, it's about something else. Something your grandmother thinks that I should share with you. I wasn't going to. But maybe it's good for you to know that I made my mistakes too. Please come in and sit down."

They sat facing each other on opposite couches, as Claire waited expectantly, and Kate didn't waste time.

"I got pregnant by accident when I was young too. I was younger than you are, I was nineteen, he was twenty. We'd been dating for a few months. I didn't know him well. I wasn't madly in love with him as you are with Reed. It was a stupid teenage mistake. I was a sophomore at Northwestern, and very innocent. I'd been pretty sheltered growing up. He was the first boy I ever slept with. His name was Ethan Henry. My father had a fit and insisted we get married. His parents agreed, and so we did. It was over the summer so we were at home here in New York, not in school. He had a summer job at a beach club on Long Island, where he lived with his parents. We were two dumb kids who hardly knew each other, and neither of us were ready for marriage or to have a child. We got married in June, when he got back from school. I was three months pregnant.

In August, we went out one night on Long Island. He was driving and he'd had some beers. I was five months pregnant, and we got in a terrible accident. He wasn't hurt, but I broke my pelvis and lost the baby. We hit another car, and a twelve-year-old passenger was killed, a little girl. My father had the marriage annulled as soon as I lost the baby, and I guess I was relieved. They told me the baby was a boy, and I felt terrible about it. I think I was in shock when I went back to school in September. Some of it is a blur. There was a trial later, and Ethan went to prison for seven years for manslaughter. I never heard from him again, and his life must have been ruined by going to prison. We never wrote to each other, and I don't know what happened to him. I always felt bad about it, him, the baby, the little girl, all of it. I put it all behind me, and a year later I met your father, and we got married after I graduated, and you know the rest of the story after that. But none of you knew the first part." Claire's eyes were wide as she listened.

"You were married before Dad?"

"For two months, because of an unwanted pregnancy. But it shows you that I did some foolish things too."

"Did Dad know?"

"Of course. I told him before we got married. I wouldn't have kept that a secret from him."

"Why did you tell me, and why didn't you tell us before?" Claire's tone was accusatory more than sympathetic.

"I never thought you needed to know. Your father and I agreed that you didn't. But your grandmother thought I owed it to you to humble myself. I'm not as perfect as you may think and I pretend."

"This is different. Reed and I are in love," she said stubbornly, but

Kate could see that she was shaken by the story. "Why did you tell me? Are you suggesting I go out and get in an accident to get rid of the baby?" she said cruelly, and Kate felt like she'd been punched in the stomach and looked it.

"I told you because I've been foolish too, and I thought you deserved to know that. Maybe you didn't though if that's all you can say." Claire looked embarrassed when Kate stood up. It had been hard enough to tell her and dredge up old history, she didn't deserve the reaction she'd gotten.

"Are you going to tell that to the others?"

"I will," she said simply, and Claire walked to the door, looking pensive, and then looked back at her mother.

"I'm sorry, Mom. That must have been hard for you to go through." It was the first sign of humanity Kate had seen from Claire since the whole mess had started about her pregnancy.

"It was hard," she said coolly. Claire had just disappointed her again. Their relationship had taken some hard hits in the past few days. Kate wondered if they'd recover from them, or if her family was starting to disintegrate. It was possible, no matter how hard she'd worked on it for years and how much she loved them.

Claire left and Kate called her mother to tell her she'd done it, told Claire the story of her first marriage.

"How was she about it?"

"Not very nice," Kate said, sounding exhausted. She hated to remember it herself. It had been a sad painful time in her life that had forced her to grow up.

"Give her some time to think about it. She's going through a lot right now too. That was a big dose of some heavy information about you." She hesitated for a moment and then went on, "Did you tell her about her father?" Margaret asked.

"No, I didn't, and I'm not going to. Some things they don't need to know, and never will." Kate sounded tense when she answered.

"It would only be fair to you, if they knew."

"It doesn't matter now. He's dead."

"But you're not. They're adults, Kate. They need to know who you are and what you've been through. That's a heavy burden for you. They're too old for secrets now." Kate thanked her mother and got off the phone. What her mother was referring to was the one secret she intended to keep. For them, and for their father.

Chapter 6

As July progressed, Anthony felt as though he was being driven to the edge of sanity by his double life. All he wanted was to be with Alicia, but he had to go home to Amanda at some point every night, and he felt dizzy every time he faced her. He was waiting for one of them to find out, and finally he knew he had to do something about it. He wanted to be honest with Alicia. He genuinely loved her and didn't want to hurt her any more than he already had. And he didn't want to hurt Amanda either.

It was a warm night and he and Alicia had taken a long, slow walk by the river to cool off. On the way back to the subway he kissed her, and realized he had never loved her more. His integrity finally took the upper hand. He stopped walking and looked at her. There was something deeply wrenching in his eyes, a bottomless sorrow she didn't understand.

"I have to tell you something," he said in barely more than a whisper. "I should have told you a long time ago, but I didn't. Remember in the beginning that I said I was seeing someone? I was, and it wasn't over. I didn't have the guts to tell you, and it's not over yet. I've been trying to figure out what to do about it. I'm so in love with you, Alicia. I don't want to risk losing you, but I think I need a little time to figure this out. I can't do this anymore, sleeping with you every night. My life is becoming completely crazy and I feel horrible about this. You're where I want to be, but there's somewhere else I'm supposed to be. I need to sort that out, Alicia, and then come back to you without a string of tin cans trailing behind me. I hope you can forgive me. I want to work it out."

"Wait a minute." Alicia stopped dead in her tracks, trying to understand what he was saying to her. "Never mind about tin cans and all that crap. *Who* are you supposed to be with, and just how much have you still been 'seeing' her? You mean like every day? Are you living with her?" He nodded, and looked like a beaten dog when he did. "Are you married?" she shrieked at him, so loud people a block away could hear her, and he cringed.

"No, of course not. I'm not that big a creep." He decided to make a clean breast of it. "I'm supposed to get married in December. I've never felt about her the way I do about you. This has been agony, lying to you. I need to figure it out, Alicia. I know it sounds like shit now, but I'm in love with you. I swear that's true." The big question was if he loved Amanda too. He wasn't sure.

"Hold on here. You're engaged to some woman you're supposed to marry in December, in *five* months? And you go home to her every night after you make love to me, and you didn't fucking tell me you're living with someone and about to get married? We've been together for almost two months, and you didn't fucking tell me that?" She was screaming at him, but he knew he deserved it.

"I don't go home to her every night. That's the whole point. I've been lying to everyone while I tried to figure it out. I need to talk to her and clean up the whole mess and come back to you if you'll have me. I want to do this right, for everyone."

"Right? Are you some kind of lunatic? You've been lying to me for two months, and now you want to do this *right*? What do you do? Make love to both of us every night? What kind of shithead are you? Who *are* you? You lying shit. Don't talk to me about 'doing this right.' Go back to whoever she is, and don't ever call me again," and after she said it, with a wild look in her eyes, she punched him so hard that he reeled backward and almost fell. Then she delivered two more punches to his chest and stomach. He was bent over as he looked at her. He had never been punched in the stomach before, and they both knew he'd get a black eye out of it, which was what she had intended. She hadn't broken anything, but she could have.

"Alicia, don't . . . I'm so sorry. I wanted to tell you. I was terrified I'd lose you."

"You just did." She was rubbing the knuckles of her right hand. It had cost her to hit him that hard, but she had no regrets. "And if you ever come near me again, I'll kick your ass from here to Brooklyn. Stay away from me!" she shouted at him.

"You've given me a black eye." He was gingerly touching his cheek.

"I meant to. I could have done a lot worse."

"It's your damn right hook. I love you. I swear I'll clean up this mess," but he wasn't sure he would, and she could sense that now too.

"Tell that to your fiancée. Best of luck, asshole," she said, turned her back, and walked away. He didn't see the tears running down her cheeks. All he saw from behind as he watched her was the proud set of her shoulders, the straight back, and the quick step as she disappeared, trying to get as far away from him as she could.

Alicia turned the corner, and then ran to the subway sobbing. Her hand was throbbing from when she'd punched him. She couldn't believe he'd done this to her. She had believed in him, and trusted him, and he'd been lying to her the whole time. The worst of it was that she loved him too, but she never wanted to see him again. He'd only left a few things there, some T-shirts, jeans, a pair of sneakers they'd bought together. She threw them in the trash in her apartment building, along with everything he'd given her, some souvenirs, a book, some dried flowers she'd saved, a pink dinosaur he'd won for her at Coney Island. She wanted no reminders of him anywhere. But the real reminders of him were her memories and the heart he had stolen from her dishonestly. She wanted to hate him, but she didn't. All she wanted to do was forget him. They had taken some pictures together in a photo booth and she threw those away too. She blocked his number on her phone, and then she lay on her bed sobbing, until she fell asleep.

By the time Anthony got home to Amanda's apartment, his eye was swollen shut, his chest and stomach were aching, and he felt sick. He didn't blame Alicia for hitting him. Knowing her abilities, she hadn't hit him with her full strength or she would have knocked him out cold. Unfortunately, Amanda was home that night. She'd had dinner with some girlfriends from *Vogue,* and he had told her he had to work late. He was bent over as he walked into the apartment, and ran into her in the kitchen, when he went to get some ice for his eye. She screamed when she saw him, and rushed to help him.

"Oh my God, what happened?" She pulled up a stool so he could sit down.

"It's nothing, I'm fine. I got mugged on the subway," yeah, by a hundred-and-ten-pound girl.

"Did they get your watch and your money?" She put some ice in a Ziploc bag and handed it to him, and he winced when he put it on his eye. Alicia had given him a good one. It was his final gift from her.

"No, I chased them off. There were three of them," he embellished the story, and he knew that if he was going to do this right, he had to be honest with Amanda too, but he couldn't. Before he canceled the wedding and ruined her life, he wanted to see how he felt about her when he didn't have Alicia in his arms every day. He needed to find out if Amanda was enough on her own. He didn't know anymore. Maybe Alicia would fade from memory and he'd be glad she did. He needed to find that out.

"Can I run a hot bath for you?" she offered.

"No, I'll take a shower." He smiled at her, but all he could think of was how beautiful Alicia looked when she was raging at him, and how wounded. It had almost been a relief when she swung at him, no matter how much it hurt. He knew he had injured her even more.

He got into the shower and let the hot water rain down on him. He realized he'd have to change gyms now. He couldn't go back there again, or to any of the places where they'd been. They'd had a whole life together for almost two months. It had been as though there was no one else in his life. Amanda had ceased to exist whenever he was with Alicia. But Alicia had come home with him, and when Amanda droned on about the wedding, it was Alicia's voice he heard in his head, her body that he longed for.

Amanda was waiting in the bedroom for him, watching TV, as he stood in the shower, crying for the woman he had just given up for her. He should have told Alicia right in the beginning, but then the last two months would never have happened, and they were the most precious memories he had now. He wondered if he would feel the same way about Amanda if he broke up with her.

He walked into the bedroom, still bent over, and his eye was turning a nasty purple. He slid into bed next to Amanda between clean freshly pressed sheets, and he lay there for a minute with his eyes closed, and felt her hand on his chest, moving slowly downward. He opened his one good eye, and grabbed her wrist more harshly than he meant to.

"I can't. They hit me in the chest and the stomach, and my eye is killing me."

"Did they hit you there too?" She looked worried and he shook his head, but if Alicia had thought of it, she probably would have.

"I'm sorry, I'll be okay tomorrow," but he wondered if he would ever be fully okay again. He had no idea how he was going to live without Alicia, with only Amanda to keep him company forever.

Anthony waited until the following weekend to visit his grandmother, who he hadn't seen in several weeks. He felt guilty about not having seen her for so long. He had neglected everyone to be with Alicia. He hadn't heard from her in the last week and didn't expect to. He knew how proud she was. He would never hear from her again, and he knew that his plan to go back to her if he canceled the wedding would never happen. Alicia would never let him near her again, and he didn't blame her for that. He had been an asshole, just as she said.

His spectacular shiner had turned into an ordinary one by the time he visited his grandmother. It was dark blue with streaks of yellow, impressive, but nothing compared to what it had been in the beginning.

"Good lord! How did you get that?" Margaret asked him, and he had stuck with the same story for everyone.

"I got mugged on the subway, by three guys."

"Maybe you shouldn't take it anymore."

"I'll be okay." He was less chatty than usual and she asked him about what he was working on, and some details about the wedding. She thought he looked distracted and thinner than usual, which wasn't explained by the mugging. She looked at him after a while, and patted his hand gently.

"Are you all right, Anthony?" He hesitated and she waited for the answer. He confided in her sometimes and she wondered if he would now.

"I don't know, Grandma. I've been confused lately," he said, hanging his head, not looking her in the eye, and then he looked at her and she saw the two pools of pain.

"What kind of confused?"

He lowered his voice as though afraid someone would hear him, but there was no one else in the apartment. "I met someone a couple of months ago. She's an amazing woman. I was so damn attracted to her. Even talking to her was exciting. She's very different. But Amanda is the kind of woman you marry. Sometimes I'm confused about both of them. I'm not sure what to do." She could see that he was in agony, and searching for answers, and she didn't know why, but she had the oddest feeling that the black eye had something to do with it. If so, this woman certainly was "very different" from the women he knew.

"It's not about comparing two women, Anthony. Don't fall into that trap. That'll only confuse you more. First of all, Amanda is 'the kind of woman you marry' if you're in love with her, enough to spend the next fifty years with her, maybe sixty if you're lucky. If you're not that in love with her, it doesn't matter what 'kind' of woman she is. All kinds of women get married, and probably all kinds of women would suit you. It's not about a job description, it's only about how much you love her. The second thing to think about is the fact that you were attracted to someone else. If you're crazy about Amanda other women shouldn't be appealing. If they are, you need to look at that, because you're going to cross paths with a lot of attractive women over the next fifty years. If you're already looking at others now, it's not a good sign. First, you need to figure out if Amanda is the right woman for you, since you're engaged to her, and if she's not, then you can check out all the others. Take a good long look at what you're getting with Amanda. Make sure it's what *you* want. And one question, just out of curiosity, about the 'amazing, very different' woman. She doesn't happen to be a female prizefighter, does she?" She nodded toward his eye, and Anthony laughed. His grandmother was a sharp old bird and she didn't buy the mugging story. Everyone else had, even his mother.

"She's an amateur, actually, lightweight, but effective." He grinned at her.

"I thought so." Margaret smiled at him. "She must be an interesting woman. She packs quite a punch."

"I deserved it," he said remorsefully, and she nodded.

"I suspect you did." She hugged him then, and he left a few minutes later. His grandmother never ceased to amaze him, and he knew she had given him good advice. She always did.

He made love to Amanda that night, for the first time in a month. He had made excuses which Amanda had been willing to accept, and he'd been out late every night, hoping Amanda would be asleep when he got home. But he was trying to feel for her now everything he had for Alicia for the two magical months he'd been with her. He tried to imagine making love to Amanda for the next ten, twenty, forty years. It was a daunting thought. She was already asleep next to him, snoring softly with her mouth open. He wondered what it would be like to look at her next to him twenty years from now. It seemed like a lifetime to him, several of them. It was hard to imagine it, or what they would find to talk about after the wedding, even if they had children. There was nothing else.

Chapter 7

One of the things Tammy loved about working for Chanel, other than the generous clothing allowance, the challenging job, and the trips to Europe, were the four weeks of vacation she was able to take every year. She kept two weeks to go on trips to interesting places during the year, often in Europe. She'd been to Prague, Croatia, skiing in Courchevel, and to South America and Mexico over the years. She combined travel in Asia with business, and loved Tokyo and Hong Kong, and had visited the temples in Kyoto. She spent two weeks on an island in Maine every August, relaxing, wearing old T-shirts and jeans, and going sailing in the small dinghy that came with the house they rented. She'd been going there for seven years, and Stacey Adams always came with her. Stacey was a busy pediatrician, forty-one years old, and needed the break as much as Tammy did. They took a stack of books, their hiking gear, and hardly talked to each other. It was exactly the kind of vacation from the pressures of their jobs that they both needed.

Stacey dealt with anxious parents and sick children all year, and Tammy dealt with the sharks in the fashion business. Maine was like being in Heaven for two weeks for both of them. Their trip was a week away, and Tammy had just gotten her mother's invitation to their family birthday dinner for Kate the day after Labor Day. The invitation from her mother was still on her computer screen when Stacey walked into the kitchen, trying to break in a pair of new hiking boots. Like a homing pigeon, she saw the invitation on Tammy's computer and stared at it for a minute.

"Let me guess," she said with a hurt expression. "You're not taking me again this year. Why am I not surprised at that?" She turned away from it, and Tammy switched her computer off. She was annoyed at herself for having left it there, but she'd gotten busy with something in the kitchen. She didn't like hurting Stacey's feelings. She was such a good person, such a kind woman, and Tammy hated causing her pain. Stacey was pretending to be busy, putting the dishes away, and Tammy walked over to her.

"You know I can't take you to dinner at my mother's." There was apology mixed with regret in Tammy's tone.

"Why not? We've lived together for seven years."

"They think we're roommates." She had even told her mother that Stacey had moved out a year or two before, afraid that she was getting suspicious. But Kate never came downtown to visit and had never met Stacey. Kate was busy too, Tammy often worked late, and traveled frequently. There was always a plausible excuse for Kate not to come to Tammy's apartment and it was easier for Kate if Tammy came uptown, which she was willing to do. As a result, she had no idea that Stacey was still living there, and even less that they were partners. No one in Tammy's family had ever suspected it. She didn't fit the stereotype of what they thought a gay woman would look like. They just thought that Tammy worked too hard to date, which was what she told them, and they believed her. She had lived a lie with them for most of her life, and for the last seven years with Stacey. They had met at an extremely discreet forum for gay women in business.

"It's pretty amazing that I still haven't made the cut after seven years," Stacey said, looking discouraged.

"I haven't made it after thirty-two." When she had first met Stacey she had promised to tell her family, but she'd never had the guts to do it. It was just simpler not to rather than having to deal with their reaction. Tammy was certain they would never understand or accept the relationship. "You know what my family's mantra is. Be perfect at everything. My mother is. My brother and sister are. They think I am."

"You *are* perfect." Stacey smiled at her. "You can't be gay and perfect?"

"I don't think so. My grandmother would probably survive it, but I don't think my mother would. She would take it as some kind of personal failure. My poor grandmother is always worried about me being an old maid."

"I'd like us to get married one of these days, and have a baby." She kissed Tammy when she said it and Tammy liked the idea too. "Do you suppose they'd let me come to the wedding?" Stacey teased her.

"Not a chance. We could hire some actor as a beard to be the groom, and you could pretend to be my maid of honor." It was sad for both of them, not being able to be open with Tammy's family, but she couldn't see it happening. Stacey had made peace with her own family when she was in college, they were crazy about Tammy, and she liked them too. Her family was educated and warm. They were unpretentious people from the Midwest. Her father was a general practitioner in a small town, and her mother had been a nurse. They had known she was gay since her teens, and accepted it. Tammy's family were sophisticated New Yorkers but much less open-minded than Stacey's and Tammy knew they would be shocked.

Stacey was more obviously gay than Tammy. Most of her patients were aware of it and didn't care. She loved wearing very elegant men's shoes, which Tammy bought her at John Lobb in Paris. She wore them with well-tailored jeans, beautifully made men's shirts, and tweed jackets she bought in London. Tammy's look was ultra-feminine and pure Chanel. She was always drop-dead chic, representing the brand, which made it all the more relaxing to live in old shorts and faded T-shirts and ripped jeans in Maine. Stacey's hair was short and prematurely gray, and Tammy's was long and blond like her mother's.

They spent the rest of the day packing and getting ready for their trip. They did errands in the neighborhood, and bought a stack of books they both wanted to read. They were a consummately harmonious couple and complemented each other, and couldn't wait to spend two weeks in Maine together.

Tammy still intended to tell her family about Stacey one day. She hadn't entirely given up on it, she just didn't see how or when she would do it. There would have to be an opportune moment, and there hadn't been one so far, in seven years. They used to fight about it. Now Stacey hardly ever mentioned it, except at times like Kate's birthday, or Christmas and Thanksgiving. She went home to her own family for the holidays, it was too depressing waiting around the apartment for Tammy to come back from family festivities she wasn't invited to. She was Tammy's dark secret, and a well-kept one. Tammy never slipped. They had separate phone lines and used their cellphones anyway. And Kate would never drop in on Tammy unannounced. It didn't even occur to her. Kate considered all the trendy areas downtown like another city. It took half an hour to get there and Kate preferred her children to visit her at home, which they did occasionally, or they met at a restaurant so no one had to cook. She hadn't been to Anthony's apartment either since he got it, and knew it would be a mess. He treated it like a college dorm room. And Claire wasn't a homemaker either in her tiny studio apartment.

Tammy always went uptown to see her mother and her grandmother. She hated the dishonesty of it, but she didn't see what choice she had. She'd made a decision long ago. She'd rather be a liar than a pariah or the outcast, as she was afraid she would be if she told the truth.

She had almost told Anthony several times when she was younger, but she wasn't sure how he would handle it either. They were all very traditional, and lived up to what their mother expected of them. They had never broken with tradition, and no one in the family had ever done anything shocking. Tammy didn't want to be the one to do that. She loved them too much to be the one to break their hearts. She wondered how her father would have reacted to it, but she had a feeling he wouldn't have accepted it either.

"Well, I guess it's tough on her, but your mother will just have to get through another birthday without me," Stacey teased her and Tammy smiled. She wished it could be different, but she knew it couldn't. And Stacey was so nice about it, which made it worse.

She called her mother and grandmother before they left for Maine, and told them they could reach her on her cellphone, if they needed to, although cell service was spotty, and there was no phone in the house they rented, which was one of the things they loved about it. No Internet for two weeks. And no TV. They could read and talk to each other at night, or play cards, or Scrabble. It was the perfect vacation for both of them.

Tammy thought her mother sounded tense when she talked to her. She had for several weeks, but she didn't know what it was about. Kate hadn't shared Claire's news yet, nor had she. Claire said she wanted to wait until after the first trimester, when she knew everything was fine, and then she was going to tell Anthony and Tammy, sometime around their mother's birthday. Kate had asked her not to do it that night, so she could enjoy her birthday without drama. She said that sharing Claire's shocking news of the baby would spoil the birthday for her, which upset Claire all over again. Claire was about to go to Aspen for three weeks with Reed, and was looking forward to it.

Kate spent two weeks with Bart at Shelter Island every summer. He rented a house there for two months, and invited his children to visit in July if they wanted to. He invited friends to come in August. Kate played hostess for him, and enjoyed it. They had to take a ferry to get there. She liked his friends who came on weekends, and the time they spent there alone. She hadn't told him about Claire's baby yet either. She was too embarrassed to do so. It felt like a double failure to her. On Claire's part to fly in the face of the rules of society, and on her part, to have failed to teach her what the rules were. Having a baby out of wedlock was not good news to Kate or anything she was proud of. It had taken all the pleasure out of having a first grandchild, now it was something she dreaded, and wanted to hide as long as she could, even from Anthony and Tammy. But the secret would be out soon, when the baby started to show, probably by October.

Kate wished Tammy a good trip to Maine when she called, and told her to be careful. She thought it was dangerous for her to go alone. What if a bear came out of the woods, or her canoe or kayak flipped over.

"I'll be fine," Tammy said cheerily. "Have fun in Shelter Island with Bart." But Kate knew there was a falseness to it this year. He had no idea what was troubling her or how upset she was and she was too ashamed to tell him, which said a lot about their relationship. There was a basic lack of honesty there, because they weren't close enough for her to confide in him, which was their unspoken agreement and the way they wanted it. It kept everything superficial. But they had a good time together, and she was looking forward to the two weeks with him, away from all her troubles in New York.

Margaret wasn't going anywhere except to a friend's in Southampton for a long weekend. She was going to visit another friend in Palm Beach in the fall, when she preferred to travel.

And Anthony was back to spending weekends in Bronxville with Amanda and her parents. He found the sound of the crickets deafening, and the heat oppressive. They had the cake and wine tasting for the wedding scheduled while they were there. He didn't care about either one. Amanda cried all day when he said he thought the cake tasted like toothpaste. It was from the best wedding-cake baker in New York, and she couldn't believe he'd said that.

It was a relief for Anthony to get back to the city every Monday and go back to work. It made him think again about what his grandmother had said about living for thirty or forty years with Amanda. It looked like a long lonely stretch of road to him. But maybe it would be better when they had children. Maybe Amanda was right about that. He was trying hard not to think of Alicia, and the more he tried, the more he thought about her. He wondered where she was, and if she was in the city. There wasn't much modeling work in the summer, and she was on vacation from Hunter until September when she'd pick up her final eight credits. He reached for his cellphone to call her more than once, but knew he couldn't. He had changed gyms after the breakup, so he no longer ran into her. He spent most of the time on weekends in Bronxville in the pool, or lying in the sun, while Amanda and her mother met with the tentmaker and the wedding planner, and her father played golf. It was the longest summer of Anthony's life.

Chapter 8

By the time Kate's birthday rolled around, right after Labor Day, she was in better spirits after two weeks in Shelter Island with Bart. She never told him about Claire being pregnant. She tried to put it out of her mind entirely and succeeded some of the time. At other times, it was much on her mind, but she never told him. There was nothing she could do about it anyway, or so her mother kept reminding her. And at Margaret's suggestion, she had invited a few of her own friends to Shelter Island too. It gave her a chance to see them since most of the time she was too busy working to see friends. Bart left for Hong Kong and Beijing immediately after the vacation on a trip for a Senate Finance subcommittee.

Relations were still chilly between Claire and her mother, but Kate had had a nice time with Bart in Shelter Island in spite of the heartaches she didn't share with him. He never suspected the grief she was concealing.

As soon as she got back, Kate had a big case with one of their major clients, which had heated up and was eating up her time, so she wasn't able to think of anything else. It was a blessing.

Tammy had had a terrific vacation in Maine, and was gearing up for fashion week in Paris in two weeks. She invited her grandmother to go with her, but Margaret said she loved September in New York, and was going to Palm Beach at the end of the month. They were all busy. They all had lots to tell each other when they met at Kate's for her birthday dinner, which she had catered by a new Thai restaurant. Margaret thought that Anthony looked gaunt, but Amanda was radiant as the wedding drew closer. She told Kate all the latest details before dinner.

Margaret was in good spirits and happy to see her grandchildren at the dinner at Kate's. Amanda commented somewhat tactlessly that Claire looked like she'd put on weight over the summer but it suited her. Claire hadn't brought Reed with her. She had come alone, and the minute Amanda commented on her weight, Kate and Margaret exchanged pointed looks across the table, and Tammy caught it. Claire looked uncomfortable for a minute, but she had passed the three-month mark, and had just had a sonogram that morning, and was told everything was fine.

She then did exactly what her mother had asked her not to do. She looked straight at Amanda and smiled at her.

"Well, there's a reason for it," she said happily. "I'm having a baby." There was total silence at the table for a minute as all of the young people stared at Claire in amazement.

"Are you serious?" Amanda asked her, looking panicked. "Are you getting married before we are?" She looked as though she was going to cry if Anthony's sister stole their thunder.

"I'm not getting married at all. We don't need to. We're happy just as we are, and now we'll have a baby." Claire acted as though they'd been married for years, and this had been a long awaited event, instead of a shocker in a now five-month-old relationship.

"Wow," Anthony said, not sure what else to say, as he watched his mother's face turn to stone, and Tammy exchanged a look with her grandmother.

"I thought we agreed we weren't going to talk about it tonight," Kate said to her youngest daughter, who pretended not to hear her.

"Are you okay with that, the baby, I mean, if they're not married?" Amanda asked her future mother-in-law. Anthony kicked her under the table, and she looked at him in surprise. "What? I can't talk about it? Claire brought it up," she said, defending herself as Anthony groaned. He could see a tornado heading toward them, and he hated confrontation, especially among his female relatives. It never turned out well.

"No, Mom's not happy about it," Claire answered for Kate. "She's furious with me in fact. She thinks it's shocking."

"My parents would too," Amanda said innocently, as Anthony closed his eyes. "My father would kill me. And my mother would probably cry for a year."

"Reed and I don't think marriage is necessary," Claire said pointedly with an edge to her voice.

"Is he willing to marry you?" Amanda continued to pursue it despite scowls of warning from her fiancé. "If he is, I'd marry him if I were you. Why expose yourself to all the nasty things people will say?" Amanda suggested. No one else said a word.

"He's willing, but I don't want to. I don't want to get married because we 'have' to, and we don't care what people will say." Kate was looking sick by then, and pushed her dinner away, as Tammy watched her and felt sorry for her. It was easy to see how upset she was and what a blow it was to her. She was furious with her sister for bringing it up tonight at their mother's birthday. It also explained why Kate had seemed so stressed recently. Tammy had wondered why.

"I'm sorry, Mom," Tammy said softly, and Kate looked at her with tears in her eyes.

"Thank you. I never realized how liberal your sister is, and how modern," she said quietly. And rebellious, she didn't add, but she thought it. "The news will be out pretty soon when it starts to show. I haven't told anyone yet."

"We've told a few friends, and we'll start telling everyone in the next few weeks when we know what sex it is," Claire said blithely.

"Do they care at your law firm?" Tammy asked her, mature, and practical, and always careful about her job. "A lot of companies wouldn't like it."

"I haven't told them yet. But Reed is one of their biggest clients. How mad could they get?" She was cocky with her response, and sensing that her news wasn't being entirely well received, even by her siblings, Claire had adopted the same aggressive tone she had been using recently with her mother.

"I'm not sure if I should congratulate you, or sympathize with Mom," Tammy said quietly.

"I don't see why you don't marry him," Anthony said, looking stunned by the whole thing. "What are you trying to prove by not getting married? How cool you are? Who cares? Why don't you just go down to city hall and get married?" He wished he and Amanda could do that, instead of being a part of the circus Amanda and her parents were planning. "Is Reed as opposed to marriage as you are?"

"He's fine either way," she said, looking annoyed at her brother.

"I think he'd actually prefer to get married," Kate chimed in. "He asked her to, and she refused." Kate had the same devastated look that came into her eyes whenever the subject came up. "I think a lot of it is delayed teenage rebellion," she said, looking at her youngest daughter.

"That's a nasty thing to say," Claire spat back at her mother.

"It's a nasty thing to do, depriving a baby of legally married parents." The birthday was a lost cause after that, and Kate stunned them all with her own story from her youth, of her first marriage. There was dead silence at the table again after that.

"Why didn't you ever tell us?" Tammy was the first to ask her, shocked at how little they knew about their mother.

"I didn't think it was important for you to know. It all happened before you were born. But maybe you should know that even parents make mistakes, sometimes very big ones. It was a sad story."

"You really don't know what happened to the guy after he went to prison? Couldn't you have found out?" Anthony said, visibly upset. It had been a distressing evening.

"I guess I could have, but we hardly knew each other, which sounds strange since I was married to him, and we almost had a baby. But when he got out of prison seven years later, I was married to your father, and two of you had already been born. I didn't really want to make contact with him again. I wanted to try to forget it. A baby and a child had died and a marriage had ended. I didn't want to revisit it, and I was happy with your dad." She glanced at Margaret then, who was giving her a stern look, and Kate sighed, as she gazed around the table at her children and Amanda, who was shocked after Kate's confession. "I think we can pretty much forget about my birthday after all this, but as long as Claire has gotten us started on a night of confessions, there's something else your grandmother thinks I should tell you. She thought I should tell you about the marriage that was annulled so you'd know that I've made some mistakes too, and she was right. The other story I'm going to share with you isn't really my mistake, but I suppose you have a right to know. If your father had lived, you would have known anyway. I've protected his memory for nineteen years, but he was human too.

"About a year before he died, he fell in love with someone else. I never knew her, but I was told she was a nice woman. He met her in Washington and fell in love with her. She worked in his congressional office. He asked me for a divorce shortly before the helicopter crash. He wanted to marry her, and I assume he would have. He loved you all very much, but he was very definite about getting out of our marriage, and I wouldn't have stopped him if that was what he wanted. You can't keep someone hostage, even if you love them. So I had agreed to the divorce. He had already seen a lawyer and was planning to remarry." The silence after that was deafening, and there were tears rolling down Anthony's cheeks when she was finished. He walked around the table, put his arms around his mother, and cried, without saying a word. It was the death of his illusions about his father, which was why Kate had never told them. She only hoped that her mother was right that they should know.

"Why didn't you ever tell us?" Tammy asked her, and Kate looked at her sadly. She had lost Tom twice, once when he told her he was divorcing her, and the second time a few weeks later with the crash. She was devastated both times for different reasons. And in the end, the good memories had lasted longer than the bad ones. But there was always the knowledge that he would have divorced her if he'd lived, which cast a shadow on how she felt about him.

"I didn't want you to think less of him. He was very nice about it, but he wanted out. It didn't matter anymore after he died. You didn't need to know and you were young. I didn't see why I should tell you, but Grandma always thought I should once you grew up. I hope she's right." Anthony had gone back to his seat by then, looking crushed. "He was a wonderful father and that would never have changed, and a terrific husband for fourteen years, until he wanted out. Sometimes that's all you get."

"But you always made him sound like a hero to us," Tammy said. Claire hadn't said a word, she didn't remember her father very clearly, but Tammy had been thirteen when he died, and a divorce would have seemed like a tragedy to her, even if his new wife was nice.

"He was a hero, to his country, to all of you, to me for a long time. But he was a human being. People change their minds, they fall in and out of love, good and bad things happen to them, they make mistakes, sometimes they hurt the people they love. It doesn't make them monsters. It makes them real. I still miss your father and I still love him, even though we would have been divorced if he'd survived. I still remember the good times, and we had a lot of them. And he gave me the three of you. I'll always be grateful to him for that."

"After everything Mom's been through, you have to make an ass of yourself having a baby out of wedlock? Is that really necessary?" Anthony said angrily to Claire, and her grandmother stepped in on her behalf.

"People have a right to make choices, Anthony, whether others approve or not. Maybe you'll make choices the rest of us won't like one day. I don't agree with Claire, but she has a right to do what she believes in."

"She believes in being a pain in the ass to Mom. That's what this is all about. She's not fifteen, for chrissake. Why can't she get married and have a baby like everyone else?"

"She doesn't want to. She's not committing a crime. She's making a choice. There's a difference. She's not doing it to hurt anyone. She believes in what she's doing, whether we like it or not. And I think that's what your mother is telling you about your dad. He made a tough choice, wanting a divorce. But he believed in it. It doesn't make him a bad man, or a bad father. It makes him human."

"It would have been a rotten thing to do to Mom," Anthony said fiercely. He had been ten when his father died, and a divorce would have had a huge impact on him too.

"True," his grandmother said to him, "but these are the chances we take when we love people. Not every story has a happy ending, and you can't always predict the way it will turn out. Sometimes there are some bad surprises in our lives."

"Thank you, Grandma," Claire said softly, for coming to her defense earlier.

"You've certainly given us all a lot to think about," Tammy said to her mother. "I'm not sure yet what the message is here, maybe to be honest with each other and ourselves. You didn't have to cover up for Dad for all these years. You didn't owe him that. And maybe the real message is to forgive each other for our differences and our mistakes." She looked at her younger sister when she said it. "I think you and Reed should get married too, but I'll still support you if you don't. You can't get married just to please Mom, although I can't figure out how you could grow up in this house with all of us, and turn out to be so unconventional."

"Maybe it's because I grew up with all of you," Claire said clearly, visibly enjoying her new role as rebel. She'd never been this oppositional or outspoken before. "Everyone in this family is so perfect all the time. The best schools, the best jobs, the best father and mother, and some of that turns out to be bullshit. Mom got pregnant by mistake at nineteen, Dad must have cheated on her and fell in love with someone else. I don't want to do what all of you do, just because I'm expected to. I'd rather kill myself than have a big wedding like Anthony and Amanda. Reed and I just want to live together, have our baby, and be happy. Half the people who get married end up divorced anyway, so why bother? Mom and Dad would have been divorced if the helicopter hadn't crashed." And then she turned to her mother. "Is that why you never wanted to get married again? I always thought it was because you were so in love with Dad."

"That's partly true," Kate admitted. "It took me a long time to get over his death. Going to law school helped. But I never want to lose someone again, by divorce, or death. It scares me to love anyone that much again. What if they died or left me?"

"Would you ever marry Bart?" Anthony asked her. He had always wondered about it and he liked him.

"I don't think so. I like him a lot and we have a good time. But I don't love him enough. You have to love someone a lot to want to spend the rest of your life with them. I loved your dad that much, but not Bart. I've never met anyone I wanted to take that chance with again. It didn't seem worth the risk."

"It's not over yet," Tammy reminded her with a smile. "You're still young enough to meet someone you really love."

"Oh I hope not," Kate said fervently, and they all laughed. "Loving someone that much is so much trouble. I'll leave that up to all of you. I don't want to do that again." Anthony was listening to her intently, and Amanda was looking miffed over what Claire had said about their big wedding. She was glad that she hadn't asked her to be a bridesmaid if that was what she thought of it, especially now that she was unmarried and pregnant. Her parents were going to be shocked by it. She had decided she wasn't close enough to either of Anthony's sisters to have them be bridesmaids. She liked Tammy better anyway. She thought Claire was shitty to her. Her disapproval of Amanda came through her pores.

"Well, it hasn't been much of a birthday," Kate said ruefully, "but it's been a great night with all of you, and I guess all these things needed to be aired. It seems Grandma was right. You're old enough now, secrets never do anyone any good. The truth is always better, as long as it's delivered gently and not said to hurt people. I'm sorry

I told you that about your father, but it shows us all that unexpected things happen in lives, and in marriages. And I'm sorry if you all feel I put too much pressure on you to be perfect, growing up and now. Believe me, I'm not perfect either. I just want the best that you can have for each of you. But in the end, I just want you to be happy. And, Claire, if you're happy doing what you are, then I guess we'll all have to get used to it."

"I'm scared too," Claire admitted. "A baby is a huge responsibility and I hope I'm up to it. Reed is wonderful to me. I'm a very lucky woman."

"I think you are." Kate smiled at her. They hadn't invited Reed that night, but Kate intended to in the future, since he was th father of her first grandchild, and living with her daughter. He appeared to be a good person with sound values. Kate would have liked him better if they'd met in other circumstances. "Any more true confessions?" Kate said jokingly as she looked around the table and no one said a word. Anthony hugged Claire when they got up from dinner, and told her what a little shit she was, but that he loved her anyway. Tammy gave her a big hug too, and they all hugged their mother, and had new respect for her. She had blown the lid right off the birthday dinner with her confessions and there had been no cake because she didn't want one.

It was nearly midnight when they all left. Anthony took his grandmother home in a cab, and she kissed him when they dropped her off. Amanda was silent on the ride back to her apartment, and Anthony sat staring out the window.

"I thought your sister was really rude about our wedding," she said. Anthony didn't say anything for a minute and then just nodded. "She should get married. Having a baby out of wedlock is really shocking." He turned to look at Amanda then.

"You heard what my grandmother said. People have a right to make choices, and even mistakes."

"That's a big one." She wondered if her parents would even want Claire at the wedding, but didn't say so.

He followed her into the apartment, and when she turned on the lights, he looked at her and knew what he had to do. He didn't know if Alicia would ever speak to him again, but even if she didn't, it didn't matter. He had finally figured out the answer he'd been looking for when his mother answered him about marrying Bart, and said she didn't love him enough. He loved some things about Amanda, and they'd had a good time for a while, but he didn't love her enough to marry her and to spend the rest of his life with her. He was bored to death with the life she wanted, and he didn't even want a big wedding. He didn't love her enough was the correct answer.

She could see that something was happening, but she didn't know what, as he stood and stared at her.

"I have to tell you something, and there's no easy way to do this. I can't marry you, Amanda. I thought I could, but I just can't do it. It's not right. I should have figured it out sooner, but I didn't. And better now than after we're married. I love you, but not enough to spend the rest of my life with you. I'm truly sorry, but I know that now." His voice was strong and even and full of regret. But he was sure.

Her mouth opened and closed several times and no sound came out at first. "Are you serious? Are you crazy? Do you know what my father has already spent on this wedding?"

"I can't help it. I can't do it. It's just not right, for either of us. I'm not the right man for you either." He was absolutely certain now.

"Do you want me to scale back on the wedding? We could have fewer bridesmaids. My father hasn't paid for the dresses yet." But the person Anthony wanted to eliminate was the bride.

"It's not about the wedding. It's about the rest of our lives. I'm not cut out to sit in Bronxville with you, or move there, or live the life you want. I'm not ready to have kids, and you want them immediately. You want a life like your parents', and that's not who I am. I want to work and play and travel and laugh and have fun and be free" and be with a woman who's so crazy about me that she'll give me a black eye when I turn her life upside down. He wanted to be with Alicia, but he didn't know if that would happen now. The one thing he did know for certain was that he didn't want to be with Amanda, just like his mother didn't want to marry Bart. Anthony didn't love her enough. He was sure of it now. It was the right answer and the one he'd been looking for.

"You're upset over what your mother said about your father. This is ridiculous, Anthony. We love each other." She sounded desperate and he felt sorry for her. Unraveling the wedding and telling her parents was going to be a nightmare. But it had to be done. He couldn't go through with it, no matter what her father had spent.

"We do love each other," he agreed with her, "but not enough to get married." He looked at her sadly for a minute, and turned around and started to walk away.

"Where are you going?"

"Back to my place," he said at the door. "I'm leaving. I can't stay here anymore. It's not right."

"Can't you at least spend the night?"

"No, I can't. I'm sorry. I'll pick up my things this week when you're at work." She didn't say anything, as tears started to roll down her cheeks, and he felt terrible. But he knew that if he tried to comfort her, he'd get trapped again, and maybe even marry her out of pity or remorse. He had to go now. As he was leaving, she pulled off the engagement ring that had been his mother's. They had had it reset in a new mounting for her. She took two steps toward him and put it in his hand. He shoved it in his jacket pocket, to give back to his mother, opened the door, and walked out.

He closed the door softly behind him, and took a cab back to his apartment. It was empty and dusty and looked unloved, and he was lonely when he got there, but as he lay down on the bed and stared up at the ceiling, Anthony knew he had done the right thing. He was free. It was a huge relief.

When Tammy got back to her apartment, Stacey was almost asleep. She'd been up with a sick patient at the hospital the night before, a six-year-old with a hot appendix, and she had just started to drift off when Tammy sat down on their bed with a big smile.

"Great news," Tammy announced as Stacey opened one eye.

"Your mom wants to march in the Gay Pride parade with us this year?" They'd never done that, and Tammy laughed at the image.

"Better than that. My little sister gave us a free pass."

"To what? Stop talking in riddles, I'm half asleep."

"She's having a baby with her boyfriend and refusing to get married. My mother had a fit over it, but my grandmother said everyone has the right to make choices, no matter who likes it or not. And my sister said she's sick and tired of being perfect. So she's having the baby and not getting married. I'm going to see my mom in the next couple of days and tell her about us. I'm giving up my claim to the perfect title too, tiara and all. And my mother admitted that she got pregnant as a teenager and had to get married, and my father was about to leave her for another woman when he died. It turns out we're not so perfect after all. We're as screwed up as everyone else, so you and I get to come out of the closet, *finally!*"

"Do you think your mom can handle it?" Stacey was wide awake by then, and sat up in bed.

"I think she can. She's so upset at my sister, I'm not even sure she'll care."

"She'll care. I'm not sure where gay ranks on the list with pregnant out of wedlock, but gay might be worse. Can't your brother do something unsuitable *too*?"

"I have a feeling there's trouble brewing there as well. He looks miserable. Anyway, get ready to meet my crazy family." She kissed Stacey, who was beaming. It was exciting news. The time had finally come to tell the truth, after seven years.

They giggled like two schoolgirls when Tammy came to bed and told her all about the dinner. It had been quite an evening, and a birthday Tammy was sure her mother would never forget.

Chapter 9

Kate was startled when her secretary told her at twelve o'clock that her son was waiting for her in the reception area, the day after her birthday dinner. She was planning to work through lunch, and he never came to her office. She went out to meet him herself. He looked somber and serious in a clean shirt, jacket, and jeans. He never went to work looking that way, he had dressed to come and see her at the law firm.

His eyes met hers with a grave expression. She knew something had happened the moment she saw him. She kissed him and led him to her office before questioning him, but she didn't need to. He told her before he even sat down in the chair across from her desk.

"I broke it off with Amanda last night after dinner," he said, looking anxious. He was certain she'd be upset with him but she could see how sure he was from the look on his face.

"Did you have an argument?" He shook his head as he sat down on the edge of the chair.

"You said exactly what I feel when I asked you about Bart. I don't love Amanda enough to marry her."

"Are you sure?"

"A hundred percent."

She sighed and looked at him sympathetically. She knew it couldn't have been easy to say to her, and she hoped he'd been kind to Amanda, as best he could be when telling her something like that. "Well, your sister and grandmother will be pleased. They both thought she was wrong for you."

"Tammy?" He looked surprised.

"Claire."

"Well, we know now how good her judgment is. What a mess she's making of her life. She should just shut up and marry the guy."

"She's making a statement," Kate said, looking tired.

"And an ass of herself. She's being a spoiled brat, to prove a point and get at you."

"It goes with the territory. How do you feel? Sad?"

"A little, for Amanda mostly. But mainly relieved. I've been crawling out of my skin with the wedding, and in Bronxville with her parents every weekend. I think I'd kill myself or become an alcoholic if I married her." Kate nodded. She could see it now too. Amanda wasn't bright enough for him. Her mother and Claire were right. She didn't try to talk him into changing his mind. And she could see that she couldn't. She noticed that he was squirming in his chair, and looked as though he had something else to say.

"There's more?" He nodded, looking very nervous, but he wanted to tell her all of it.

"I met someone three months ago. I fell madly in love with her, which was my first clue that Amanda wasn't the right woman for me. I haven't seen her in a month, and she swore she'd never see me again. I lied to her, and didn't tell her I was engaged. We were together for almost two months, and then I told her. I needed time with Amanda to see how I felt about her. I haven't seen the other woman in a month. She probably wants nothing to do with me, but on the off chance that she'll forgive me and talks to me again, I wanted to tell you that I'm in love with her. I'm sure of it now. She's wild and smart, and she won't put up with any shit from me. She gave me the black eye when I told her about Amanda." His mother looked shocked at that. Domestic violence was not an acceptable means of communication in her opinion.

"Does she have a name? A job? A family?" He nodded.

"Alicia Gomez. She's thirty years old, and putting herself through Hunter College. She's a lingerie model to pay her rent, and wants to become an actress, and she's probably a good one. She was born in San Juan, Puerto Rico, and grew up in Spanish Harlem, and she's three quarters Puerto Rican and a quarter Chinese." He had handed it all to her on a silver platter, and she looked as though she had seen a ghost over his head.

"Are you serious?"

"I am. She's got incredible drive and spirit, and she's smart as a whip."

"She must be to catch you. Where did you meet her or shouldn't I ask?"

"At my gym."

"And you're in love with her? Or in lust with her? Something tells me she must be beautiful with that combination."

"She is. And I am both, in love and in lust. I actually think you'd like her, Mom, if you can get past all the obvious things I know you'll object to."

"You must think I'm a snob and a racist," she said unhappily.

"No, but I know what you liked about Amanda. Her family's social position and respectability. Alicia is the exact opposite of Amanda. She's had to fight for everything she has, and she's very independent. I tried to send her a text this morning, and she's blocked me. I don't know if she'll ever speak to me again."

"Well, let me know how it goes." She didn't object to anything he had said and he was stunned. "Your grandmother is right. You all have the right to make choices, whether I like them or not."

"Except for Claire. She's being an idiot and ridiculously immature." She didn't disagree with him.

"Even Claire. I don't like the decisions she's making, but she has a right to make them. We'll just have to live with it. I like her man a lot though. It's something at least. So we'll see about Miss Gomez, if she forgives you. It sounds like you behaved very badly with her," Kate said sternly and he nodded. He felt like a kid in the principal's office.

"I did. She has every right to be pissed."

"But not to give you a black eye, I don't approve of that."

She got up and came around her desk and kissed him.

"I meant what I said last night. I just want you all to be happy, and safe. I'm going to have to give up my ideas of what I thought would be good for you. I thought Amanda would be a good wife you could rely on, but I guess she's not for you."

"She really isn't, Mom." He remembered the ring then, pulled it out of his pocket and handed it to her. "I'm sorry we screwed up your engagement ring, changing it for Amanda."

"It's okay. I wanted to give it to you anyway, for when you get married one day. Your dad would have wanted you to have it." She walked him to the door of her office and hugged him again.

"Let me know how it turns out," she smiled at him, "and duck this time. Don't just let her hit you." He grinned at his mother, and a moment later he was gone and she went back to her desk. Her secretary came in a minute later.

"Do we have any Tylenol, Advil, aspirin, arsenic, heroin, something? I have a blinding headache." Her calm exterior hid a tidal wave of stress.

"I have Advil in my purse. I'll bring you two."

"Thank you," Kate said as she sat down at her desk and put the engagement ring in her purse.

She could hardly keep up with them, canceled weddings, illegitimate babies. Her perfect children were certainly far from perfect. And she couldn't even imagine what Anthony's lingerie model was going to look like or how she'd behave. If she even agreed to see him again, which was by no means a sure thing, according to him.

Her secretary brought her the Advil and she took two, and she brought her a cup of tea after that. Kate could only imagine how Amanda's parents were feeling, if she had already called them. They would be furious, but three months' notice to cancel a wedding was reasonable. And if Anthony didn't love her enough to marry her, there was nothing to discuss. Thank God he hadn't gone through with it. The wedding had sounded like a three ring circus. In some ways, Kate was relieved too. She just hoped that things turned out right for him, and that the Puerto Rican girl wasn't even worse. These were certainly interesting times in her family. A lingerie model, or even an actress, was not what she had wanted for her son, but the debutante hadn't worked out either, so it was a free-for-all now. She could hardly wait for the next chapter. More than ever, their lives were beginning to feel like a bad movie.

She got a pained email from Amanda's father an hour later, bemoaning Anthony's breaking the engagement and canceling the wedding. He said that he was sending Amanda and her mother to Paris for a few weeks. This was going to be very hard for Amanda, and he didn't mention what it was costing him to cancel the wedding. But Kate knew that if it was not meant to be, it was better for both of them that it was over.

Her secretary stuck her head in the door then, to remind Kate that she had a meeting with opposing counsel and his associate on the big lawsuit that was brewing. They would be meeting in the conference room. Kate had forgotten it completely.

"Thanks for telling me. I may need more Advil before that's over." She returned some calls and answered emails, ate half a sandwich, and at two o'clock she was ready for the attorneys' meeting, and took Ed Buckman, one of her associates, with her. The meeting lasted for two hours of ranting and raving and threats from plaintiff's counsel, and by the time it was over, she wanted to kill someone. She wasn't sure who she disliked more, the opposing counsel, or his partner. From what she could see they were both arrogant, angling for a big settlement, and had a losing case and they knew it. They were from one of the most powerful law firms in the city and thought they walked on water. She wanted to snarl at them when they left the room, but she waited until they were well out of earshot before telling Ed what she thought of them, and he agreed.

"I've known Jack Hirsch for twenty years. He's a complete asshole in the courtroom, but the new guy, his partner, Scott White, is tough as nails. He's going to give us a run for our money on this one, even though they don't have squat to work with, and their client is a bigger jerk than they are and is lying through his teeth."

"We're tougher than they are," Kate said staunchly. "They have a crap case and they know it. I'm not offering them a penny."

"I love working with you, Kate," Ed said, and smiled as he went back to his office. He loved a good fight, and Kate was one of the best. She was a killer in the courtroom and at the negotiating table. Her depositions were famous for making people squirm.

Kate's headache was even more intense by the end of the day, when Tammy called her.

"Want to have lunch tomorrow?" Tammy asked her. Kate checked her calendar, and saw that she was free.

"Sure, I'd love to."

"That was some birthday party last night."

"Your brother broke up with Amanda today, and canceled the wedding."

"I thought something was going to happen when they left." She didn't tell Tammy about the other woman. It might never happen anyway. Kate wasn't even upset about it yet. There were too many other things on her plate, at work and at home. She couldn't let herself think about it or she'd get depressed, and she needed her wits about her for work, and to deal with Claire.

She set a time and place for lunch with Tammy the next day, and left the office at seven-thirty, after reading the discovery files again for the new case. It was shaping up nicely in spite of the hostile meeting with the two opposing lawyers that day. She was willing to go to the mat on this one, and wouldn't agree to a settlement easily. She thought they'd win if they went to trial, which wouldn't be for another year or two. But litigation would be expensive for her client to win the case. This was just the beginning. She was thinking about it on the way home, when her mother called her on her cell in the cab.

"Are you holding up all right?"

"I think so. Anthony broke up with Amanda today," she said in a tired voice.

"I know. He called me. He mentioned another woman to me a couple of months ago. I thought it was a bad sign."

"You were right about Amanda. She bored him to death."

"Do you know anything about the other woman?" Margaret asked her.

"Only that she grew up in Spanish Harlem, is a lingerie model, and gave him a black eye. She's not speaking to him, which is the best news I've had all day. I'm not even upset. My family is falling apart, Mom. You were right about that too. Suddenly they're acting out all over the place. Tammy is the only one left standing. I'm having lunch with her tomorrow."

"Well, there are no surprises there. You can rely on that," she said confidently. "She's the most solid of your children. She always has been. Oldest child syndrome. She takes care of everyone else."

"She's the only sane one left. Anthony and Claire seem to be losing their minds," although Anthony seemed sensible and sure of his decision.

"Try not to let it upset you. They'll come around and straighten up again."

"I hope so. I feel like everything's upside down right now."

"They're the same people they always were. They're just making different choices than you would have wanted them to make."

"There's a major understatement. A baby out of wedlock and an underwear model? What's next? I'm afraid to answer my phone."

"Try to get some rest. You sound exhausted."

"I am. I'll call you tomorrow," Kate promised and they hung up.

By the time Kate got home, Anthony had been trying to reach Alicia all day. She had blocked both her phone and her email to him. He couldn't think of any other way to reach her to tell her that he had broken his engagement and it was over with Amanda. He had sent Amanda a text earlier that day to see how she was. She said she was going to Paris with her mother, and he was relieved. He didn't want her to be destroyed by this, he just didn't want to marry her. It would have destroyed him. He was certain of that now.

He tried Alicia's Skype account and she didn't answer. She didn't respond to FaceTime or WhatsApp. He was dead as far as she was concerned. He had no way to reach her, and after work, he went to her apartment building, checked that her name was still on the bell, and sat on the stoop waiting for her. By eight o'clock, there was still no sign of her, and he could see that there was no light in her windows. He wondered if she was out with another man, and then he saw her, coming down the street in jeans and flat shoes with her bag of schoolbooks in her hand. She stopped ten feet away when she saw him.

"What, are you stalking me now? Get off my front steps or I'm calling the police." Her voice was harsh and she looked angry. She sounded like the street fighter she had been as a teenager. He remembered her promise to kick his ass if he ever came near her again, and he believed she would.

"I just wanted to tell you that it's over. I ended it. I broke the engagement, if it makes any difference to you."

"It doesn't. I don't care. You're a piece of shit, and you lied to me."

"I know I did. It was stupid and wrong and cowardly. I was too afraid of losing you."

"Well, you did, now go away and leave me alone, or I'll get a court order against you."

"Or give me another black eye?" he said, wanting to put his arms around her but there was no way he could. She would have killed him.

"You can have another one of those too, if you want."

"Can we just talk for a few minutes? I only wanted to tell you how sorry I am. I really mean it."

"Now you've told me, so get lost." She was wearing her street fighter face and looked at him with disgust.

"Alicia, please . . ."

"No! You think I'd let you do that to me again? I don't trust you. Why should I?"

"Because I'm an honest man who made a really stupid mistake and I love you."

"That is the worst bullshit excuse I've ever heard. You're pathetic *and* a liar."

"I'm not lying to you now."

"Congratulations. What do you want from me?"

"Another chance," he said, realizing how pathetic he sounded, but he meant it.

"I'm not stupid, Anthony. Why would I do that?"

"Maybe because you loved me too."

"I did. Past tense. I don't give second chances. You blew it."

"And what does that get you? The Toughest Girl of the Year Award? You can kick everyone's ass? Can't you be human about this?"

"You weren't. What you did was disgusting."

"Yes, it was. It was a shit beginning, but I'm free now. We could do it better this time, if you give me a chance."

"If you lied to me again, I'd have to kill you. And you're not worth it."

"Are you seeing someone else?" He felt sick as he asked her.

"That's none of your business." She had been crying over him for over a month, but she would have died rather than tell him, and she liked seeing him standing there next to her front stairs, begging her for forgiveness and another chance. She wasn't going to give it to him. She had too much self-respect for that, and she was too scared he'd hurt her again. No one had ever hurt her as he had. She had never loved any man as she had him. She had let her guard down, and he had burned her. The last thing she wanted was to give him the opportunity to do it again.

"Can we go for coffee somewhere?"

"No, we can't. Now get out of my way, I have homework to do." He couldn't stand arguing with her anymore and she was winning. He took three long strides toward her, and pulled her into his arms and just held her there. She tried to take a swing at him, but he wouldn't let her this time. He was ready for her. He didn't hurt her or even try to kiss her, he just held her as gently but firmly as he could, and he was stronger than she was.

"I'm in love with you. I've thought of you every waking moment since you walked away," he said holding her tightly.

"I was in love with you too. You broke my heart. I'm not giving you another chance to do it again," she said, struggling to get out of his grip.

"I won't. I swear."

"I don't believe you, and I hate you," she said, but the fight had gone out of her. He could feel it, and he kissed her, gently at first and then passionately when she responded. They clung to each other like two drowning people, their bodies pressed together. He could feel her heart pounding against him like a bird in a cage, and he moaned just holding her. He had thought of her a million times since they had left each other. Her books were all over the sidewalk, and he picked them up, and handed them back to her, as she stood looking at him with tears in her eyes. She walked up the front steps then, and he followed her, and she didn't stop him.

They walked to her front door, and she unlocked it with shaking hands, and the moment they were inside, he slammed the door closed with his foot and she was in his arms, and they were pulling each other's clothes off. She stopped for an instant to look long and hard at him. "If you *ever* lie to me again, I'll be gone so fast you won't know what hit you." He nodded, and by the time they got to her bed, they were both naked and their lovemaking was even more white hot than he remembered or maybe it was even better than it had been, because they had missed each other so much. It went on for hours, loving her was exquisite agony and being with her was the culmination of all his dreams. When they finally lay together, spent, in a tangle of sheets, she smiled at him, and he felt as though he had died and gone to Heaven.

"I love you, Alicia, thank you . . . thank you . . ."

"I love you too," she said softly. "You wouldn't be here now if I didn't."

They lay there talking for a long time, until he was aroused again, and then they made love until the sun came up. It was the longest and happiest night of his life, and hers.

Chapter 10

Kate met Tammy at one of the restaurants in easy walking distance from her office. Claire preferred the fancy French one, and Tammy preferred the simpler Italian restaurant with pasta and good salads. Tammy was already seated when Kate got there, out of breath, and ten minutes late.

"I'm sorry I'm late. Work is out of control right now. Everyone comes back from their vacation happy and relaxed, and they all want to sue each other."

"Well, I'm not suing anyone." Tammy smiled at her. She looked healthy and tan after her vacation in Maine with Stacey. They'd done some sailing, kayaking, and canoeing, and a lot of hiking. It was the perfect counterpoint to their busy lives. Tammy had to leave for Paris soon, for fashion week, and the Chanel show of ready-to-wear. "Thank you for making time to have lunch. That was certainly an interesting dinner the other night. I'm sorry it all happened on your birthday."

"I should have known it would. The opportunity was too tempting for Claire to resist. What do you think of her news?"

Tammy thought about it before she answered. "I think it's too bad she's being so stubborn about it. I think she's going about it all the wrong way. Everyone would be happy for her if she were getting married. As it is, everyone will be shocked. What's the point of that? I don't know why she's so adamant about not getting married."

"Neither do I. I think Reed would rather get married too. Girls her age seem to have babies all the time now without getting married. I don't see what it proves."

"How's Anthony doing after the big breakup?"

"I haven't talked to him today, but he was very sure about his decision yesterday when he came to my office to tell me. I'm disappointed for him, but he can't marry her if he doesn't love her."

"He's been looking nervous and unhappy for a while. I don't think Amanda even noticed it. She was so busy planning the wedding."

"I think that may have been what scared him off, and apparently he met someone else a while ago, which threw him for a loop. What about you?" Kate looked seriously at her oldest daughter. "Are you okay after all the revelations the other night?"

Tammy nodded. "In a way it's very freeing, to realize that things weren't perfect for you and Dad either. Maybe your telling us that gave Anthony the courage to break up with Amanda and cancel the wedding. It was liberating for me too," she started down the slippery slope, and was praying that she'd say the right things. "Actually, that's why I wanted to have lunch with you today."

"Liberating in what sense?" Kate looked puzzled as their pasta came. Tammy didn't touch hers. She was too nervous to eat.

"There's something I've wanted to tell you for a long time. I should have years ago," as she said it, her mother looked at her, mystified. "Mom, I'm gay," she said without lowering her voice. She didn't want it to be a secret anymore.

"You mean as in happy?" Kate said, and Tammy almost laughed. "I don't think people say that these days."

"No, gay as in homosexual. I'm a lesbian, Mom." If she had taken a gun out of her purse and shot her mother, she wouldn't have looked more shocked.

"Are you serious? Is this a joke?" Tammy was beginning to think she had made a terrible mistake telling her, but it was too late to turn back. She had to keep paddling now. They were going over the waterfall, and there was no way to stop.

"Yes, I'm serious, and no, it's not a joke. I never wanted to upset you by telling you, so I've been lying to all of you. I've been living with a woman for seven years."

"As lovers?" Kate looked as though she were about to faint into her plate. The idea that Tammy was gay was so preposterous that she looked as though she didn't understand what she was saying.

"Yes, if you want to put it that way."

"Were you always gay?"

"I figured it out when I was about fifteen, maybe sixteen. I didn't act on it till I got to college. In high school, I was afraid someone would tell, and I knew you'd be upset. How are you now?" Tammy felt as though she should take her mother's blood pressure, and added to everything else that was happening, she was suddenly afraid it would be too much, and she'd have a heart attack. Kate didn't look angry, she looked stunned.

"I think I'm all right. Why didn't you ever tell me?" She seemed hurt.

"I didn't want to disappoint you. I wanted to tell you when I was in college, but I never had the guts. And then once I was working, it was easier not to say anything. When I had to, I lied. I don't want to lie about it anymore. When you told us about you, and Dad, the other night, I thought it was time to be honest with you about myself. I live with a wonderful woman. She deserves to know you, and be included when I am. It's been very hurtful for her that I've been hiding her for all these years." Kate nodded, trying to be gracious about it, as she tried to rewind the mental film of Tammy's life and look for the clues she had missed.

"Did you ever date men?" Kate couldn't remember any, but there was always some explanation for it. She just thought that Tammy had never fallen in love yet and was a late bloomer.

"No, I didn't. I never wanted to. Some women figure it out later than I did. A lot of them marry and have kids. I'm not attracted to men." She said it so simply that there was nothing Kate could say. She looked sad for her more than angry or disappointed. And she felt as though she was seeing her daughter for the first time, or had just been told she had a terrible illness. Tammy hated the pity in her eyes.

"Do you want children?"

"Maybe. I've never been sure. Stacey, my partner, wants them, but she's used to them. She's a pediatrician. I've never been around kids so they scare me a little. And it is a huge responsibility. I'm not ready for that yet."

"Is she the roommate you had several years ago?" Tammy nodded.

"I told you she moved out, but she never did. I'm so tired of lying to you, Mom. I know this is a big piece of news to drop on you now, especially with Claire and everything going on with her, and Anthony, but I want to be honest with you. I've wanted that for a long time."

"It's right that you should be. I'm your mother. I just wonder what I was doing or thinking that I never even thought of it as a possibility. In high school, I thought you were shy. In college, I thought you were discreet. And since then I figured you were too busy working to have a life. How the hell did I miss something like this?" She reached out and touched Tammy's hand. "I'm so sorry, I really am. Can you ever forgive me? I've been blind and out to lunch for your entire life," she said as they held hands.

"I'm also a damn good liar." She smiled at her mother, and their pasta was cold by then. Neither of them had touched it, and they started to dig into their salads. But Kate wasn't hungry. She was too shaken by what Tammy had shared. Her oldest daughter was a lesbian. Her youngest daughter was having a baby out of wedlock, and her son was in love with a lingerie model who had grown up in Spanish Harlem and was part Chinese. All put together, it was overwhelming, and she tried to focus on just Tammy now. Kate felt as though the walls were coming down around her. She felt like Alice in Wonderland down the rabbit hole.

"If you decided to have a baby, how would you do it?" Kate asked her. "Would you adopt?"

"We could. I think we'd be more likely to get a sperm donor, and one of us would get pregnant, probably me, since Stacey is nine years older than I am. It might be harder for her to get pregnant." They had discussed it before, and Tammy was still nervous about it. She didn't feel equipped for motherhood yet. Unlike her sister, she was cautious and still unsure. "I wouldn't want to do it unless we got married, not like Claire." She smiled at her mother. "Now that same-sex marriage is an option, it's a possibility. But I'm in no rush to get married."

"None of my children are, it seems," Kate said wryly. "Thank you for being so open with me now. It's a lot to think about. I'd like to meet Stacey sometime."

"She's wanted to meet you for seven years." Tammy was impressed by how her mother had risen to the occasion. She could see that she was struggling with it, but she was trying, which was all that mattered. It was a start.

"What's she like?"

"Smart, funny, patient, kind, a terrific doctor. She works very hard. Her family is from Ohio, and they've been very accepting of both of us."

"You know them?"

"I've met them a few times. Her father is a doctor. I think it was hard for them in the beginning, but they've known about Stacey for a long time. Her mother says she's known about Stacey since she was little. She wanted to play with her brothers' toy trucks all the time. She has a brother, and another one who died. They're just regular people, and they're okay with it. She told her brothers before she told her parents. She's the oldest, so they expected a lot from her."

"You were the girliest girl I've ever seen," Kate said with tears in her eyes. "You still are." Claire was much less frilly than her older sister, although she was sexier. Tammy was fashionable and chic.

When they left the restaurant, Tammy hugged her mother and thanked her for being so understanding. She called Stacey from the cab on the way back to her office and told her it had gone fine. Her mother had been wonderful although she was shocked at first, and she promised to arrange a meeting soon. She wanted to give her mother a chance to digest everything before they met. She'd had a big dose of reality all at once, and she was getting it from all sides.

When Kate got back to her office, she looked dazed. She walked past her secretary without even noticing her, who walked in a few minutes later to check on Kate.

"More Advil?"

"No, actually, I think a week in Bellevue would be nice." Her whole world was coming apart at the seams. She couldn't help questioning what kind of mother she had been. Claire was defying all the values she'd grown up with. Anthony had just canceled his wedding to what had seemed like the perfect girl. And Tammy was gay and she'd never noticed. Where the hell had she been while she thought she was being such a good mother? She had missed all the clues and the signs of who they really were and what they wanted, or needed. When her secretary left the room, she dialed her mother's number. Margaret answered on the second ring and sounded

distracted, which meant she was painting, but she answered anyway when she saw Kate's number come up.

"Can I come by after work?" she asked bluntly.

"Is something wrong?"

"Is anything right at the moment?"

"Are you okay?"

"I guess so. Is there a choice?"

"Come whenever you want."

"I'll try to leave the office early."

She left at five-thirty, and got to Margaret's apartment at six,
which was early for Kate. She couldn't concentrate on her work
anyway, she had too much on her mind. And now one more very
major thing.

She kissed her mother absentmindedly when she walked in.

"Do you want a glass of wine?"

"Do you have anything stronger? Vodka maybe?" Margaret
pulled a bottle out of the freezer, poured some over ice and handed
it to her.

"What happened today?"

Kate sat down in her mother's kitchen, took a sip of the stiff
drink, and looked at her mother. "Tammy's gay."

"Wow," Margaret said, looking stunned too, "I completely missed
that. It never even occurred to me. Some shrink I am."

"She's been lying to us for years. She's been living with a woman
for seven years, a pediatrician."

"What did you say to her?"

"What can I say? It's who she is. They might get married and they might have a baby, but Tammy's not sure. She's always been more cautious than Claire or Anthony, and she takes longer to make decisions. But what I want to know is where was I when all this was happening? I was so busy worrying about what schools they went to, doing homework with them so they'd get into good colleges, and trying to keep my head above water, I missed everything else. I feel like this whole family, which I thought was so solid, with my supposedly perfect kids, was a house of cards, and it's all flat on the ground now like pick-up sticks. Their lives are in shambles and so is mine."

"It looks like that right now. They're all in a transition of some kind, but their foundation is solid. That's what you gave them, Kate. They'll build it all back up again, stronger than before. They're all the same kids you knew, they've just made very different choices from the ones you thought they'd make. You can't make those choices for them. It's up to them now. And nothing about Tammy has changed. She just likes women instead of men. That doesn't change her value system. She's the most solid of your children. That hasn't changed."

"Why didn't I notice it?" she asked, taking another sip of her drink. "Do you mind if I get drunk?"

"Actually, yes, I do. I'm still your mother. I'm cutting you off after this one. You've earned it though." Kate felt as though she had lost all her familiar landmarks. Everything had crumbled, and a flood had washed it all away. What was left after this? And how were her grandchildren going to grow up now? One without a legal father, and another, if they had any, with two mothers? She felt as though everything she had built for the past thirty years had vanished suddenly. The family she loved and had been so proud of had disappeared, and strangers had taken their place.

"I'd like to meet her partner," Margaret said quietly. "She sounds interesting."

"I'm sure she is. And intelligent. Tammy told me she went to Harvard, undergraduate and med school." Tammy had gone to Brown. They were obviously both very bright women. "It's funny how it all happens at once, isn't it? All three of them," Kate said wistfully.

"That's how life works, the good and the bad. It comes in bunches, like grapes. They'll settle down again, in the right places. It sounds like Tammy already has. Claire needs to grow up, and Anthony has to figure out what he wants, and not just follow what he thinks you want for him. I think that's what happened with Amanda. You thought she was perfect for him, and he believed you."

"Well, he's following his own path now. This girl couldn't be more different. He says he's in love with her. I want to meet her too, if she goes back to him. He didn't think she would."

"She gave him a hell of a shiner," Margaret commented. "She sounds like a handful. Maybe that's what he wants, or needs. Amanda was too bland. She didn't challenge him."

"What do I know?" Kate said as she finished her drink. Her mother had been sparing with the vodka, with a lot of ice. "I don't even know what I want anymore. Or what I need."

"You need some sleep, and to worry less about your children. It doesn't stop them from doing what they want anyway. You have to trust that they'll figure it out for themselves."

"They're not doing much of a job of it at the moment."

"Yes, they are," her mother disagreed with her. "Anthony got out of what would have been a disastrous marriage, Tammy told you the truth about herself, and Claire found herself a good guy, even if she's going about it the wrong way, in our opinion. But that's not a bad start. It could be a lot worse."

"Could it?" Kate was feeling a little drunk even after one drink, but she'd eaten almost nothing for lunch with Tammy's stunning announcement. "I'd better go home," she said, standing up, and put her arms around her mother. "Thank you for keeping me sane. And now I've got this damn huge case to deal with, and the lawyers on the other side are driving me crazy. I hate plaintiffs' attorneys, they're such jerks. They're going to nitpick us to death on this case."

"It'll keep you busy. You need that right now," her mother said wisely. "Or your children will drive you crazier." She smiled at her daughter.

Kate picked up her briefcase and kissed her mother goodbye, and left a minute later. She took a cab home, and as soon as she got there, she lay down on her bed and stared at the ceiling. She was still lying there, when the doorman buzzed her five minutes later and said there was a delivery for her. She walked to the door and a delivery man handed her an enormous arrangement of flowers. She couldn't imagine who would send them to her. Bart had sent her flowers earlier in the week for her birthday. He always sent her red roses. And this was a spectacular arrangement of pastel colored flowers. It looked like a painting. She set it down on the hall table, tipped the delivery man, and opened the card after he left. "Thank you! We can't wait to see you! Love, Tammy and Stacey." She stood staring at it for a long time, and smiled. Maybe the world wasn't coming to an end after all. The flowers were beautiful, and Tammy hadn't changed. She was as elegant and gracious and thoughtful as ever. And she was a loving daughter. Kate was still smiling when she lay down on her bed again, fully dressed, and fell sound asleep.

Chapter 11

As soon as Tammy had broken the news to her mother about her sexuality, Stacey was consumed with anxiety about whether or not Kate would like her. She was sure she wouldn't. Her hair was too short and too gray, her clothes were too masculine, she hadn't worn high heels since her high school graduation at eighteen, but maybe she should buy some. She looked in the mirror, stared into her closet in despair, borrowed a dress from Tammy, and looked like a man in drag in it or a kid on Halloween, and burst into tears. She was driving Tammy insane, with a thousand questions, and her fears about Kate's reaction to her.

Tammy decided that the only way to deal with her anxiety was to get it over quickly. She called her mother and asked if they could come for a drink in the next few days. She didn't think that Stacey would survive a meal without hyperventilating. Her normally calm, confident, level-headed partner, her tower of stability, was collapsing, as though her entire life depended on the meeting with Kate.

"Of course," Kate said, surprised to hear from Tammy so quickly. She knew how busy she was, constantly in meetings at Chanel and working late. She assumed that that part of her life was true, even if the stories about her personal life hadn't been. "Thank you for the flowers by the way. I've never seen anything so beautiful. I'm going to try your florist."

"I'm happy you like them," Tammy sounded pleased. "It was Stacey's idea. She sent me some too, after I told you about us. She's waited seven years for this, and she's going to have a nervous breakdown if she doesn't meet you soon. I want to put her out of her misery, before she gets a facelift, starts having Botox shots, and buys a whole new wardrobe. She's driving me nuts. She's afraid you won't think she's good enough for me. She's a lot smarter than I am, and a wonderful person."

"So are you," her mother said lovingly.

"I really hope you like her, Mom. It's important to both of us." Kate could hear the love in her voice for the woman she lived with. She had waited sixteen years to tell her mother, seven of them hiding her partner from her, and now she wanted Kate's stamp of approval on her life. It had been a long painful wait for both of them.

"Are you free tomorrow around five o'clock?" Kate offered. It was Saturday.

"That's perfect. Stacey sees patients on Saturday until four o'clock. It'll give us time for her to change, and for us to get uptown."

"I'm looking forward to it. Tell her not to worry. I'm on board now. All you had to do was tell me," she said calmly, as both of them wondered silently if Claire and Anthony simultaneously going off the deep end had made it easier. Tammy hadn't done anything dramatic, she had just told the truth, which was dramatic enough in her case. Her siblings had made life changing alterations, and changed directions completely. Tammy was still quietly and sanely on her familiar path. And Stacey was a sensible intelligent woman. She was sure her mother would see it the minute they met.

She told Stacey about the meeting when she got home from work that night. She was instantly panicked.

"Oh God . . . oh no . . . so fast? Maybe we should wait. Maybe I should take a Xanax when we go up there. Or have a drink before we go."

"Oh great. If you walk in like a zombie, or show up drunk, I know she'll love you. Just be yourself. I told her how terrific you are. She knows I love you. All you have to do is meet her now, and we can relax after that."

"Beware of what you wish for. I've waited seven years for this, now it seems like a terrible idea. What if she hates me? What then?"

"Then I dump you and find someone else she'll like better, or maybe I stop being gay?" Tammy suggested and Stacey laughed.

"Okay, okay. But should I try to wear one of your dresses?"

"Only if you want her to fall down laughing when we come through the door. I don't know how you do it, but you can take a Chanel dress and make it look ridiculous. Just wear jeans, my mom probably will. I'm not getting dressed up."

"She knows you, you don't have to prove anything," she said miserably.

"Neither do you, you've already got everything it takes to impress her. We're on your side."

"You don't understand. This is like meeting your future mother-in-law, only much, much worse. What if she thinks I'm gay?" Stacey said, starting to relax, with Tammy's encouragement.

"She won't, she never thought I was. Why would she think that about you? Are you, by the way?" Tammy was laughing, and Stacey grinned in spite of herself.

"Of course not, I'm straight all the way. Why would you say something like that?"

"Just a rumor I heard, something about your shoes."

"Will she think I'm weird for wearing men's shoes?" She stared at her feet and then at Tammy.

"Let me clue you in. She knows you're gay, you can go dressed as GI Joe if you want."

"One of my five-year-old patients asked me the other day if I was wearing my daddy's shoes." She smiled and Tammy laughed.

"Smart kid. Very strong gaydar for a five-year-old. I wonder how my brother is doing. I haven't heard from him since Mom's birthday dinner. I sent him a couple of texts today, saying I hope he's okay, and I haven't heard back."

"He's probably hiding out somewhere," Stacey suggested.

"My mother said something about his meeting someone a while ago, and it threw him. I wonder if he's with her."

"That would be pretty fast, but you never know. Maybe that's what gave him the courage to break up with his fiancée."

"He needs time to figure out what happened," Tammy said thoughtfully, "and how he got so far down the road with the wrong woman."

"That's easy to do sometimes." Tammy knew Stacey had spent

ten years with a sociopath before leaving her and meeting Tammy. She was a doctor too, and totally insane. And then Stacey met Tammy six months after they broke up. "Some relationships are so right on paper that you talk yourself into them. I did that with Mercedes. Two doctors, how perfect—only one of us was nuts."

"Amanda's not nuts, but she and my brother had nothing in common. My grandmother and sister were right on that. My mom got caught up in all the fancy social bullshit and thought it would be good for him and civilize him. My brother's a sweet guy, but he's always going to be a geek and an artist at heart. I hope the next woman is the right one for him. He deserves it. At least I don't have to worry about what to wear to the wedding. We could have worn matching tuxedos. We have a great one at Chanel this season." Tammy laughed.

"I wouldn't have been invited," Stacey said.

"You will be from now on," Tammy said gently. "I'm not going out without you anymore. That's over." Stacey looked touched.

"You get a pass for fashion events, though. I couldn't handle it." She rolled her eyes and Tammy laughed. It was a whole new day for them.

As it turned out, the next day Stacey had an emergency in the office. A one-year-old who had rolled off the changing table, and needed to have her forehead stitched up. Stacey had no time to change properly when she got home, she put on loafers instead of running shoes, changed her shirt, and they were out the door to go uptown to meet Tammy's mother. Before they arrived, Kate stood looking around her apartment, waiting for them. Tammy had texted that Stacey had had an emergency and they'd be ten minutes late.

She tried to guess what Stacey would be like. It was like meeting a daughter-in-law seven years after the wedding. It was a done deal by then. Everything about the situation was new to her, and Tammy was the bridge between them. She straightened the books on the coffee table again. The flowers they'd sent her were on a table in front of the window and looked beautiful. Kate had changed three times, and finally settled on white jeans and a pink shirt. She didn't want to overdress. They were fifteen minutes late when they rang the bell. Kate nearly jumped out of her skin, and ran to open it. Tammy hugged her before she even saw Stacey, and then she saw a tall, thin, shy young woman, with delicate features, deep blue eyes, and prematurely gray hair in a short pixie cut. She was wearing a white shirt and jeans.

Tammy introduced them, and without hesitating, Kate reached out and hugged her. Stacey started to cry. Two minutes later, they were all hugging and crying, and Kate felt as though she were adopting a child.

"I've waited so long to meet you," Stacey said in a choked voice.

"Me too, I just didn't know it," Kate said in a voice filled with emotion. She hadn't expected Stacey to be so simple and human and warm, but it shouldn't have surprised her knowing Tammy.

"God, you two are such sissies. Man up," Stacey said as Tammy handed out tissues for all of them, and they laughed.

"Would you like a drink?" Kate offered, and wondered if she should have had food for them, but none of them could have eaten. It was too emotional.

"Water would be fine. I'm on call this weekend. I'm sorry we were late, I had to stitch up a one-year-old." Kate could see her easily in that role, and being great with kids. She had eyes filled with compassion, and a gentle style, with laugh lines near her eyes.

They sat down in the living room, and she brought out some of the albums of Tammy as a little girl. Stacey loved it, and they laughed at some of the pictures. Tammy looked angelic in most of the pictures, and she was always carrying her favorite doll.

"You sure were a girly girl," Stacey commented with a loving look. "I looked like Dennis the Menace as a kid. I carried a tool kit for about two years, and took my parents' TV apart and nearly electrocuted myself. I set fire to a Brillo pad stuck in an outlet to get a spark to light a cigarette in my room when I was fifteen. I don't think anyone was surprised by how I turned out. They're just surprised I didn't wind up in jail. I stole my father's car and drove to Cincinnati from Columbus when I was fourteen. My younger brothers were scared to death of me." Tammy knew that one of Stacey's brothers had been gay too, and had died of AIDS. Stacey had had her share of heartbreak. It was what had made her decide to go to medical school. She'd spent a year with Doctors Without Borders, working in an AIDS clinic in Africa. They talked about it briefly with Kate, who was vastly impressed by Stacey. She was a very impressive woman, and the bond between her and Tammy was obvious.

The time sped by as they talked, and at seven o'clock Stacey got a text from her answering service. She had an eleven-year-old boy in the emergency room with a broken arm, and she looked apologetically at Tammy and her mother.

"I have to go to work, but this has been so wonderful." She

turned to Kate then. "Would you come to dinner at our place some-time? I'm a terrible cook, but I buy great pizza and spaghetti and meatballs, or sushi." Kate hadn't been to Tammy's apartment for years and felt guilty about it now.

"I'd love it." She smiled warmly, and they hugged before the girls left, this time without tears.

"Thank you for everything . . . for this . . . for Tammy," Stacey said softly.

"Thank you, Stacey." Kate suddenly felt like she had a lot to be grateful for. Things weren't as bleak as she had thought only a few days before. "You should take Stacey to meet your grandmother," she said to Tammy.

"I will. Stacey wanted to meet you first." They hugged again, and the two women got on the elevator, as Kate walked back to her apartment, thinking about the time they had spent together. Stacey was a wonderful addition to Tammy's life, and now to Kate's. A whole new chapter had begun.

She was still thinking about them that night when Bart called her. He had a meeting in New York on Tuesday and wanted to know if she was free. She had been so busy and overwhelmed lately, they hadn't spoken in days, since her birthday. But a lot had happened since then, Anthony's breakup and Tammy's revelation.

"What's up? You've suddenly gone quiet on me," and her texts had been brief and read like fortune cookies. And she wasn't up on his news either.

"A lot has been going on," she said. She hadn't told him about

Claire's pregnancy and the debacle over that, and now she didn't feel comfortable telling him that Tammy was gay. That still felt somewhat private. The only thing she felt at ease telling him was the news of Anthony's wedding being canceled, which he would hear anyway. But her reluctance to share more intimate news with him told her something about their relationship, which she already knew. Their relationship was easy, but had remained shallow. Anything deep or too personal, she kept to herself. She let him see the pretty parts of them now, involving all three of her kids. Although Tammy's relationship with Stacey was anything but messy. It was adult and mature, and as solid as any marriage, but it would be considered unorthodox in some people's eyes, and most likely his. His children weren't huge successes in life, compared to hers, but their problems were more ordinary and run of the mill. She felt too vulnerable at the moment to share most of it with him.

"That's too bad about Anthony's engagement," Bart sympathized. "Is he heartbroken?"

"I don't think so. Amanda overdid the wedding, and I think it gave him cold feet. He's not ready."

"Maybe they'll patch it up later," he said, trying to sound optimistic.

"I doubt it." He was surprised by how philosophical she was, but so much else had happened in the last two months that Anthony's canceled wedding was the least of it.

"So how does your dance card look for Tuesday?"

"I have a late meeting at the office, but I should be home by eight or nine." She didn't want to tell him she was busy, but she wasn't enthused about seeing him, which surprised her. She usually was. She just wasn't in the mood nor to put a good face on it.

"That's perfect. I won't be free till then either. And I have to leave the next morning at six A.M. for a meeting in Washington. I just thought that it would be nice to spend the night together." It was basically a very high end booty call, and usually she didn't mind, but this time when she hung up, she realized that she did. It suddenly occurred to her that it would have been nice to have someone she could really talk to, whose problems and interests were similar to her own. His children had never been a high priority to him, and he didn't pretend they were. He was honest about it. But it bothered her that these days the only adult she could confide in was her mother. It seemed a little strange at her age.

Margaret had always doubled as best friend, particularly since Tom's death, but Kate was missing some male perspective in her life, which she didn't get from Bart, since their common goal had been to keep things light. She wondered now if it was a little too light, to the point of not being real. Real life was what she had been dealing with, oppositional children, a hostile unwed pregnant daughter, her concern about her children's poor or risky decisions, and discovering that one of her children was gay. You couldn't tell those things to a stranger, or a man you slept with once in a while.

Bart lived in another city, they were both busy, and she was no longer even sure how exclusive their relationship was. She had no idea what he did when he wasn't with her, or who he went out with, and it bothered her. They were too old to have a relationship based mostly on sex and the occasional nice dinner. She didn't want to complain to him about it, but in the past few weeks, since their two weeks in Shelter Island, it had occurred to her that she was telling him none of the heavy things that were going on in her life. He was in the outer circle, not the inner sanctum. As long as her children had appeared to be perfect, it was fine. But now it wasn't. No life was as perfect as it appeared from the outside.

Stacey and Tammy took Margaret to brunch at The Carlyle on Sunday. It was a treat for her, and had been Stacey's idea. Afterward Kate and her mother discussed what a lovely and very impressive person Stacey was.

Kate spent most of the day working, preparing for a tough week in the office. It was clear to her that for the next two months, she was going to be buried, getting ready for impending trials. There would be no playtime in her life, just work. It happened that way sometimes and went in waves.

Anthony checked in with her on Sunday night while she was working at home.

"I was beginning to think you had run away and joined the circus." He had been MIA for several days, and she figured he had been in hot pursuit of his amateur boxer, the underwear model with the mean right hook.

"Not quite. I've been working things out with Alicia." She noticed immediately that he sounded happy. More so than he had in months with Amanda.

"Has she forgiven you?"

"Almost. I'm working on it. She doesn't trust me yet, but that's fair. I'll have to prove to her that she can."

"That sounds reasonable." It appeared that she was the kind of woman who wasn't willing to be treated badly by anyone, which Kate approved of. She was that way herself, ever since Tom. It was why she kept serious relationships at bay, and figured she didn't need one. But they were a lot younger and had their whole lives ahead of them, with everything that entailed, marriage, kids, heartbreaks, divorces, good times and bad times, joys and bitter disappointments. "Am I going to meet her?"

"You will," he said vaguely. "It's too soon now."

"Have you heard from Amanda?"

"We texted a couple of times. She sounds okay. She's in Paris with her mom. Maybe this is a relief for her too. The wedding got to be overwhelming. If I ever do get married, I'm going to city hall. I don't need or want all that fanfare and pretentiousness. Her father was going to spend a million on it."

"At least," Kate agreed with him.

"That's sick. I'd rather have the money to start a company."

"I think she liked it, and he wanted to indulge her."

"I guess," he said, sounding baffled. "I just wanted to let you know I'm alive."

"I'm happy to know it," she said. A few minutes later, they hung up and she went back to work. Kate wasn't hearing much from Claire these days either. She was giving her mother the cold shoulder. She could live with it, although she was sorry not to be more supportive of the pregnancy, but Claire wouldn't let her. She was still proving a point, and Kate didn't want to cater to it, and didn't have time to do so. She had sent her half a dozen helpful books on pregnancy, as a loving gesture, and Claire hadn't even thanked her.

Monday at the office was as stressful and hectic as she'd expected. Tuesday was worse. She had another meeting on their big case with Jack Hirsch and Scott White as opposing counsel. She was seeing a lot more of them than she wanted. They were trying to wear her down, and she was developing a severe aversion to Scott White, the other partner on the case. She thought he was good looking and arrogant, and too cocky for his own good. His comments to and about her client were sometimes downright rude. She didn't like her client much either, but she had to be professional about it.

She noticed that White stared at her a lot to unnerve her. She had a strong urge to tell him to get over himself and behave. He thought he was God's gift to the legal profession. He was a few years younger than she was. He fit the bill as tall, dark, and hand-some, and looked a little like Tom, but she was impervious to him. Good-looking men didn't impress her, and she considered him a huge pain in the ass. Most of their meetings so far had been time wasters. It wasn't working. It just made her angrier and tougher. She had half a dozen other big cases on her desk, not just theirs.

She was sitting at her desk reading discovery files at home, when Bart showed up on Tuesday night, as planned. She hadn't dressed for him, she hadn't had time. She was in work mode, only got home from the office half an hour before he arrived, and hadn't had time for dinner.

She realized that in the beginning of their relationship she would have used the half hour to dress for him and do her hair, and look relaxed when he arrived. But she had too much work right now. She looked distracted when he finally showed up, half an hour late himself, but ready for playtime. She had hours of work left in her briefcase.

"You look busy," Bart said jovially when he saw the files spread out on her desk. She poured him a Johnnie Walker Blue Label on the rocks. She was out of gin, and couldn't shake him a martini.

"This month is a nightmare," she confessed, sitting down next to him on the couch, "and next month will be too. I hate these damn frivolous cases."

"So do I. We need to change the laws governing that in this country. Anybody can sue anybody here and it costs them nothing, with contingency lawyers, and the plaintiffs don't have to pay legal fees. They should."

"Amen to that. So do something about it, Senator," she teased him.

"I have a few other things on my plate right now too," he said, stretching his legs out in front of him. He always relaxed when he was with her. They never talked about their problems. He was there for pleasure. That was the farthest thing from her mind tonight. She hadn't even had time to brush her hair before he got there, and he realized his timing wasn't ideal showing up mid-week. "Ready to take a night off?" he whispered as he leaned over and kissed her. She wasn't, she was still stressed from the office, but she didn't want to say it to him. She was thinking of getting out of bed to go back to work, after he fell asleep. She didn't know what else to do, in order to finish her work. But she was definitely not in the mood for playtime. That was the trouble with hit and run sex and romance. Sometimes it was the wrong time, and if she wanted that kind of relationship, you had to take it when you could get it, convenient or not, and be ready to act like a geisha who had nothing else to do.

"Kids okay?" he asked her, as she poured him a second drink, and tried not to look at her watch as she did, but he saw her do it.

"Perfect," she said by rote. That was definitely not the truth. But she knew it was a courtesy question, not a real one. Anthony and Claire were somewhat precarious at the moment, but she didn't want to go into it, and she didn't want to tell him she had met Tammy's female partner of seven years, which finally explained why she hadn't been dating. Her lack of apparent dating life wasn't about work, it was about sexual orientation, and a secret Kate had no intention of sharing with him. She had a feeling he'd disapprove. He was very old school about some things, and Catholic, and was opposed to same-sex marriage. Kate had been too, and now her view had changed overnight with Tammy and Stacey.

"What have you been up to?" he asked pleasantly.

"Just work." She smiled at him. He kissed her again, and half an hour later, she followed him to her bedroom, and for the first time with him, she felt like a hooker. In real life, if they lived together or dated seriously, she would have told him that she had too much work to do to think about sex at the moment, but he only had nine hours to spend with her, and she couldn't be picky, and didn't want to let him down, or refuse him.

She took a quick shower, put on a pink satin dressing gown with nothing under it, and slid into bed beside him, knowing how he expected the evening to end. It was why he stayed with her. He kept condoms in her bedside table, which always made her wonder if he was sleeping with other people. She wasn't. He was the only partner she'd had for six years, and the sex had always been very good. Not earth shattering, but good, and satisfying for both of them.

He pulled the tie of her satin dressing gown loose once she got into bed. He had already been there when she slid in beside him, and he dropped the pink satin gown on the floor and felt the silk of her body as he kissed her, and slowly convinced her this wasn't such a bad idea after all. Their lovemaking was quick that night, and he'd been drinking before he got there. It didn't affect his performance, but he was sound asleep and snoring seconds after rolling off of her. She looked at him lying there next to her. He was a handsome man but he suddenly felt like a stranger, and she felt like a trick. They had talked for half an hour at most, had sex for ten minutes, and at six A.M. he'd be leaving to catch his plane back to Washington. It was a total of forty minutes of interaction. She wondered how much hookers charged for that, or if they had a minimum if he spent the night. She never used to think of that with him, but now she did. Something was missing. The fire had gone out of it for her, and maybe for him too.

She got out of bed while he was sleeping, retrieved her dressing gown from the floor and went back to the living room to read discovery files, and went back to bed at midnight.

He woke her when he got up the next morning at five. He showered and shaved, and she had coffee and toast waiting for him in the kitchen when he was dressed. She knew he ate breakfast on the plane. He was hopping a ride on someone's corporate jet that morning with the people he'd been at the meeting with the night before. The others had stayed at a hotel, but he wanted to stay with her. And in previous years she'd enjoyed it, but not now. She wasn't sure why, whether it was him or her, or time had just caught up with them. Shelter Island had been fun when she wasn't working, but this wasn't, when she had so many cases to deal with.

"Is something wrong?" he asked her as he sipped his coffee. "I feel like we're missing something. We were both tired last night," he said and she nodded. "Are we played out?" he asked, wanting her take on it, and she wasn't sure either.

"I don't know. I have a lot of work right now," and family problems galore.

"Relationships like ours have a shelf life, you know," he said calmly. "We may have hit our expiration date. I'm getting that feeling. Six years is a good run, if that's where we are now." He didn't seem sad or emotional about it, he just wanted to know, in case he needed to change his route and make other arrangements for his free time.

"I don't know. Maybe we have hit our expiration date," she said, surprised to hear herself say it. But the sex didn't feel right anymore. It was sex and nothing more. It had never been love, but it had been real affection for a while. She had felt something change that summer in Shelter Island too, and tried to ignore it. And she'd been upset about Claire. But it wasn't getting better. If anything it was worse, with the pressures of their real lives. It didn't feel cozy between them now, just mechanical and a little cold, which wasn't what she wanted. She didn't just need to get laid, she wanted to feel somewhat loved, even at her age and in her circumstances. At fifty-five, she wasn't totally ready to give up on tender feelings for a man she slept with, and he seemed to have none for her. Just respect and companionship and appreciation of her body, which was all he had to give. It had never been different, only a little warmer and more fun. But lately, with her family falling apart, she needed more emotional support. He didn't even know about it, and she wasn't inclined to tell him.

"I think we've kind of done it, Kate," he said as he finished his coffee. He hadn't had time to eat the toast. "I'm going to miss spending time with you, but I hate dragging things out once they reach this point. We should quit while we're ahead and still like each other." She nodded agreement, and was startled by how quickly he was willing to shed an alliance they had shared for six years. He was ready to toss it in the trash like a used condom, and she didn't stop him, which startled her too.

Two minutes later, he stood in the doorway, his overnight bag in his hand, smiling down at her, and kissed her.

"Thank you, Kate," he said, which was meant to encompass six years of sex, weekends, nights, conversation, and a few vacations. "You're a great woman. Stay in touch. It was fabulous," he said with a wave and a smile and got on the elevator, and that was the end of Bart Mackenzie. She wasn't even sure how she felt about it, sad or nothing. It had ended within a matter of minutes. At the first hint of autumn in the air, he had shut it down, and moved on. It told her how little she had meant to him, but she had never really let him into her life either. This was all it was ever meant to be. A casual affair with a handsome senator who lived in another city. There was no real substance there and never had been. She closed the door behind him, and went back to her desk. She had two hours to spend on the work she'd brought home from the office.

She wondered if she'd ever hear from him again, and decided she probably wouldn't. They would be friendly when they met by coincidence somewhere. She had seen lots of women do that with him, and now she was one of them. She was a woman he had slept with for a while. He had taught her one thing, that if she slept with another man one day, which was never a sure thing at her age, she wanted it to be someone she loved and who loved her. Sleeping with a man she didn't love, even in a comfortable arrangement like hers with Bart, just made her feel cheap. It was funny how, at every age, in the end, love always mattered. It was the only thing that did. The rest was just smoke and mirrors.

Chapter 12

September and October were every bit as busy and hard as she had expected them to be and sometimes more so. Trials to prepare, depositions to do, discovery to study, witnesses to do research on, new cases, old cases, conferences, meetings, her partners to consult. Work rained on her like a hailstorm. She loved it, but she had no time for anything else, and even worked on the weekends. It gave her no free moments to think about Bart Mackenzie, and after a few weeks, she realized she didn't care. He hadn't called and she'd thought he wouldn't. She was part of his archives now, no longer "active." She barely had time to talk to her children, although they all seemed to be fine. Stacey's being introduced to the family had deepened their relationship, according to Tammy. Stacey still had to meet Tammy's siblings, but she had met her mother and grandmother, which was the most important.

Claire's pregnancy was advancing, and she said it was beginning to show in October. Kate made a point of calling her regularly, to demonstrate some interest, and Claire was still being cool and bratty. Kate was hearing very little from Anthony, but he sounded happy when she did. Her mother spent three weeks in Palm Beach with an old friend, which alleviated Kate's guilt about not having time to see her, but she knew her mother understood.

The rest of the time, every waking moment was spent on work. They heard depositions in October for the case being handled by Jack Hirsch and Scott White, who was continuing to be a thorn in her side, and was visibly enjoying it. He interrupted her depositions constantly with objections and tried to get away with everything he could during his own. Jack Hirsch was lazy and old, and happy to let Scott run the case. That irritated Kate too since she could run rings around Jack, but Scott used some of the same tricks she did. It was like a game of chess, and they were equally matched. She always made a point of dressing well for depositions, to intimidate the people they were deposing. Sometimes it worked. She wore six inch heels, and Chanel suits she bought with Tammy's discount. Jack Hirsch was overweight and his suits were old, and Scott White showed up looking like the cover of *GQ*. She was sick to death of him and couldn't wait until the depositions were over. She knew there would be settlement battles after that. She had depositions in other cases scheduled in late October and November. She could easily see herself working like a slave until Christmas. She was used to it, but after a while it became wearing, and the strain started to show. She was tired, and hoping to wrap up several cases by the end of the year.

The last day of depositions in the case was November first and Scott bowed with a little flourish in her direction when they had heard the last one. It ended at six o'clock. At least that was done, and she hoped to see less of Scott White in future until the settlement conferences started. She was sure they would let her sweat it for a while before Scott contacted them. She had plenty of other cases to deal with in the meantime. She nodded at Scott and Jack, walked out of the conference room, and went back to her office.

She left at six-thirty with a briefcase crammed full of work, and when she got to the lobby she saw that it had been snowing all afternoon. She hadn't noticed it. She hadn't worn boots since the weather forecast had said it wouldn't snow until the weekend. All she had was a pair of running shoes in her desk, and the six inch heels she was wearing. She was too tired to go back up to her office and put on the running shoes, and all she had to do was cross the street in front of the building, to hail a cab going in the right direction. She could manage that in heels, and decided to brave it.

When she got through the revolving door, she realized the temperature had dropped dramatically, and the streets were covered in ice with snow on top of it, and salt sprinkled here and there to keep people from slipping. It was like walking on an ice rink, as she crossed the street with the light. She was glancing around for a cab, and as she approached the curb, she didn't see a sheet of black ice. She slid across it at full speed, and fell knees first onto the curb, as her shoes, briefcase, and handbag went flying. The pain in her knees was excruciating, and she couldn't stand up in stocking feet. She didn't even know where her shoes were, and hoped that no one would steal her purse, as she felt powerful arms lift her off her knees and help her hover over her shoes which someone had put next to her. She was fighting back tears and trying to catch her breath when she put her shoes on, and looked up to see that Scott White, her archenemy, had rescued her and was holding her up. When she glanced down again she saw that her knees, shins, and the palms of her hands were bleeding. The pavement and the ice had torn the skin, and the salt she had fallen onto had ground itself into the skinned areas. Both knees were bleeding profusely, with salt lodged in the wounds.

"Are you okay?" Scott asked her with a worried look. He continued to hold her up with one strong arm around her, and the other supporting her elbow. He had a solid grip on her and could feel her shaking.

"I'm fine," she said in a trembling voice, and he could see that she wasn't.

"I'm not letting go of you," he said in a firm, reassuring voice. "Do you want to go back to the office?" She shook her head trying not to cry, as people gathered around them and stared at her. She had made a spectacular landing on all fours. Someone handed her her purse, and another person put her briefcase next to her. Her knees hurt like hell, but she didn't think anything was broken since she was standing. She suspected that if Scott hadn't been holding her up, she might have fallen to the pavement again, or fainted. "We need to take you somewhere to clean you up," he told her. "If I hold on to you, do you think you can make it around the corner? There's a small hotel where I meet clients before our depositions with you."

"Yes . . . really . . . I'm fine . . . this is so stupid . . . thank you . . ." She didn't care that she had wanted to strangle him all afternoon and for the past several months in the depositions. He had saved her, and he was being very gallant about it.

They inched their way along on the treacherous ice, while she kept her hold on her briefcase and purse in one bleeding hand. She almost slipped again, but he had a strong grip on her, and just around the corner was the tiny hotel she had never noticed. They had cleared a path with salt on it, and her legs were still shaking as he led her into the lobby and deposited her in an overstuffed leather chair. They both surveyed the damage. There was blood everywhere from her knees to her feet, and the palms of her hands were bloody too. It was all over the beige cashmere coat she was wearing.

"I think it looks worse than it is," she said, embarrassed.

"I hope so," he said. "You look like someone tried to kill you."

"I didn't know it was snowing and had gotten so icy."

"The shoes look great on you. It was almost worth it." He smiled at her. "Now, don't move, we'll get you patched up in a jiffy." He acted as if they were long lost friends, instead of fierce opponents, but she was grateful to him. She'd still have been lying on the street if he hadn't been there to help her. He disappeared for five minutes, as people walking by glanced at her sympathetically, and a clerk at the front desk came to ask if she needed a doctor or an ambulance. She assured him that she was fine, and her friend was helping her. Scott came back then, with a roll of bandages, some cloths soaked in warm water, and antiseptic.

"You look like you're about to deliver a baby," she said, slowly regaining her composure.

"I hope not, although I could if I had to. I was a paramedic in the

Navy before I went to law school." He quickly and gently got rid of the excess blood with the damp cloths, her sheer stockings had literally been torn to shreds and disappeared. He applied the antiseptic, and expertly bandaged her badly skinned knees where the blood was coming from, and her hands. The bandages were neat and well done, and she stood up unsteadily but gratefully when he was finished. He went to dispose of the cloths in the men's room. He'd gotten what he needed from the hotel employees' first aid station and was back two minutes later. "Can you walk?" he asked her. "You looked pale when we got here."

"I'm feeling a little wobbly, but I'm okay. Scott, really, thank you."

"I don't think you broke anything, but you may need to get the wounds cleaned. There's some salt in them, but I didn't want to mess with it without gloves," he said and she thanked him again. "You had a nasty fall. How do the knees feel?"

"They hurt a lot," she said with a sheepish expression. "I feel really stupid."

"Don't. It can happen to anyone. Can I take you home?" he asked, looking both helpful and hopeful at the same time.

"If you put me in a cab, I'll be fine."

"I'll have the doorman get one. It's still snowing." It was the first big snowfall of the season. Scott spoke to the doorman, and ten minutes later, he had a taxi and helped Kate back out to the street, with his arm around her. He carried her briefcase for her and helped her gently into the cab. She smiled up at him.

"I can't thank you enough."

"I'm sorry it happened, but I'm glad I got to talk to you. I hate all this warlike posturing. There should be a time-out for lawyers, so we can shoot the shit with each other. It's all bullshit and playacting anyway. I've been wanting to talk to you since we started," but it wouldn't have been proper, so he hadn't. Now he had the perfect excuse. "If you need to have the bandages changed, call me. I do house calls," he said and she laughed. She was surprised by how friendly he was, and how easy to talk to. She had pegged him as an arrogant son of a bitch, with strong narcissistic tendencies, but he didn't seem like that now. "Seriously, I hope you'll be okay, and it doesn't hurt like hell tomorrow."

"I'm usually tougher than this," she said, still embarrassed.

"You don't need to be. I thought you were very brave." He stepped back then and waved, and the cab took off toward her address, moving cautiously on the icy streets, with snow tires. She closed her eyes and leaned her head back against the seat. She felt slightly sick, but a lot better than she had when she was on her knees on the pavement. She was still thinking of Scott White and how nice he had been.

She was even more surprised when he called her the next morning. It was Saturday, and she was hobbling around the house with her bandages. Her knees and hands still hurt a lot.

"I'm calling to check on my patient," he said cheerfully. "Do you need a bandage change? An amputation? A Mickey Mouse Band-Aid?" She laughed when she heard him.

"I'm fine. It hurts like crazy, but it's okay. I'm going to take a hot bath and soak my wounds. I went straight to bed last night. I was still kind of shaken up when I got home."

"I'll bet you were. You had a nasty fall. You're lucky you didn't break an arm or a wrist. It was nice having a chance to talk to you, like human beings. You're a noble opponent, Counselor," and a beautiful woman, he didn't add. He'd been admiring her since he first saw her. "Would you have a drink with me sometime?" He went straight to the point, and she hesitated. She felt as though she owed him a debt now, and he was much nicer than she would have expected. But he was still the opposing counsel in a lawsuit.

"I don't think we should. We don't want either of our clients accusing us of a conflict of interest. How about a raincheck for when it's all over?" She tried to sound natural about it.

"I'll hold you to it," he said seriously. "I hope it's over soon. Our client is such an asshole. At least yours is a better guy. I hate cases like this. They waste everybody's time. It's all about ego and greed, vengeance and showing off. It's a waste of our collective talents," and he thought hers were considerable.

"I know. It's a lousy case. I keep hoping he'll drop it, but I can tell he won't," Kate said with a sigh.

"You're right there. I'm going to hold you to that raincheck. And park those shoes until next spring, or at least don't wear them outside."

"Believe me, I won't. Strictly snow boots from now on. See you at the settlement conference, Scott."

And then he thought of something else. "Do you need anything? It's a mess outside. You shouldn't go out and risk falling again." He sounded sincere and she was touched.

"No, thanks, I'm all set. I've got enough food here to get me through the weekend."

"Call if you need anything." He gave her his cell number. "The Mickey Mouse Band-Aids are kind of cute. I have Cinderella too."

She was laughing at him. He was an entirely different person from the sarcastic, supercilious attorney who had made the depositions a living hell. It reminded her that you really never knew who people were in their private lives.

"You can show me the Cinderella ones at the first settlement conference." They both laughed at the thought.

"Our clients would love it, especially mine. He eats children for breakfast. See you soon." They hung up and Kate smiled, thinking about him for a minute. It was nice hearing from a man, even about something as innocuous as this. It had been well over a month since she and Bart had parted ways. It was for the best, and he was right. It had played out, but she missed him occasionally, and a little male attention. Although Scott White certainly wasn't an option. He was a rival attorney in an active suit and younger than she was, but he had been an efficient rescuer, and it had dissolved some of the animosity and tension surrounding the case. He was human after all, though she was sure he would still be a fierce and aggravating opponent when they met again with their clients. It was his style. But hers wasn't warm and fuzzy either. It was all posturing, as he'd said.

She stayed in bed for most of the weekend, and came up with an idea. She'd hardly seen her children for the past two months, and she wanted to have them come for dinner. They were all leaving town for Thanksgiving. Reed was taking Claire to the Turks and Caicos for some sun, Tammy had promised to go visit Stacey's family in Ohio, and Anthony was going to San Juan with Alicia to meet her father and assorted other relatives. Kate still hadn't met her, and hoped to soon. A small dinner in the next couple of weeks would get them all together, and give Kate a chance to meet Alicia.

She texted all of them asking for dates that worked for them, and by the end of the weekend, they had agreed on a date. She was going to serve sushi and Mexican food, which they all loved. There would be eight of them, her children, their significant others, Kate, and their grandmother. It sounded like fun, and distracted her from the ache and burning of her hands and knees.

Claire had called her when she got her mother's text, wanting to know what the dinner was about.

"Do you have more confessions for us?" she said with an edge to her voice.

"Not at all. It's just dinner, since you're all going to be away for Thanksgiving." Claire relaxed after that. Reed was coming too.

Anthony called her late that night, nervous about it. "Is this so everyone can meet Alicia?"

"It's a nice sidebar and we all want to meet her, but the only purpose is to be together and enjoy each other's company."

"Oh," he sounded surprised. "What should she wear? She's worried about it."

"Whatever she wants, jeans, whatever. It's just the family for dinner, Anthony, there's nothing behind it." He sounded relieved, and the conversation was brief.

Kate was looking forward to it. It was going to be interesting to see how the group blended, with three new partners in their midst. Her family was changing. Margaret was curious too, and they only had ten days to wait.

Chapter 13

The day of the dinner with her children, Kate bought flowers, put them all around the apartment, and enjoyed arranging them herself. She put an embroidered tablecloth on the table, brightly colored napkins and a set of red plates she used once in a while. It looked festive and she put a chocolate turkey at each place, just as she had when the children were little. She had champagne for those who wanted it, and good French wine for dinner. By the time they all arrived, it felt like a party. Tammy and Stacey got there first, and thought the table looked lovely.

"I can never do that and make everything match," Stacey said. "It looks like Martha Stewart did it," she said admiringly. The candles matched the decor too. Tammy was used to her mother doing beautiful table settings when she entertained and even for the family when she had time, but it was new to Stacey.

"Tammy is good with things like that too," Kate said, smiling at both of them. "And you can cure a sick child. You can't do everything. We all have our talents." She was happy to see Stacey again, she had done the seating carefully, and had used place cards to seat them, trying to guess who would get along best with whom. She had gone all out, and had bought a fabulous cake for dessert, and a huge box of chocolates.

Reed and Claire were the next to arrive. The baby was showing now. She was five months pregnant, and she could feel it move. She put her sister's hand on her belly several times to feel a kick, but didn't invite her mother to. She still had an attitude with Kate, because she had been critical of her getting pregnant and their not getting married. Claire could hold a grudge forever and apparently intended to, but she was pleasant with everyone else.

Margaret said something to her about it before dinner, when Kate was out of the room tending to something in the kitchen. "What you're doing to your mother isn't fair. She wants the best for you, and she had a right to be upset by your news."

"I have a right to be upset by her attitude, and by her being judgmental about me," Claire said coldly. She was being intentionally petulant with her mother, which seemed very wrong to Margaret, and childish, since she was about to become a mother herself.

"You don't need to abuse her, Claire. You've been very rude to her since July. Why do you want to hurt her?"

"She hurt me being so angry about the baby, and trying to force us to get married. She's embarrassed that I'm pregnant. She's not happy for us."

"She'll adjust to it, but she won't if you continue to be nasty to her. Sooner or later, she'll stop trying, and then you'll regret it."

Margaret knew her daughter and Kate had her limits as to how much abuse she was willing to take. Margaret could sense that Kate had reached hers. Claire didn't comment, but showed no sign of relenting and went cold whenever her mother was near her. Reed was embarrassed by Claire's behavior, and tried to compensate and whispered to her when they sat on the couch.

"Why do you always act like a brat around your mother? She's perfectly nice to us. You don't need to punish her."

"Whose side are you on?" she said angrily.

"The adults' side," he said firmly. "Why don't you join us? It's a winning team." He was disappointed by her childish attitude, but he loved her in every other way. He was more in love with her than ever, particularly as the baby's birth got closer. It was only four months away. Claire had already started decorating the nursery. It was a boy, which made Reed even happier. Stacey came over to sit next to Claire, and asked her about the due date and how she was feeling, which touched Claire. She warmed to Stacey immediately, although she had been shocked when Tammy had called her and said she was gay, after she'd told Kate. Claire was meeting Stacey for the first time that night. They chatted while Tammy and Reed talked business.

Anthony and Alicia were the last to arrive, half an hour late, but the Mexican food was staying warm in the oven, and the sushi was in the refrigerator, so Kate wasn't worried about the dinner.

"She changed outfits six times," Anthony whispered to Tammy when he kissed her, and she laughed.

She introduced him to Stacey, and they talked videogames. She said she had been addicted to them in college, and once she started playing she couldn't stop. She knew several of his games and loved them.

Anthony was immediately caught up in the swirl of family activity, and after he introduced Alicia, he forgot about her momentarily, teasing his sisters, and chatting with Reed and Stacey, while Alicia stood shyly at the edge of the group. Kate saw what was happening and went over to her. Alicia had worn a cream-colored skirt and sweater, which showed off her figure and was perfect with her café au lait skin.

"All the kids' partners are new to us," Kate said warmly, "so you're not the new girl at school, they all are. Don't feel like the Lone Ranger. I met Stacey two months ago for the first time, and Reed this summer. I've heard a lot about you," she smiled and lowered her voice, "I'm glad things worked out. He's crazy about you." Alicia beamed when she said that, and was relieved to see that Kate had worn a skirt, and so had Tammy, so she'd guessed right about her outfit. As she glanced at Kate's skirt, she noticed her legs and gasped.

"Oh my God, what happened to you?" Her legs were still black and blue from knee to ankle, she had huge scabs on her knees, and Alicia saw that she had scabs on the palms of her hands too.

"I fell on the ice when it snowed two weeks ago. I felt really stupid. I was wearing six inch heels." None of her children had noticed her legs, but they saw Alicia's expression and looked down. Stacey was horrified.

"Why didn't you call me? Did you see a doctor?"

"No, nothing's broken, just bruised and scraped. The opposing counsel in a deposition I'd just finished bandaged me up. He's a former Navy paramedic."

"That must have hurt, Mom," Tammy said sympathetically. Claire said nothing, yet again to prove a point. It was getting old, and Anthony told her to shape up and be nice to Mom. He was happy to see his mother talking to Alicia. She had been terrified to meet her. And Margaret was quick to join the group, and chat with Alicia too. By the time they sat down to dinner, Alicia felt totally at ease, and was talking animatedly with all of them. At dinner she was very funny about where she went to school, and Hunter College now in her final semester. They were impressed that she was determined to get her degree, even at thirty. She was obviously smart and persevering, and hardworking.

"Where did you go to college?" she asked Stacey, who looked instantly embarrassed.

"Don't ask her," Tammy intervened. "I feel stupid every time someone asks her. She went to Harvard, and graduated summa. She's obviously some kind of alien. Normal humans can't do that."

"Holy shit! Really?" Stacey nodded, and Alicia looked profoundly impressed, but Stacey was modest and unassuming about her achievements. Kate smiled, watching the interactions at the table, and was pleased that everyone got along. They gobbled up the food, the conversations got louder and louder and the wine flowed. Margaret was happily part of it, and Kate had Anthony and Reed opening more wine.

"Nice group," Kate whispered to her mother.

"I told you the family hadn't fallen apart. It just looked that way for a while. It's different, that's all," Margaret responded.

"You have to admit, it's a little unorthodox," Kate reminded her.

"That's what families are about. No family is normal these days. There is no such thing, even in Disney cartoons." Kate patted her mother's shoulder and handed Anthony another bottle of wine to open. Alicia looked comfortable in their midst. She had an incredible body and Tammy asked her how she kept it that way. She said she did kick boxing and had gotten Anthony into it. She said she had taken lessons from a pro at a gym as a kid. "I could kick any boy's ass in the neighborhood, which came in handy where I lived." Anthony handed his phone around with a video of her boxing on it, and everyone was impressed. They were all different, from different backgrounds, with a variety of talents, but the mesh worked well. The only disappointing member of the group was Claire, who was quiet a lot of the time, and only wanted to talk about her pregnancy. She was totally self-involved.

"Can't you talk about anything else?" her brother finally scolded her. "You're not the first woman on the planet to have a kid. How's your job?"

"Fine," she said, looking sullen. "I can't wait for my maternity leave. I'm taking three months off."

"I'm fascinated," he said, and rolled his eyes. Kate thought it was good for her to be back in the fold of her family, and not pampered by Reed all the time. He treated her like spun glass and hung on her every word. And felt her belly for every kick.

Stacey asked her if she was signing up for Lamaze classes, and Claire said they sounded boring and she didn't need them since she wanted drugs at the delivery anyway. Stacey said she might find the classes helpful and Claire brushed her off.

Tammy asked Alicia about her modeling, and she explained that she did it to pay the rent, but was trying to be an actress, without much success so far, but she was determined.

"She's a genius with computers," Anthony said proudly, "she understands all my games."

"I'm glad somebody does," Tammy said.

"I do!" Stacey piped up. "I have a lot of them. They're brilliant."

The teasing and talking went on for many hours. They demolished the cake, and Kate ran out of wine. They switched to champagne, and Anthony and Reed drank tequila shots after dinner and Alicia had one too. They were a lively group, and finally left at one-thirty in the morning. The living room was a mess and Kate was delighted. The evening had been a huge success and they all liked each other, which was a major coup. Reed made a date with Anthony and Alicia to try their gym. He had been extremely congenial, and with no family of his own he really enjoyed Claire's, in fact more than she did.

Margaret had gone home earlier and slipped away quietly, and Kate disappeared to the kitchen after a while to clean up, and not intrude on the young people, who were showing each other videos and photographs on Instagram, and all spoke the same language. Alicia talked to everyone. Claire finally warmed up and stopped talking about her baby. They were better than ever, and one happy family again, with partners who got along. And Kate didn't care that some of them were gay, or about where Alicia had grown up, and despite his enormous success, Reed was happy to be part of a simple evening, and was able to roll up his sleeves and join the fun. There was nothing pretentious about him. It was Claire who was getting too big for her breeches and overly impressed with herself. Her brother tried to put her in her place whenever she did. She talked about Reed's plane and everyone at the table booed and hissed at her, and Reed said it belonged to his company and he didn't own it. It was good for Claire to be back among real people who didn't care what she had now, or how spoiled she was becoming. It wasn't attractive.

"Wow, Amanda would never have survived with this lot," Kate commented to Tammy when she came out to the kitchen to check on her mother and help.

"I really like Alicia," Tammy said admiringly. "She's a live wire, and she's good for Anthony. She doesn't take any shit from him, and she gets his geek side."

"I'm glad someone does, and I like her too." Kate smiled at her, happy with how it had turned out.

They all promised to do it again soon, Alicia wanted to have them to dinner at Anthony's apartment, and Tammy and Stacey wanted to host a family dinner too.

Kate was thrilled with the evening, and it took the sting out of losing them all for Thanksgiving, which had never happened before. She was going to spend it alone with her mother. But she was determined not to spend a lonely Christmas. She had gotten them all to agree to Christmas Eve dinner together at her place again. Kate was hosting it, and everyone was excited at the prospect. She didn't mind losing Thanksgiving so much, if she had them all with her for Christmas. It was the first Christmas that Stacey was going to be in New York, to spend it with Tammy, and now her family. It had been a long wait, but well worth it. The day after Christmas,

Reed and Claire were flying to Saint Bart's for the last trip they would take before the baby. She'd be too pregnant to fly after that.

Alicia's eyes were alight on the ride back downtown, and not just from the tequila. She could drink most of the men under the table as well as kick their asses, and was proud of it.

"Your family is fantastic!" she said happily and Anthony beamed at her.

"They loved you." He had never felt that way with Amanda. Alicia was part of everything, and the center of the excitement. She wasn't intimidated by anyone in the group, not even his mother, who had been very kind to her.

"I love your mom," she said, smiling at him.

"Yeah, me too. I've got to hand it to her. She's made a hell of an adjustment in the past four months." It was a major understatement, but she had done it, because she loved them. They made it all worthwhile.

Kate spent Sunday cleaning up the kitchen, putting things away, and tidying the apartment. They all called to thank her, and she reminded them about Christmas Eve.

It seemed hard to believe but the people they had added, the eclectic group of partners they had chosen, made things better, not worse. They were all close in age, however different their backgrounds. It was a fantastic mix. And her mother was right. There were no normal families anymore. Normal was accepting whatever cards you were dealt, and how well you played the hand.

Chapter 14

The first settlement meeting about the case Kate and Scott White were on opposite sides of was scheduled for the Monday before Thanksgiving. After consulting with her associates, their decision was to get rid of the case if at all possible. It was taking up too much time, a trial would take months of preparation, would cost a fortune, and juries were unpredictable. She and her partners set a ceiling for the amount they were willing to throw at the unworthy opposition, and Kate hoped that Scott and Jack Hirsch would be able to convince their unpleasant client to settle for that amount. She was counting on Scott now that she knew there was another side to him, after he had rescued her when she fell.

She wore slightly lower heels to the meeting. She saw Scott lean down and check discreetly, and give her an almost invisible thumbs-up, and she laughed. They didn't talk to each other before the meeting. She didn't want to do anything to jeopardize the settlement of the case, or be accused of improprieties later that might overturn whatever decision had been reached.

The meeting got under way quickly. Both the plaintiff and defendant were there. Kate's client was being pleasant and polite and non-inflammatory. Scott was invariably rude and insulting, calling people names so that he had to be reprimanded frequently. It was tedious dealing with him. The meeting droned on for four hours, the opposition offering fresh accusations of malfeasance to strengthen their argument, which Kate knew meant nothing, and was only done to try to increase the settlement.

The defendant's side finally made their offer, and left the conference room, so the plaintiff and his team could discuss it. It was all about a business deal which had gone sour. Money invested had been lost, and the plaintiff was trying to recoup his losses inappropriately by accusing Kate's client of everything under the sun, most of it lies. She didn't think a jury would buy it, but it could take years to resolve if they went to court. The logic of doing so made no sense, and Scott had tried to convince his client of that also, to no avail. His client was a street fighter who had nothing better to do, was bitter about the failed deal, and had billions, so money wasn't the issue. In reality, the settlement, whatever it was, made no difference to him. It was more symbolic. He wanted his legal costs paid for too. And his lawyers were charging him a fortune.

Scott came out of the conference room a couple of times to go to the men's room, but Kate could read nothing on his face. They were called in at last, and Kate was feeling optimistic since it had taken them so long to discuss the offer, and she expected to hear that their offer had been accepted. Instead, Scott addressed her, standing in front of her the moment she sat down.

"Miss Morgan," he began, looking pompous again, which was his official persona, when representing his client. "Or is it Mrs.? What exactly is your marital status?" he asked haughtily, and she almost laughed.

"It's Mrs. I'm a widow. I don't see what that has to do with this case." His client had said "rake them over the coals." He hadn't added details, so Scott had thrown that in, allegedly to embarrass her, but he was actually curious himself.

"*Mrs.* Morgan," he emphasized, "do you have any idea how insulting your offer is to my client? Do you and your colleagues not understand the suffering and humiliation he experienced when the deal failed? Are you not cognizant of how sloppy your client's practices are, how *fully* responsible he is for the money my client lost? Are you not mortified by making us an offer like this? So paltry, so pathetic, so completely without merit? You should be ashamed of yourselves." His glance took in her partners seated in the room. All the big guns were there. It was a ridiculous speech, an affront and highly offensive, but she knew it was what his client expected from him. She would have hated Scott if he hadn't knelt at her feet bandaging her knees two weeks before. It was the only way she knew he was a real human being, and not the total horse's ass he'd been hired to be for his client.

His insulting speech went on for half an hour, while her client looked unhappy and started to lose patience, and her partners looked furious. It was all a long-winded way of his client saying no, and refusing the settlement. They had to go back to the drawing board, but neither her partners nor their client were willing to offer more.

She managed to say quickly, that if the offer was refused, they would go to trial, which no one wanted to do.

"Is it war then?" Scott asked her, sounding theatrical.

"If you want to call it that. It's a trial, Mr. White. If we can't make a deal, and we've made our best offer today, then we'll go to trial as I just said. We will leave our offer on the table for seventy-two hours, for your client to reconsider. After that, our offer will be withdrawn."

"I understand," Scott said for the benefit of the court reporter typing a transcript of the proceedings, so they couldn't say later that they didn't know the deal would be off the table in seventy-two hours. It was a tedious business, and Scott looked as fed up as she was.

Kate and her partners waited for opposing counsel to leave with their client. They took their time. As Scott marched past her stone-faced, he whispered almost inaudibly, "I'm sorry." No one heard him but Kate. She showed no reaction other than a barely perceptible nod.

As soon as they'd left, her partners exploded. Their client looked discouraged. It was an incredible waste of time and money. They'd probably go to trial on it in a year, maybe two. They were prepared to. The heat might have gone out of it by then. Sometimes litigation like this was settled on the courthouse steps the night before the trial, or the morning of it. But in the meantime, they had to prepare for a trial.

She didn't hear from Scott afterward. It would have been inappropriate and there was nothing left to say. It was all in his client's hands.

The following day, Kate had dinner with all three of her children at Le Bernardin, one of the best restaurants in New York, before they left for their respective trips on Wednesday, either to see their de facto in-laws, or in Claire's case to get some sun. Since Reed's parents were both deceased, and he had no siblings, he liked going away for holidays, and was thrilled to have Claire to spend them with now. He was looking forward to Christmas Eve at Kate's. He seemed hungry for family connection.

Anthony was looking forward to going to Puerto Rico with Alicia. He had met her mother who lived in the Bronx now in a tiny apartment. He could see where Alicia got her looks. Now he was going to meet her father and his second family in San Juan. She had five half brothers and sisters, all younger than she was, in their early to mid-twenties.

And Tammy was going to Columbus, Ohio, with Stacey, where her parents and brother and his family lived. She had met them all before and enjoyed them. Then they were going to Sun Valley, Idaho on Friday for the weekend to ski.

Anthony and Tammy felt guilty leaving their mother, and Claire didn't say anything. She was quiet and sullen through most of dinner, which Anthony told her had become really boring. None of them had brought their partners along. It was family only, so they could speak more freely, and Anthony called Claire a spoiled brat several times. He finally had enough and snapped at her at the end of dinner.

"I don't see why you need to be a bitch to Mom. She doesn't like you having a baby out of wedlock and showing off about it, and not getting married. She's entitled to her opinion. Most people, particularly of her generation, feel that way, so why do you have to be such a bitch to her? Frankly, I don't think it's cool either. I wouldn't do what you're doing, and Alicia wouldn't either. We talked about it. And neither would Tammy, I know her. So why do you have to be the odd man out and be so shitty to Mom on top of it? I just don't get it. Couldn't you at least be a little apologetic, out of respect for her? Would that cost you so much?"

"I'll get married when I *want* to, not when I *have* to. No one can dictate to me when I should get married. And I don't owe anyone an apology for living my life the way I want to. I support myself, so I don't owe anyone anything," she said nastily, as Kate looked pained.

"No, you don't," Anthony corrected her. "Reed supports you, and you're damn lucky he does. You're living like the Queen of Sheba, and being snotty to Mom on someone else's dime." Claire's face turned red.

"This isn't about money," she argued hotly.

"No, it's not. It's about manners, and traditions, and morals, and respect for how you grew up, and everything Mom did for us. You don't pay that back by snubbing her because she's upset that you're having a baby out of wedlock. She has every right to be upset about it. People are going to say nasty things about you, and that hurts all of us because we love you."

"I don't give a damn what people say," she snapped back at him.

"Apparently. So Mom should be humiliated by your bad behavior, AND have you be nasty to her on top of it? Wow, what a cool deal for her. I hope your kids will be nicer to you than you are to her." Claire had tears in her eyes but she wouldn't give in, and didn't look at Kate, who had tears in her eyes too. Claire suspected her mother would be crying and didn't want to see her tears. "You're being a jerk," he added.

"That's enough," Kate stepped in then and they stopped.

"What are you doing for Thanksgiving, Mom?" Tammy asked her. "Are you going to a restaurant with Grandma?"

"No, I'm cooking squab from a French recipe at home, with all the fixings, including chestnut stuffing. And then we're going to a movie. And don't forget our Christmas Eve dinner."

"We're going to Saint Bart's," Claire chimed in to get out of it. Anthony gave her a furious look.

"No, you're not," he said. "Reed told me you're going the day after Christmas, so you'd damn well better be there on Christmas Eve with the rest of us, or I'll kick your ass," he threatened her as he had when they were teenagers.

"Why don't you have Alicia do it?"

"I will, and believe me, that would be a lot worse for you than if I did it. She's hell on wheels." Tammy laughed at the thought, and dinner wound down after that. They'd had a nice time together, in spite of Claire. Then they all kissed and hugged and wished each other a happy Thanksgiving, and went their separate ways. Reed had a car and driver waiting outside the restaurant for Claire. Anthony and Tammy shared an Uber, and Kate went uptown in a cab.

She wondered when Claire was going to relax again, and if she ever would. Or if she was trying to separate from her mother and the family. At least she had shown up.

They all called to say goodbye and thank her the next day, and that night she was studying her French cookbook so she didn't screw up the squab. She started cooking early Thursday morning, and Margaret arrived at eleven. By some sheer miracle, the squab was absolutely perfect and a golden brown when Kate served it, with a delicate sauce, chestnut stuffing, wild rice, and an assortment of vegetables. She even made popovers which she knew her mother loved.

"I think this is the best Thanksgiving meal I've ever had," Margaret said happily. "I can't believe you cooked it."

"Neither can I," Kate admitted. She had bought small apple, pumpkin, mince, and pecan pies for dessert, and made whipped cream to put on top. They both had a sliver of each, and Kate served cappuccino with dessert.

"That was a four-star meal," Margaret said when they sat on the couch after dinner.

Kate missed the kids, but as long as they were coming for Christmas, she was happy, and willing to give them up for Thanksgiving. She was planning to use the weekend to catch up on work, do some things around the apartment, and some reading. She had already started Christmas shopping, and wanted to do more of that too. She had found a pink cashmere sweater for Alicia, a good-looking tweed jacket for Stacey, and a pair of cuff links for Reed. She was working her way down a list for her own children. She wanted to do some shopping with Claire for the nursery, but she didn't seem to be interested in doing it with her. Claire was determined not to share the experience with her mother, to punish her.

Kate was putting some linens away when her phone rang on Friday morning at ten o'clock. She assumed it was her mother, scurried down the ladder she'd been using and answered. There was a male voice she didn't recognize at the other end. He asked for her, and then she knew who it was. It was Scott White.

"Happy Thanksgiving. Jesus, was that ever a nightmare at the settlement conference on Monday. I'm sorry I was so rude to you. I get paid to do that by my asshole client, kind of like a Mafia hitman." She laughed.

"It's too bad he won't take the offer. We won't go higher."

"I told him that, and you shouldn't. Just please don't tell me that I can't cash in my raincheck until after a trial. That could take years. How about when the settlement bullshit is officially over? We won't have any professional dealings before the trial after that for months, probably a year. Will that do it?"

"I suppose so," she said cautiously. She didn't know why he wanted to have a drink with her, other than to complain about his client.

"How was your Thanksgiving?" he inquired.

"Nice. Quiet. All my kids were away with their significant others. I missed them. I had lunch with my mother."

"That's nice of you. How many kids do you have?"

"Three. Do you have children?" she asked, faintly curious about him.

"No, I don't. I've never married. I'm an old maid." He laughed.

"These days you can have children and not be married," she said, thinking of Claire. "It's not too late." She guessed him to be in his mid to late forties, still young enough to have kids.

"I'm forty-eight and I'm not dying to have kids. That looks scary and stressful to me," he said. "And I'm getting a little old to start a family, with a woman half my age. Somehow that has never appealed to me."

"Sometimes it is stressful," she admitted, thinking of the past few months with her own. "But it's worth it. It's not easy though. It is when they're little, and not so much so when they grow up."

"I'll take your word for it. That's what my parents said. I believed them."

"What did you do for Thanksgiving?" It was odd talking to him like they were friends. He seemed to want to be, ever since he had bandaged her knees.

"My mother passed away a few years ago. My father moved to New Zealand and bought a farm there. It's too far to go for holidays. And he doesn't come here. So I have dinner with a group of friends every year. All people who have nowhere else to be. There are a lot of us, around twenty. It's fun. I made the turkey this year."

"I cooked squab, which my mother was astounded I didn't ruin. I was shocked too. With chestnut stuffing," she said, sounding proud of herself. "I'm usually a lousy cook, but I got it out of a French cookbook."

"I'm impressed. What are you doing the rest of the weekend?" He seemed as though he had nothing to do. He obviously didn't have a family to be with from what he said, so it was nice that he'd spent the holiday with friends.

"Work, errands, maybe some Christmas shopping," she answered.

"Could we agree that the settlement attempts are over so I can cash in my raincheck for a drink, or dinner and a movie?"

"Why don't we give it a couple more weeks to be sure it really is over."

"Okay, I draw the line at Christmas. Deal?"

"Deal," she agreed.

"How are your knees, by the way? I couldn't tell, you had on dark tights at the meeting." He had obviously looked carefully, which surprised her.

"They still hurt a little and I'm black and blue, but otherwise they're fine. You're a good paramedic."

"What are you doing over the holidays?"

"Christmas Eve with my kids, after that nothing."

"I'm going skiing in Vermont for the New Year. I can't wait. Do you ski?"

"Not lately. I can't afford to break a leg. Too many people depend on me. And I'm not a great skier. I like ice skating better."

"Where did you grow up?"

"Here, in New York."

"I grew up in Montana, glued to a horse. I came east for college, and stayed, other than my time in the Navy. This is home now. When my father moved to New Zealand, it changed things. He has a good life there and he loves it, but it's just too far to go and it's not for me. I'm happy for him though. He's in his seventies and it's given him a new lease on life. But my life is here."

They talked for a while longer, and then they hung up. She thought about him afterward. He was so different from his brash, aggressive style as an attorney. She liked him better in private life, although she could see he was a good lawyer. It was nice chatting with him and learning more about him. She could easily imagine him on a horse in Montana, but now he was definitely a big city boy.

She spent the rest of the weekend doing the small tasks around the house she had wanted to do. She did some work, read a novel, and missed her children. They had texted her on Thanksgiving, and she had facetimed Tammy and Stacey. It was a peaceful holiday and a nice break. By Sunday night, she was ready to go back to work again, and looked forward to it. Weekends were lonely without kids or a man in your life. She'd been wrestling with it for years, and work always filled the void.

As it turned out, she'd been right to tell Scott to wait until they considered the settlement period totally over. The week before Christmas, she got a call from Jack Hirsch. They wanted another meeting. Her own team was fed up by then, and thought it was pointless. But they couldn't refuse, so Kate set it up.

Jack and Scott walked in with their client, and Scott was stone-faced and barely greeted her. He definitely had two personalities, his professional one, and the one who had called her twice and bandaged her knees.

Jack took the lead this time. He droned on forever about how insulting their offer was, how insensitive they were, how badly the plaintiff had gotten screwed over by their client's incompetence, and how gravely he had suffered. Kate nearly fell asleep in the meeting, and let her mind wander. They'd heard it all before. Then at the end of his monologue, he said that in spite of how insulting the offer was, their client had decided to accept it, to avoid the headache and expense of a trial. Kate snapped her attention back to the proceedings, and looked at Scott with a quizzical expression. He nodded and smiled.

"Well, I'll be damned," Kate said under her breath, and one of her colleagues laughed when he heard her. The offer had been off the table for some time, but her client agreed to honor his offer. All of the attorneys stood up and met to shake hands, and the plaintiff walked out without a word to any of them. Good sportsmanship was definitely not his style. Their own client thanked them and left a few minutes later. He was relieved to be rid of the lawsuit and so was Kate.

The attorneys all stood around talking, and Scott made his way to Kate. "You were right," he said softly, "I didn't think we had another round in us."

"It's always better to wait and be safe, and not shut the door." She was grateful that her client was willing to reinstate the offer, just to get the matter over with.

"You know what this means, don't you?" She smiled at Scott and he looked puzzled.

"You don't have to see your client again—until his next lawsuit. He sues everyone. We've been up against him before on other matters."

"I don't care," Scott said, smiling down at her. He was tall, with dark hair and green eyes, and very good looking, which didn't really matter. "It means that my raincheck is now valid, and fully redeemable. What are you doing tomorrow? Let's have a drink to celebrate, and don't tell me we have to wait till the deal is signed. That's bullshit."

She laughed. "Okay, tomorrow. Deal." She felt silly having a drink with him, but she felt awkward reneging on a promise, and he'd been so persistent about it. "Where?"

He mentioned a bar a few blocks away from her office. It was nicer than most of them, and had a restaurant too. "Six o'clock?" It was earlier than she usually left the office, but she was willing.

"Bring your coupon with you. It's not transferable."

He laughed at that. "As though I would transfer it to someone else. I would kill them first. This is *my* raincheck, and I intend to use it. We've earned it."

They all disbanded with enormous relief a few minutes later. Kate's managing partner said it was the best Christmas gift they could have, to settle the case and get rid of it.

And now she had a date for a drink with Scott White to celebrate. It seemed silly to her, but she had nothing else to do, so what the hell. He'd scraped her off the sidewalk and bandaged her knees, so the least she could do was have a drink with him. She owed him that. And he seemed like a decent guy.

Chapter 15

Kate forgot she was having a drink with Scott the next day when she dressed for work, so she wore a gray skirt and a gray cashmere sweater, and realized once she was at the office that looked seriously drab. She had worn a warm gray coat over it, since it was freezing outside. She also had on her gray suede boots with high heels. She looked very serious and lawyerly. She didn't even have a scarf with her to jazz it up. But it wasn't a date anyway, she reminded herself. It was a drink between lawyers to celebrate the resolution of a case, after a lot of grief along the way, for the lawyers on both sides.

She arrived right on time, and found Scott sitting at the bar. He looked happy to see her, and the maître d' led them to a quiet corner table. Scott suggested champagne, which sounded good to her and appropriate for a celebration. They toasted each other when it arrived.

"So you're a widow," he said gently. "Long time? Short time?" He hoped it wasn't too recent.

"Very long time. Nineteen years. Twenty in January. Helicopter accident. He was a congressman." That told him all he needed to know, except that Tom was divorcing her, which she wasn't going to tell him.

"You must have been a kid when it happened."

"Young enough. I was thirty-five, with three kids, who were thirteen, ten, and seven. I kind of hung around for a year, trying to figure out what to do, and then went to law school."

"After he died?" He seemed surprised. He had looked up her law school graduation from Columbia and saw it was only sixteen years earlier, so he figured her for early to mid-forties, at most. "I thought you were younger than I am, by a few years. I'm forty-eight, as I mentioned."

"That's very flattering, but no, I'm ancient. Fifty-five." He could Google it anyway, there was no point lying, and this wasn't Match .com or computer dating. "Do I have to give the drink back now?" He laughed.

"Definitely not. I don't care about age. It's hard enough meeting someone you want to see again, let alone worrying about whether the numbers match up."

"I'm seven years older than you are. If you're considering me for a date, I'm too old for you," she said bluntly.

"Am I too young for you?" he asked her directly, looking anxious.

"I'm not sure I ever want to date again. I had a six-year, superficial, on and off, long distance dating relationship that ended a couple of months ago. As he put it, we had reached our expiration date. It just kind of petered out. We didn't see much of each other, and it never went very deep."

"Did you want it that way?" He wasn't afraid to ask questions, and he wanted answers. She wasn't sure if she was auditioning or not. But in her mind, she wasn't.

"At the time, yes. My kids were younger, although the youngest was in college, and my son had just graduated, but they came home a lot, and I like being available for them. He wasn't big on kids, and I didn't expect him to be involved with mine. I kind of kept them apart."

"It sounds like you played it safe, emotionally. Not too involved." She nodded.

"I've never had a big deal relationship since my husband died. I had my kids. They kept me busy, and happy."

"And now?"

"Not always so happy," she said honestly. "It's harder when they get older. I see them when I can, and they're not too busy. It's an adjustment once they're out of the house. I'm still trying to figure it all out. But that's not an excuse to get in over my head in a dating relationship. It has to be the right person, and I've never met that person. I wasn't looking for it." In fact, she'd been hiding from serious commitment, most of the time.

"Neither was I," he admitted. "I've had some long term relationships, one in particular that lasted for eight years. We lived together, but it was never quite right. We finally agreed to give up and move on. Time passes quickly. And we lead busy lives. Suddenly you wake up and you're forty-eight, and forgot to get married. The right person just never came along. I'm okay with it. I have a good life."

"Forgot to get married, or didn't want to." She turned the tables on him.

"Maybe both. I'm not convinced I'm cut out for marriage. And if I don't want kids, there's not much reason for it."

"I kind of feel that way too about marriage. I'm not going to have more kids. So I have no incentive for marriage. I like time to myself now too. That's hard to explain to people who don't need that. I gave up all my time and energy to my kids for a lot of years, now it's kind of nice to be lazy once in a while, and do what I want when I'm not working, I work most of the time."

"Yeah, me too," he said, looking pensive. "We lawyers are a strange breed. The good ones are all workaholics. I don't think you can do it any other way." She nodded.

"I agree."

"Which leaves no time to date," he concluded with a grin, "or not like normal humans do anyway. Women don't like it when you come home with a briefcase full of work. But I love what I do."

"So do I," she smiled at him, "except with clients like yours. Fortunately, most of them aren't that way. I couldn't have been a lawyer while I was married. My husband's political career was too demanding. He needed me on deck all the time, especially during campaigns."

"I would hate that," Scott said, looking at her admiringly.

"I didn't love it either, but it was the deal. I always knew he wanted to go into politics. He loved it."

"Were you happy with him?" It was a tough question from someone she barely knew. She didn't answer for a long time.

"I don't know why, but I'll answer you honestly. I was. He wasn't. He wanted a divorce right before he died. There was someone else. I just told the kids recently. They never knew. My mother thought that I should be honest with them, instead of covering for him, which I always did. It's twenty years later, and she thinks they have a right to know. My mother is a psychologist."

"I'm sorry I asked, but I'm intrigued by you. Wife, mother, you're a great lawyer, politician's wife, obviously for a long time."

"Fourteen years."

"You do everything so well. You're alone, and you were alone for a long time with three kids. I don't know how you've done it all."

"You just do it. And then one day your kids tell you what you did wrong."

"Can you tell them to go to hell?" She shook her head.

"No, you can't. They get bitching rights forever about how you screwed up their lives. They're yours forever, for better or worse." She smiled, thinking of Claire.

"That scares me to death. I'm sure I'd do a lousy job, and they'd never forgive me. That's why I never wanted kids. I'm too selfish anyway. And I'm always working."

"I've always got one who is pissed off or hates me, and one or two who love me and think I'm great. It hurts, but it's the way it works. I like perfect scores. In fact, one of their complaints is that I expected too much of them, and wanted them to be perfect. They're probably right. I thought they *were* perfect. And recently the whole house of cards came tumbling down, and it turns out that they're human, and not perfect—and so am I. It's been a hell of a shock. But we're getting things put back together now. It's a little more real, and maybe easier to manage. I think I raised the bar too high for all of us. I figured that if everything and everyone was perfect, nothing bad would happen to us, but that's not the way it works. Bad things happen anyway." He nodded, absorbing what she was saying, and he was impressed. Nothing appeared to be out of order with her. She seemed in perfect control of herself, her environment, and didn't have a hair out of place.

"You're an impressive woman, Kate. I couldn't do what you've done. It was a lot easier being by myself."

"Lonely though," she said simply, and he nodded.

"That's the problem when you get older. It's not so terrific being alone. And if you wait too long, no one wants you. The dilemma of timing. I hope your kids realize how awesome you are, and appreciate what you gave up for them," he said, truly impressed with her.

She laughed. "That's not part of the deal. They're not supposed to notice, and they don't."

"So what's the score at the moment? How many love you, how many don't?" He was fascinated by her and her family and what she said. She seemed like the most practical, realistic, enchanting woman he'd ever met. He had suspected it in the office, but she was even better than his fantasies about her.

"One hate, two loves," she said without hesitating. "That's about par for the course. At two hates, I panic. Right now, we're okay." He laughed and they both noticed that it was already eight o'clock.

"Can you stay for dinner?" he asked cautiously. She seemed like a bird who would fly away easily if you grabbed for her, and he didn't want to rush her, and lose her so soon. Kate could stay for dinner, but she wasn't sure if she should. She hesitated. "We can do it another time," he said, so she didn't feel pressured, which was all she needed to feel comfortable. She was having a nice time with him.

"No, let's do it now. I can stay." She smiled at him, and he liked being there with her. She wore a faint musky perfume, he could just barely smell it. He wanted to lean closer to her so he could, but he didn't want to frighten her or seem weird. It had a mysterious Oriental scent to it. It was as bewitching as everything else about her. She was a feast for the senses. He couldn't imagine how any man would want to leave her, her husband in the past, or the man she had recently broken up with because they'd reached their "expiration date." Scott thought he must have been crazy to let her go.

They talked about other things during dinner, his time in the Navy, her time at Columbia law school, working to become a partner of the firm while she raised three kids and how she did it, her mother the artist and psychologist, who sounded fascinating too.

"My life in Montana as a kid was so mundane compared to yours. I was an only child in a small, simple place. It was a good life. I didn't really start to see the world until I was in the Navy, and then I wanted to go everywhere. I was thinking about going to med school, but it took too long, so I went to law school instead. It was the right decision. I love the law. I think about going out on my own one day, but I like the convenience and protection of a big firm, with everything at your fingertips and important clients. As a corporate lawyer, I think a big firm is the way to go."

"I'm happy where I am too." She looked satisfied as she said it. There was nothing disgruntled about her, or unfulfilled, and he liked that about her. She was happy with her lot in life, despite everything that had happened to her. That was rare, he knew.

They had finished dinner by then and he didn't want the evening to end. "What happens now that I've used my raincheck up, a double since we had dinner too. Is that it? Do I get another chance?" She thought about it and smiled, still not sure what he wanted from her, a date or a friend.

"You don't mind that I'm seven years older? Are we friends?"

"We are now, I hope, but I have to be honest with you, truth in advertising, I'd love to be more than that one day. And seven years is nothing. It's small change." He didn't want to terrify her, but he wanted to make it clear, he didn't want her as a pal, although he would have settled for that. He was wildly attracted to her, and had been since the first time he saw her across the room, and he didn't give a damn how old she was. "I wouldn't care if you were ninety, you're the most beautiful, exciting woman I've ever met." What he said was very flattering but she couldn't believe it. She was just an ordinary person, a widow with three kids, and a lawyer. She never saw herself as exciting or special, but it seemed kind of fun that he did. She smiled at what he said.

"I really think you deserve another raincheck after all that, or several of them."

"Do you like movies?"

"I love them, ballet, theater, not opera, and staying home. I'm a homebody."

"So am I." He looked pleased. "That's hard to sell on a hot date."

"Maybe that's why I don't date much."

He got her home at eleven. They'd been together since six o'clock, and the time had flown. They had learned a lot about each other. He kissed her lightly on the cheek when he left her in front of her building with the doorman watching, and he continued on in the cab. She went upstairs feeling pleased. She'd had a very nice time. It didn't have the panache and sophistication of an evening with Bart, or even Tom, but Scott was a smart, extremely astute man in the same field she was. They had a lot in common, and she was completely at ease with him, and could be open and honest about everything. That was a first. She didn't have to "be" anything or anyone for him, except herself.

Kate's dinner for the whole family with their partners on Christmas Eve was even more fun than the first one before Thanksgiving. She had decorated her apartment and a tree and put everyone's presents under it. She made eggnog, and served that and champagne when they all arrived. She had invited them for six o'clock. They opened presents at seven and sat down to dinner at eight. Everyone loved their gifts, and the children always gave Kate lovely ones that meant a lot to her. She had chosen all of theirs with great care.

She had ordered a family style meal from an excellent Italian restaurant. They delivered it on time, and the girls helped her serve it, even Claire. She had given Claire several outfits for the baby, along with presents for her, and Claire was excited. The baby was two and a half months away now, and she was huge. It was going to be a big boy. She was excited about her trip to St. Bart's with Reed the day after Christmas too. It would be their last trip before she became a mother.

The food was plentiful, and the conversation loud. Reed had brought some terrific French wine. It was a real family Christmas with all eight of them at the table, and everyone was in great spirits. Then Anthony said he had an announcement. They all looked at each other, and Alicia, sure that he was going to say he was getting engaged. His wedding date with Amanda had been a few days before, and they had all wondered if he was sad about that, but he didn't seem to be. He looked jubilant now. Kate was afraid that an engagement would be too fast. They had only known each other for six months, but he stunned them into silence with what he said.

"They've asked me to open our new corporate office in New Delhi. It's a fantastic career opportunity and I can still design games. They're moving a big chunk of our videogame design and production department there. I'm moving to India in January," he stood beaming at them, "and I'm taking Alicia with me," he added. "She just finished school at the end of the semester. There's a huge film industry in India, and they love exotic women. We already have the name of an agent, and she's going to audition there for some parts in feature films." He looked like he was about to explode he was so happy, and Kate felt it like a blow and didn't want to show it. He was going so far away. It felt like a terrible loss to Kate. Margaret looked at her immediately, and understood.

"How long will you be going for?" Kate tried to sound upbeat about it, and happy for him. But her son was moving to India. She would hardly see him anymore. He had grown wings. She was pleased for him, but sad for herself, selfishly, and she knew that was wrong.

"Just two years," Anthony said. "We're coming back in June or

July for a three-week vacation. And if we haven't killed each other by then, we want to get married while we're here. So get ready for a wedding." Alicia smiled broadly at that. "We want to start a family after that, but not until we're married." He looked at his sister pointedly, to register his disapproval again of what she was doing. Their family values hadn't been totally lost on him.

"You can meet the baby then," Claire said, smiling happily. "He'll be three months old in June."

"Does she think of anything else anymore?" he said in a low voice to Tammy. "She's getting to be as bad as Amanda was with the wedding."

"I think it's some kind of hormonal thing. Pregnant women get obsessed with their babies, even if it's boring as shit for the rest of us."

"So that's our big news," Anthony concluded. They were moving to India in January, and getting married in June or July. Kate felt a little better knowing the move was only for two years, not forever, like going away to college, and they would be coming back in six months to get married. But January was only a few weeks away.

"I think your mother and I should come to visit you in India," Margaret said with a light in her eyes. "I've been wanting to get back there for ages, and now we have the perfect excuse."

"After the baby comes," Claire added. "I want you both here till then." She glanced from her mother to her grandmother and Anthony rolled his eyes.

"I can hardly wait till the baby comes out and you get your brain back," he said to his little sister, and Reed laughed. Claire rarely talked about her work anymore. Reed read baby books and she read nothing. She was thinking about Lamaze classes in January, but she still wasn't sure. She felt certain she could get through the delivery without them, with drugs. It couldn't be that bad.

"Any of you who want to come to visit us are most welcome," Alicia stood up and said. She had high hopes for launching her movie career there, and possibly a better shot at it than in the States.

"Why don't you two come too?" Kate leaned over and said to Tammy about a trip to India, and Tammy glanced at Stacey, who looked noncommittal.

"We might have other plans next year," Tammy answered vaguely, but it was certainly the biggest piece of news at the table, and everyone said they were going to miss them, and Kate most of all.

They stayed until midnight and then everyone went home with their presents, after hugging and wishing each other a Merry Christmas. Some went to midnight mass, Alicia and Anthony and Reed. Claire was too tired. Stacey wasn't a churchgoer and Tammy stayed home with her. Margaret always said it was too late for her. And Kate wanted to clean up after dinner. Margaret stayed back to talk to Kate for a few minutes after the young people left. "Are you all right about Anthony leaving?" She worried about her, she was so attached to her children.

"Do I have a choice? It's for his job." She sighed. "At least he's not going forever, and it's very exciting for him, for both of them. It's a wonderful opportunity. I would never stand in the way of that. They all have to grow up and so do I." She had no doubt in her mind, Alicia was the right woman for him. She encouraged him in just the right ways and gave him strength. She didn't drain his energy the way Amanda had. And if they decided to get married next summer, Kate was fine with it, and she told Anthony that before he left that night. They had her blessing, and he thanked her and hugged her tight. He appreciated how supportive she had been of all the changes in his life in the past six months, even when she didn't agree with him.

Kate sat alone in the living room after her mother left. She turned off the lights, and sat looking at the tree all lit up, remembering what it was like when they were little, assembling bicycles and doll carriages for all three of them to discover on Christmas morning, after Santa Claus left them during the night. They had been the best years of her life. But she couldn't let the story stop there. They were the early years, when Tom was alive and still loved her. And there had been all the years since, and now these last few months where they were all starting to take flight, in directions she had never even dreamed of, into skies far from where she could even see them. She couldn't protect them anymore, or keep them safe. She had to trust that their wings were strong and would carry them as far away as they chose to fly from her, and back again. These were the years she had dreaded long ago. They had finally come. Her babies were gone. Men and women had taken their place, with ideas that she didn't always agree with, like Claire's.

It was all different now, but the house was still standing, and it was strong. From now on, they would come and go, and she would be there for them, and they would be there for each other. Their foundations were built on rock, and the family was as strong as she had hoped. It was all she had to give them of real value.

Chapter 16

Scott called Kate two days after Christmas, and invited her to dinner and a movie. She accepted happily. She was quiet when he picked her up, and he thought she seemed different. He asked her if anything was wrong.

"Not really. My kids are growing up. My son announced on Christmas Eve that he's moving to India for two years. It's a wonderful opportunity for him. I'm just going to miss him. He's coming home next summer for three weeks, possibly to get married. His moving away like that is a big change. I have to get used to it. It kind of shocked me. We've had a lot of shocks in the past six months, but this is a big one and a good one. But even the good changes can be hard." He nodded, trying to imagine what it felt like for a mother to watch her children move away. He had done it to his parents when he left Montana. He had never realized how much it must have hurt them. And then his mother died later. He'd had a happy childhood with them, and he still missed them at times, especially now with his father so far away. He had never thought of it before from their perspective, when he left for college and never moved back, and how hard it must have been for them. He had only thought of it from his point of view. He had never before realized the selflessness it took to let one's children go and fly away, because it was what they wanted.

"None of your kids are married yet?" Scott asked her and she shook her head.

"Not yet. Almost. Anthony was supposed to get married this month, and he canceled the wedding in September. He fell in love with a different girl. She's going to India with him. Stupidly, I would have objected to her before. And I think she's lovely and the right girl for him. I would have picked the wrong one, for all the wrong reasons. He found a better one, for him, which is what matters. They're thinking of getting married next summer." She thought about telling him the rest then, but she wasn't ready to share it with him yet.

They went to a movie that made them laugh, and had dinner afterward. They talked about a million different things until the restaurant closed, and then he took her home. She didn't invite him up, and he didn't suggest it. They were still learning about each other and having fun. Kate no longer cared about the age gap between them, it seemed irrelevant.

He was going on his ski trip four days later. He planned to leave the morning of New Year's Eve. She was going to stay home cozily in her pajamas, which was what she had done for several years. She used to go to parties on that night, but she felt that people tried too hard, and it was never as much fun as she'd thought it would be. She liked staying home better.

When he dropped her off at her place, he wished her a happy New Year and said he'd call her from Vermont. She'd had another lovely evening with him, and he kissed her gently on the lips before he left her. It was a heady promise of things to come, if everything worked out right.

The next morning, Tammy called her.

"We just got a wedding license, Mom." She sounded breathless. "We've been wrestling with a decision. It changed things once Stacey met the family, and we're not a secret anymore. We want to get married and try to have a baby, and we want to do it in the right order. Neither of us care about a wedding or a big white dress. We have the wedding license now. We want to get married in two days, on the thirtieth. Will you be my witness?" Tears filled Kate's eyes. She was going to be the witness to her daughter's gay marriage, and if what she had always said to them was true, that all she wanted was their happiness, this was the proof of it. This was the happiness Tammy wanted.

"I'd be honored," Kate said, with raw emotion in her voice.

"We have an appointment at noon in city hall. We're going to the sperm bank tomorrow. Stacey knows how to do the insemination since she's a doctor. It's pretty simple. We want to do it on our wedding day. It probably won't work the first time, but we'll try." It was a little more mechanical and more detail than Kate was ready for, but she was touched to be included and part of the wedding. It was a little startling to realize that her first child to get married was going to be her daughter marrying another woman. But they had been together for a long time, and Kate had come to love Stacey. She was an honorable woman. "Do you think Grandma would be our other witness?"

"You can ask her. I think she'd love it."

"I'll call her," Tammy said, sounding excited. Kate called her florist as soon as she hung up and ordered a bouquet of white Phalaenopsis orchids for each of them. She didn't know what they were wearing, but brides needed bouquets, and she wanted them to have them. The florist asked her if one was the tossing bouquet, in which case they would make it smaller. It was a standard question.

"No, two brides, two bouquets, same size, one for each of them."

"Are they twins? Is it a double wedding?"

"No, they're marrying each other. My daughter is marrying her partner, and I want the bouquets to be gorgeous."

"Of course," the woman at the other end said nervously. "We'll deliver them to you at nine A.M. on the thirtieth."

"Perfect, thank you." She made a reservation for lunch at La Grenouille afterward, and the rest of the details she left up to them. She took two blue handkerchiefs out of a drawer. And she got the string of pearls Tom had given her when Tammy was born out of her jewelry case. Margaret called her a few minutes later.

"We're witnesses day after tomorrow, I hear. This is so exciting." Margaret sounded genuinely happy for them, and Kate was too. She didn't have to fake it or pretend. And she wouldn't have to at Anthony's wedding next summer either. She would be truly happy for him.

"I'll pick you up at eleven A.M.," Kate told her mother.

"What'll we wear?"

"Something nice. I just made a reservation for lunch afterward at La Grenouille for the four of us."

"They don't want Claire and Anthony there?"

"I don't think so. Tammy would have mentioned it. It seems to be just the four of us."

Kate picked Margaret up at eleven A.M., on the day of the wedding. They were both wearing mink coats, and Kate had a navy wool dress under hers, Margaret a gray suit. They were meeting the girls at city hall. She had the florist boxes with the bouquets in them, the pearls and the blue handkerchiefs.

"We should have picked Claire and Reed up and gotten them married too. Maybe they would have given us a group rate," Margaret said and Kate laughed. The ironies of life were exquisite sometimes.

Tammy and Stacey were waiting for them in the lobby of city hall, as Margaret and Kate hurried in, carrying the boxes. Kate opened both of them and handed a bouquet to each bride. They were truly beautiful. Tammy was wearing a white Chanel suit with a white coat over it, and a very chic little white Chanel hat with a wisp of white veil over her eyes. She looked spectacular with her blond hair in a bun, and Stacey was so happy she looked like she was about to burst in her Saint Laurent tuxedo pantsuit, with black patent leather men's dress pumps, a white tuxedo shirt from Charvet in Paris, and black satin bow tie. Kate reached into her purse then, and brought out the pearls. She put them around Tammy's neck and clasped them in back.

"Your father gave them to me when you were born. They're yours now, on your wedding day." There were tears in Kate's and Tammy's eyes when they looked at each other. And then Kate reached into her purse again and pulled out the two pale blue lace handkerchiefs. "Something borrowed, something blue, I'm lending one of these to each of you. So you have to give them back for good luck." Margaret stood by watching approvingly, and patted her daughter's arm.

"When you do it right, you really do it. I'm proud of you."

"I'm proud of all of us." It was five to twelve by then, and they went to the room where they'd been directed to go. They had the wedding license, and there were two urns of white flowers as they walked into the room. Another couple was just leaving. The bride had on a tight white lace wedding dress, and a veil, and they were beaming.

"Good luck," they whispered to the foursome. Kate could never have imagined that this would be such a happy day, but it was. It felt just right to all four of them, and most of all to Tammy and Stacey.

The clerk officiating made a very nice little speech about marriage, and got their names right. They had signed the papers to change their names when they got the license. They were both taking the name Morgan-Adams, which combined their last names. He pronounced them wife and wife, without batting an eye. He had done that often by now, and told Stacey she could kiss the bride. She handed her bouquet to Margaret, and kissed Tammy. She had handed her bouquet to her mother when they exchanged rings. Tammy was wearing a narrow diamond eternity band and Stacey a wide gold one. They had bought them at Tiffany the day before. Collectively, they had thought of everything. A photographer stepped up to take their picture, and Kate said in a stage whisper, "Take lots please!" and they all laughed. It was the happiest day Kate could remember in a long time.

They were back on the steps of city hall at twelve-thirty, having posed for a few extra photographs in the lobby, and Kate took photographs of the bridal couple with her cellphone, and the father of another bride took a few of all four of them, and then they got in the car Kate had hired with a driver who drove them uptown to La Grenouille for lunch. Both girls handed her back the blue handkerchiefs in the car, to return what had been blue and "borrowed," for good luck at the wedding, and all four women walked into La Grenouille wearing broad smiles, looking elegant and radiant.

They had a spectacular lunch in the exquisite restaurant, and Kate ordered Cristal champagne. They left at three-thirty. It had been a very special day for all four of them. Tammy thanked her mother for making it so perfect.

"You two are what made it special," Kate said with deep emotion, and meant it.

She gave them the car to take them home, and she and Margaret went uptown in a cab, and talked about the wedding.

"I don't know why Claire doesn't just do something like that,"

Margaret said. "It was very sweet and relatively painless. And you made it so nice for them. I'm very proud of you," Margaret said tenderly.

"Thank you. You're beginning to sound like me about Claire," she said with a sigh. "But she's not going to do it. We just have to accept it."

"She's making such a point of not getting married. It's so childish," Margaret said, annoyed with her. It wasn't worth the energy she was putting into it, or the people she was upsetting to have her way.

"The girls looked so pretty, didn't they," Kate said happily. Tammy's suit and coat had been gorgeous, and classic Chanel. And the pearls had looked just right.

Kate dropped her mother off at her building and Margaret turned to smile at her. "Well done." Kate smiled and waved as they drove away, and when she walked into her apartment she had a text from Tammy, telling her what it meant to her to have her mother be a part of it, and make it all so lovely for them. They would never forget it. She had texted her brother and sister too to tell them they had just gotten married. Both responded immediately to congratulate them.

Tammy took her chic Chanel hat and laid it down carefully on a table when they walked into their apartment. She wanted to save the hat and her bouquet forever. She was so touched that her mother had brought the flowers, and Stacey loved hers too. Tammy thought she'd wear the dress and coat again. She had worn white satin Manolo Blahnik shoes with rhinestone buckles that she had bought the day before when they went to Tiffany for their rings.

They had pulled everything together in a single day, once they decided to do it, and Kate had added the little extra touches that made it more special.

"It was magical, wasn't it?" Tammy said as she sat down on the couch, still in her wedding dress after she took off the coat.

"I never thought a city hall wedding could be so much fun. And lunch was fabulous," Stacey said and sat down next to Tammy with a look of gratitude and disbelief. "I never believed we'd get here, did you? Marriage at a pretty little wedding. Your mom and grandmother there as our witnesses. I keep thinking I must be dreaming." She looked happy and peaceful.

"I thought it would happen, I just didn't know when or how," Tammy said, smiling at her.

And now they had the rest to do, which had been the whole point of the wedding before they did it. They'd actually been carefully selecting their sperm donor for three months, but they both wanted to be married before they did it. And the one they wanted had made a sperm donation yesterday, just for them. He was Swedish-American, with blue eyes and strong masculine features, six feet four, and a medical student at NYU. He looked surprisingly like Tammy, as though he could have been her brother, and he looked a little like Stacey too. They were both tall and angular, and Stacey had been blond before her hair turned gray when she was twenty-five.

The vial was waiting for them in the refrigerator, since they'd picked it up at the sperm bank, and Stacey had been instructed how to use it. You didn't need a doctor to do it, but it was convenient that she was one. There would be no slipups, and Tammy trusted her to do it more than anyone. It was the final seal of their vows and their bond on this very special day.

"Why don't you go change," Stacey said gently. "We're not doing this in a Chanel dress," she said and Tammy laughed.

She came back a few minutes later in her nightgown with nothing under it. Stacey was reading the directions again. She had three needleless syringes, in case there was a problem with any of them. It was a completely painless procedure, which only required directing the sperm upward with the syringe internally, just as it would happen during normal sex. It just came out of a syringe instead of a penis, but the process was simple and similar. There were no hormone shots involved or medication. Tammy was only thirty-two, and had no history of fertility problems. All they needed was the sperm.

"I'll get out of my tuxedo and be back in a minute," Stacey said. She was back five minutes later in her nightgown too. Tammy looked at her, and they both had the same idea at the same time. Since they lived together, they had the same cycle and the time was right for her too. They were both ovulating at the exact moment. Tammy had checked that morning. It was why they had wanted to get married on that day, so Tammy could get pregnant on their wedding day, if it worked the first time. They realized that they might have to try for six or eight months, or even a year for her to get pregnant. This was only the first try, but if it took, Tammy loved the idea of conceiving on the day they married. And she finally felt ready to get pregnant, after months of thinking about it.

"Why don't we both do it?" Tammy voiced what they were both thinking and hadn't said.

"Is that too weird? And I want to be sure there's enough sperm for you," Stacey said, but she could already see that there was more than they needed, even a lot more, just in case they spilled some. "There's no point doing it halfway, we want this to work. My eggs are nine years older than yours. We have a much better chance of you getting pregnant." They had known that for some time.

"You're only forty-one. Women your age get pregnant all the time."

"I know. I see the results in my practice. Half of the kids I see have mothers over forty now. Some of them have to work at it with IVF and hormones. I don't know if I'm over the hill yet or not." But her periods were as regular as Tammy's.

"Let's do it. That way maybe at least one of us might get pregnant. It could be you." They hadn't planned for that, and Stacey thought Tammy would handle it better. She couldn't see herself nursing nine months from now. But she suddenly loved the idea of both of them doing it on their wedding day. "Should I do it to you?" Tammy asked her.

"I'll tell you how. I can probably do it myself. Most women do, they don't have a doctor to help them. It's a very simple process. You just fill the syringe from the vial and shoot it up there."

Stacey carried the vial into their bedroom, while Tammy laid two big bath towels on the bed, and they lay down next to each other, and pulled their nightgowns up. Stacey carefully filled two syringes to maximum capacity, and there was even a little more left over. She inserted the first one into Tammy, pushed the plunger, with Tammy's pelvis tilted upward, and told her to lie there for a while. Then she used the second one on herself as Tammy watched. After that she used what was left for a little more in each syringe for a "top-up." It was all done in a matter of minutes. Stacey put two pillows under Tammy's hips and told her to lie still, and did the same for herself.

"It's probably an old wives' tale, but they say that helps with conception. It gets the sperm swimming in the right direction. I don't know if it's true or not, but why not try it? Let's stay here for an hour to be on the safe side." They both had their bottoms on pillows, and lay next to each other chatting excitedly.

"What if we both have twins?" Tammy asked her.

"Then I'm divorcing you immediately, and you're on your own, kid." She laughed too. "It's taken me forty-one years to decide I could handle one. I'm not sure about two, but if we're doubly blessed, I'll deal with it and figure it's God's will. Four and I'm out of the picture. I know what we're going to be dealing with. I see these little monsters every day. We won't get a decent night's sleep for the next ten years."

"At least we'll have our own in-house doctor. We won't have to go to the emergency room every five minutes. When will we know if this worked?"

"A couple of days past two weeks, more like three. We can use a home test, and I'll confirm it with a blood test."

"This is so exciting, isn't it? I hope we both get pregnant."

"I think I hope so too," Stacey said in a serious voice, and when they looked at each other, they were both crying. Their emotions were overwhelming. They lay next to each other and held hands for a while, and then Stacey leaned over and kissed her.

"This is the best day of my life, Tammy. Just because of you, even if this doesn't work this time."

"It's the best day of mine too."

There were no words left after that. They just lay next to each other, holding hands, thinking about what might happen.

Chapter 17

Kate was still floating on the cloud of the wedding the day before when she got up and made coffee on the morning of New Year's Eve. She stood in her kitchen thinking about the girls and how happy they had been. It had really been a perfect day. Her phone rang as she was thinking about it, and she was startled when it was Scott. He was still so new in her life, and his calls were always a surprise.

"Hi? Where are you? In Vermont?"

"No," he said, sounding disappointed. "There's a huge storm in New England. The roads are closed. We had to cancel. I know this is very rude and last minute, but I thought I'd check in with you and see what your plans are for tonight."

She laughed at the question. "Bed, my pajamas, and a movie on TV."

"No champagne and popcorn?"

"I forgot them."

He was sounding more cheerful by the minute. "If I provide the popcorn and champagne, and maybe a pizza, could I crash your party? Or will the bouncer stop me at the door?"

"Hmm . . . let's see, I have to think about it. What kind of pizza?"

"You name it, and it's yours."

"Wow, that's tough to resist." She liked the idea of spending New Year's Eve with him. She was really enjoying his company, although they had only had two dates so far, and one kiss. But the kiss had been first rate, and the dates were fun too. "Okay, you bring the pizza, maybe half mushroom, half margherita?"

"Or one of each. This is a big night."

"Okay, so you get the pizza and popcorn. I probably have a bottle of champagne here somewhere, and I'll talk to the bouncer and make sure that they let you in."

"Fantastic!" he said, suddenly delighted that he hadn't gone to Vermont. He'd rather spend the evening with her. "You sound very cheery by the way. What have you been up to since I saw you?"

"My oldest daughter, Tammy, got married yesterday. It was a really sweet wedding at city hall, and we had lunch afterward at La Grenouille."

"Was that expected?" He sounded startled. "You didn't mention it the other day."

"No, it was kind of last minute and a surprise. But a very nice surprise. My mother and I were her witnesses. It all came off very nicely."

"Do you like the groom?"

"Very much. I'll explain it to you tonight when I see you." She didn't want to tell him over the phone. And she wouldn't have told Bart at all. But she wasn't ashamed of it now. She was very proud, and she wanted to tell Scott all about it. She wondered how open-minded he was, but she was about to find out.

"See you later. Are you seriously going to wear pajamas?"

"I was going to," she said, happy with their plans.

"Well, don't change anything for me. What time does the party start?"

"When you get here."

"How about seven-thirty? We can eat early, and then start watching movies. We can get two in by midnight."

"That's perfect." She was smiling and humming to herself as she put her coffee cup in the sink, and went to figure out what to wear that night. It had to be something a little cuter than pajamas. She hadn't had a date on New Year's Eve in ages. She had only spent it with Bart once in six years. He was always in the Bahamas as a houseguest, or on a friend's yacht in the Caribbean, or skiing in Aspen with one of his kids, if they were around. They had never spent major holidays together. And she was excited to be spending the evening with Scott. It was a totally unexpected gift.

She found a pair of lounging pajamas that seemed right for the occasion, checked that she had a bottle of champagne, found two and put them in the fridge. She could make them a salad. Scott was bringing the rest.

He rang the doorbell at exactly seven-thirty after she had the doorman let him come up. He was carrying two shopping bags and two pizza boxes, and he kissed her on the lips before he started unpacking what he'd brought. He had a small tin of caviar on ice, with sour cream, lemon, and chopped egg. He had brought popping corn, and she slipped the pizza boxes in the oven to keep warm. She'd made the salad, and he had brought light-up necklaces and bracelets and sequined glasses with the year on them, and then he pulled out a pair of pajamas with hearts. He had admired hers as soon as he saw them. They were very glamorous compared to his.

"Where can I change?" he asked as she laughed at him, delighted with everything he had brought. Pizza, caviar, popcorn, and champagne sounded fantastic. He had improved on the theme. She pointed him toward the guest bathroom, and he was back two minutes later in the pajamas with hearts. He looked half sexy and half Bozo the Clown. He had brought slippers with fleece and he was wearing them.

"You are the best date I've ever had for New Year's Eve and the best dressed," she said and meant it. "Thank you for the caviar." She put it on a plate with the little mother of pearl spoons one was supposed to use. "This is so fun!"

They ate the pizza while it was warm, with the salad she'd made, and they both ate the caviar. He had decided he'd rather have red wine than champagne. They were saving that until midnight, and they sat at her kitchen table having a feast.

"So tell me about the wedding. Who did she marry? Was it a spur of the moment thing?" He wanted to know more about her kids. And she wanted to tell him.

"Yes, to all of the above. Do you remember I told you that our family had gone through a lot of changes in the last few months? Well, this was one of them. It actually started in July. It's been a very unnerving five months. I'll preface it by saying that pride cometh before a fall. I've always been very proud of my children. Great grades. Great schools. Terrific colleges. No problems with them. No alcoholics, no drug addicts, great jobs and careers, nice boyfriends. You couldn't ask for better children. I've always said I have perfect children. So . . . this summer I got it right between the eyes. My youngest daughter started dating a client of the law firm where she works, which seemed like a bad idea to me, and I'm sure does to you too."

He nodded. "It's against policy at our firm," he responded.

"Mine too. And hers."

"Is he an asshole?"

"No, he seems to be a really nice guy, nicer than my daughter at the moment. Two months later, she announced to me that she's pregnant, and refuses to get married. He wants to marry her, and she won't. She thinks it's an archaic tradition, and entirely unnecessary. Her brother and sister are furious with her, and so am I. The father is Reed Bailey, by the way." Scott opened his eyes wide and looked impressed. "In any case, she's refusing to get married, is knocked up, and is barely speaking to me, and hates me at the moment."

"That's your hate-you kid." He smiled at her.

"Exactly. Meanwhile my son was engaged to be married this month to a seemingly lovely girl. Prominent, very social family. Debutante, not that it matters. Nice parents. Ridiculously elaborate wedding costing a small fortune, but the sort of girl parents think they want their sons to marry. I will confess that I was all for it, although I realize now that she's not very bright, and very boring. But still, very proper. Meanwhile, he fell in love with a Puerto Rican Chinese lingerie model/actress from Spanish Harlem who he met at his gym and called off the wedding in September. I can live with that better than the baby out of wedlock. And while I was reeling from all that, my oldest daughter, a senior executive at Chanel and a really lovely person, told me that she's gay and has been living with a woman for seven years, while I never suspected it for a minute. I was clueless. So first you have to wonder who the hell are these kids, really, and then what kind of mother am I that they pull all this shit, and I don't know what's going on. My youngest kid has no morals, and my oldest is gay and I had no idea." He looked sympathetic as she told him all this over their pizza. It was a relief to tell him. "I'm not sure who I was madder at, them, or myself."

"Don't be so hard on yourself. This shit happens to people."

"But all three of them? All at one time?"

"It sounds like you had a bitch of a summer."

"I did. But I've come to my senses about some of it. As crazy as it sounds, I think my son did the right thing. I've met the girl, and she is perfect for him, and a nice person, smart as a whip and just got her degree from Hunter, at thirty. He's being transferred to New Delhi in three weeks, and she's going with him with my blessing, to try and further her acting career. She's ambitious and works hard. They want to get married next summer, as I told you the other day. So much for the debutante. I guess she's as dull as my other kids say. My son will have beautiful children with the new woman, but most of all, I think she's the right woman for him. He lied to her and didn't tell her he was engaged when they started dating. He was juggling both of them, trying to make up his mind, and when the Puerto Rican girl found out, she gave him a black eye. I'm against domestic violence, but I don't blame her.

"I'm glad my oldest daughter finally had the guts to tell me the truth. I thought she was working too hard to date. The woman she lives with is remarkable, summa cum laude from Harvard, a pediatrician, Doctors Without Borders, and a really wonderful human being. Tammy's been hiding her for seven years. I met her and I love her.

"They got married yesterday at city hall, and they want to have a baby. I was a witness at the wedding, and my mother was the other one. They decided three days ago to get married, so yes, it was a surprise, but not really. Not nearly the surprise it was when Tammy told me she's gay. They have my blessing too.

"The youngest one, Claire, is in my black book at the moment. I don't approve of illegitimate children, when there's no reason for it, and I don't think marriage is an irrelevant archaic tradition. I believe in it profoundly. So that's what I did this summer. I got the shit kicked out of me by my kids. But at least two of them are in pretty good situations now. It's not what I wanted for them, but their choices are right for them, and I respect that. The little one needs to have her ass kicked, and if her father were alive, he'd go berserk. So there it is." Scott was staring at her as she told him the story of the last five months and he looked stunned.

"I repeat what I said to you the last time I saw you. You are an *amazing* woman. Any one of those situations would have unglued me while it was going on. It's why I never wanted to have children.

It would have killed me. I don't know how you dealt with it, and three at once. Kate, you're a saint."

"No, I'm not," she said fervently, "I'm a shit mother. My daughter has no morals, my son is marrying an underwear model instead of a debutante, and I had no idea my other daughter was gay, which she's known since she was fifteen and she never told me, and I never noticed. What kind of crap mother is that?"

"A very human one, who is juggling five million balls in the air and three overactive kids. But you can't do everything for them. I agree with you. Sounds as if your youngest should have her ass kicked, not because she's knocked up, but because it sounds like she's giving you a hard time, which you don't deserve. All I can say is fucking Wow, Mrs. Morgan. You are one hell of a woman." He leaned across the table and kissed her hard on the mouth. "Hats off to you. I think you're the mother of the century. I probably would have bought a gun and shot them all. They are very, very lucky kids to have you. Not only did you survive all their shit, but you were open-minded enough to meet their lovers and boyfriends and girl-friends and partners, check them out, get to know them and reverse your opinion where appropriate. A lot of people wouldn't do that. You're giving your kids even more respect than they deserve, and they'd damn well better do the same for you.

"Funnily enough, I was going to ask you tonight if your kids would be upset that you're going out with me, or about the difference in our age, which you seemed to care about and I don't. But after hearing all that, I don't give a good goddamn what they think. You need a break, and if they give you any shit about me, they can address their complaints to me directly and leave you out of it. They shouldn't say a single word to you about anything you do, after what you put up with in the last five months. Kate, you are the most incredible woman I've ever met. I think you're fantastic, and I hope your kids do too. If they don't, they don't deserve you."

"How did I get so lucky? We took that crap case, against that asshole you represent, and hate too, and I wind up spending New Year's Eve with a guy in pajamas with hearts on them, who brings me caviar and pizza and light-up jewelry and thinks I'm terrific. I hope I deserve you. Not only that, you bandaged my knees for me when I fell flat on my face."

"I think we're both lucky." He smiled at her. "Now finish your pizza so we can watch a movie. And where do I find a pot to make the popcorn? It's showtime." She pointed him in the right direction for the pots and pans, cleared the table of their leftovers, and poured him another glass of wine.

The popcorn was ready a few minutes later and she poured it into a bowl, melted some butter to put on it, grabbed some paper napkins and his bottle of red wine, and steered him toward her bedroom to watch the movie.

"Where are all your kids now, by the way? Do they drop in on you?" He didn't want to create trouble for her, or embarrass her.

"Never," she answered his question about drop-ins. "They always call first and only come here when invited. I guess they're all celebrating New Year's Eve with their friends. Anthony is getting ready to leave for India, Claire is probably staring at her belly while Reed Bailey waits on her hand and foot. And the newlyweds are at their apartment, trying to get pregnant by a sperm donor."

"You deserve a vacation. Or a year off, or something. Meanwhile you actually do great work at the law firm and always make perfect sense. I'd be drooling in a corner by now, sucking my thumb."

"I've considered it, or a career in alcoholism."

"Screw all that. We are going to party tonight." He went back to get the light-up jewelry and put it on her, and the light-up glasses that had no lenses on himself. They turned off the lights, and he pulled her close to him as he lay next to her, and she smiled. She had never had a night like this with Bart Mackenzie, or any other man. "Thank God that fool you were dating thought you guys had an expiration date, or you'd probably never have gone out with me."

"I probably wouldn't," she said, smiling.

"I should probably write him a thank-you letter."

"Just don't vote for him if he ever runs for President."

"Another politician?"

"A senator, from Massachusetts."

"Am I boring for you? I'm just a lawyer from another law firm." He looked worried.

"So am I. I'm not a movie star. I'm just a lawyer, and a very mediocre mother."

"Bullshit," he said and kissed her again, and this time he gently ran a hand up her silk pajama top, and found her breasts with one hand, as she moaned softly. He had a delicate touch and was very gentle, and then he slid his hand down into her pajamas, and she turned toward him, and did the same. They hadn't made their movie selection yet, and forgot all about it as they discovered each other's bodies. He looked at her then with a question in his eyes, and she nodded. He had what they needed, in the pocket of his pajamas, and a minute later, they lay naked, as he admired her body, and she couldn't get enough of him. He was aching with desire for her, and she wanted him desperately.

He was the best lover she'd ever known, and they came together with such force that Kate could hardly breathe as she clung to him. They went on making love for a few minutes because it felt so good, they didn't want to stop.

"Oh my God, Kate . . . what are you? Lover of the year . . . mother of the year . . . why didn't I find you sooner? And why did we wait for that crappy case to settle before we did this?"

"Because we have ethics, and integrity," she said, still breathless.

"Fuck that, I want you . . . I hope you don't get tired of me, because now that I've found you, I'm never letting you go. I don't want to meet your children for a while, I want you to myself." It was what she wanted too. It was her turn now. She had earned the right to a life of her own, not constantly worrying about her children.

"You should meet my mother though," she said, as she cuddled up next to him, naked on the bed as he admired her long graceful body that hadn't been touched by age yet. "My mother is fantastic."

"No, *you're* fantastic." He picked up the remote on the bed and went through the list of movies and they picked one. They shared the popcorn, and halfway through the movie, he wanted her again. He couldn't keep his hands off her, and his body away from her. It was as if they were magnetized to each other. Now that they had found each other, they couldn't get enough. They paused the movie twice to make love, and when they glanced at the clock on her nightstand, it was five minutes to midnight. They switched the channel to the ball in Times Square, and watched it.

"This means something, Kate. We're starting the year together. Let's make it a good one, for *us*." He sensed that she needed more of that in her life, not just constantly giving to others. He suspected that her children had been spoiled in every way possible, materially, and above all emotionally, and with all the time and energy and thought and love she devoted to them, and it sounded to him that they didn't give enough back, which was the nature of children. He wanted to do that for her now, and to let her lavish some of her love on him. He needed her too. He had waited years to find the right woman, and he finally had. "This is going to be a very special year for us. Your daughter is going to have her baby, and maybe the other one will too, and your son will have his sex bomb in New Delhi, and an exciting job. It'll give us more time for each other." They both loved that idea. He had understood everything quickly. And she was ready for him. She had been waiting for him and didn't even know it.

"If I hadn't fallen on the ice that day, I never would have gotten to know you, and how sweet you are. You're a shit in the courtroom, you know." She grinned.

"So are you," he said to her.

"Thank you," she said meekly.

"You know what I just realized?" he said, looking thunderstruck.

"What? We ate all the popcorn?"

"No, I haven't made love to you since last year." It was 12:04 of the new year, and she laughed, but a minute later she was breath-less again and wanting him, and he was inside her. They made love again and again that night, trying to make up for lost time and the years when they didn't have each other. They fell asleep as the sun came up. A new day was dawning, a new year, and a new life for both of them.

Chapter 18

Scott and Kate woke up at noon on New Year's Day. He woke up first and lay smiling next to her, watching her as she slept. He didn't know what he'd done right in his life, but he had finally found the woman he always knew he wanted and didn't think existed. Real, kind, warm, loving, honorable, he could see all those things in her, and talented and smart as well. She was beautiful inside and out. He couldn't wait to learn more about her.

He went to make coffee for them, and looked at the framed photographs around the apartment. They were all photographs of her children, or of her with them. They were a handsome bunch but they had been giving her a run for her money lately, and he thought it should stop. At their ages, they needed to do more for her, instead of expecting her to do for them. He had already gotten the picture. He was probably going to like them, if they were anything like her, but he didn't want them to hurt her. She was a strong woman but he could tell that inside she was vulnerable and fragile, and they probably didn't suspect it. She was the workhorse they counted on, the safety net they expected to be there for them, and she always was. And now, he wanted to be the safety net for her. Just being with her made him feel like more of a man, and he wanted to take care of her, if she'd let him.

"Good morning," she said in a sexy voice from the doorway, her long blond hair draping over her shoulder and covering one breast, while he could see the other. He was in her living room, naked, and they were totally at ease with each other. It was as though they had been together forever, not just for one night.

All her kids sent her texts while they were having breakfast, to wish her a happy New Year. He was pleased to see that. They weren't totally without feeling or respect for her. They were just used to taking everything she had to give. Until now, she gave her all to them.

She called her own mother when they finished breakfast, and Scott was impressed by how close they seemed. Margaret said she was having lunch with the newlyweds that day and invited Kate to join them, but Kate said she was seeing a friend, which surprised her mother. She didn't see friends much anymore, just family. Between her job and her kids, she never had time for anything else. But she was going to make time now, for Scott. It was the only resolution Kate had made the night before, and it was a good one.

It was snowing when they looked outside, and they wanted to go for a walk in the snow.

They took a shower together and dressed reluctantly. They hated to leave the nest they were making, but they wanted exercise and air, and they went for a long walk in the snow, and then came home, pulled off their clothes and wound up in bed again. It was where everything had started, and they didn't want to leave it yet. They slept in each other's arms that afternoon, and made dinner, and then went back to bed again.

They stayed home all weekend and he hated to leave her to go back to his apartment on Sunday night, and by midnight he was back at hers.

"You've cast a spell on me," he accused her. "When I get ten feet away from you, I'm miserable. I might have to give up work." He had brought a suit back with him, so he could leave from her apartment to go to his office in the morning.

They both had early morning appointments, and left together. Their offices were only five blocks apart so they could share a cab.

"Are you free for lunch?" he asked her and she nodded. "Good, then let's go back to your place and make love."

"I thought you were going to feed me," she teased him. But in the end, they did what he'd suggested and went back to their offices after lunch, looking like they had a guilty secret. They returned to her place that night, and she had to bring home a mountain of work. She tried to keep her mind on it, but she couldn't for long, as he came to check on her, kiss her, or run a finger down her neck until she shivered.

"They're going to fire me if I don't get my work done," she said but didn't really care.

"They can't afford to. You're the best thing they've got." She had two cases set for trial, and she had to start to work on them. He was in the same situation. He had a massive workload, but they agreed that they'd figure out how to balance it all eventually.

Being with Scott was taking the edge off Kate's sadness over Anthony leaving. She hated knowing that soon he'd be so far away. But Margaret was insistent they should go to visit him, and Kate was beginning to think that would be a good idea after Claire's baby was born. She didn't want to leave until then. They had just come back from Saint Bart's, and Claire couldn't travel after that, until after the baby.

By the time Anthony was ready to leave, Claire only had seven weeks left until the baby was due. She was starting to call her mother more frequently again. She was asking her advice about the delivery and the nursery. She was getting increasingly anxious, and finally admitted that she was scared. What if she died? What if the baby did? What if there was something wrong with him? They knew it was a boy, and had seen it on the sonogram. But what if the birth hurt too much or she couldn't handle the pain? Kate tried to reassure her but Claire had too much time on her hands, and she was panicking, imagining every possible nightmarish scenario.

"Maybe you should have kept working till the end," Kate said, unable to reassure her. "You've got too much time to think and scare yourself silly." Kate wasn't quite as easy to reach as she used to be. She was spending every night with Scott. He was staying at her apartment, and she tried to keep her nights free for him. Claire now wanted all her time, energy, and attention, and Kate was less willing to give it to her, which frightened Claire even more. Kate wanted to be there for her, but not every single hour of the day.

Claire wanted her mommy. She acted like a frightened child. And Kate had Scott now and loved him too. Her children still knew nothing about him.

"What if I can't reach you when I go into labor?" Claire said one day in a panic. "You didn't answer your phone last night."

"I must have been asleep, or maybe my phone was in the charger in the other room," which it often was now, so she and Scott could sleep through the night, or make love without being disturbed. Her children weren't babies anymore, and she needed time to herself. They could also call on her landline in an emergency, and they hadn't so far. Claire could do that if she went into labor.

"Your kids are used to having access to you at all hours of the day and night," Scott commented with surprise one day over breakfast. All three of them had called her between one and two A.M., and she was usually up working. Now she was with Scott at night.

"Yes, they are," she admitted. "They'll get used to the new order of things." He nodded. He didn't want to pressure her about it, but she needed better boundaries with them, and she knew it too. But so far it hadn't caused a problem between them. Nothing had. Everything was going so smoothly between them that it was hard to believe he hadn't always been there. "When do you want to meet them?" she asked him.

"Not yet. I want time for us first."

"I'm giving a farewell party for Anthony on Friday." They were leaving for New Delhi two days later. "They won't be all together here again until next summer."

"I'll meet Anthony then," he said firmly. "And the girls in a while."

He wanted to meet Tammy and Stacey first. They sounded like the easiest to him. He was annoyed at Claire before he'd even met her, because she was so demanding and gave her mother such a hard time. Although he was curious about Reed Bailey and eager to meet him when the time came.

Kate was already sad about Anthony leaving. She was grateful she had Scott in her life now. Without him, she would have been devastated to have her son so far away. She was less sad than she would have been, because Scott was with her so much, so supportive and kind and caring. She felt like the luckiest woman in the world. It had only been three weeks, but they felt like the best three weeks of her life.

"Okay," Stacey said handing the test stick to Tammy, so she could pee on it. This was the earliest day when a pregnancy would register on the home test. Stacey had just done hers and hadn't looked at it yet. They were going to look at them together at the same time, and see if the insemination of the donor sperm had worked for either of them. Tammy peed on it, and then they waited for it to process. And then they both stood in the bathroom holding their sticks, and stuck them out at the same time. They saw Tammy's first. It had two dark pink lines. And then Stacey's. The same two dark pink lines. They stared at each other in disbelief and Tammy screamed as they threw their arms around each other and jumped up and down. It had worked. Their double insemination with the same sperm had worked. They were both pregnant.

"Oh my God, I'm pregnant," Stacey said and sat down on the

edge of the tub feeling dizzy. It had been a last minute decision. They had always agreed that Tammy would be the one to carry a baby, and now they both were. "What if I get too sick to work? My practice will fall apart."

"No, it won't," Tammy said calmly. "This will be fantastic. It will be like having twins."

"You have no idea what that's like. Mothers of twins come into my office all the time, crying and ready to kill themselves."

"Two babies are not going to kill us. We can afford them, and we can hire a nanny to help us."

"I don't want to nurse. I don't have that instinct." Stacey was panicking.

"I'll nurse both of them," Tammy said, and put her arms around Stacey to calm her. "It's going to be wonderful. It's what we've wanted for all these years, and now our dreams are coming true." It was real now, and Stacey had never been so scared in her life, but she loved Tammy, and there was something so exciting about it at the same time. Using all of the sperm for both of them had been a daring thing to do, and it had worked. Now they just had to wait nine months to see what motherhood was like. "Can we tell my mom?" Tammy asked her with wide excited eyes. She wasn't scared at all, although she had been before they made the decision to do it. This was what they wanted, they were married, and they would both be pregnant at the same time.

"We should really wait until the end of the first trimester to make sure everything is all right before we tell people," Stacey said with a serious look on her face.

"Just my mom?" Stacey couldn't resist the pleading look in Tammy's eyes, and Kate had been so good to them and so supportive. She smiled as she nodded. "We can tell her quietly at Anthony's farewell party on Friday night. She's going to be so happy for us. Are you happy, Stacey?" Tammy was worried about her. She looked shocked.

"I am happy, but I'm scared shitless."

"I'll take care of you, I promise," she said lovingly and Stacey's heart melted. She was usually the stronger one but this time it was Tammy.

"Oh, baby," she said and kissed her, and held her in her arms for a long time. "This is the bravest thing we've ever done," Stacey said wisely. It was unbelievable. Their dreams really had come true and they were both going to be moms, and going to give birth.

The party for Anthony went off as smoothly as everything Kate did for them. She had all his favorite foods, set a beautiful table, had flowers everywhere. The whole family had come, and the significant others. Everyone gave them little gifts to use on their travels and Anthony was so excited he could hardly contain himself. Alicia already had an agent and three auditions lined up. Everything was going smoothly. Kate smiled as she saw her family gathered around her. She hadn't seen them since Christmas. She had been with Scott every night since New Year's Eve, and he was going to stay at his place that night for the first time in three weeks. He had texted her that he was having withdrawal symptoms, and she missed him, but she loved being with her children too. She wanted to introduce him to them soon, so they would know he existed and could get to know him, and would be a little less demanding of her time.

Claire was following her around like a whale in high heels at the dinner. After barely speaking to her for seven months, she was in full panic mode now, and acting like a four-year-old. She wanted her mommy. Kate hadn't seen her since Christmas. The baby had gotten huge, and there were still seven weeks to go.

Kate was alone in the kitchen for five minutes after dessert was served, a cake she had ordered with Anthony and Alicia on it dressed in Indian garb. She was getting the ice cream out of the freezer when Tammy and Stacey walked into the kitchen and closed the door with a conspiratorial look. "Is something wrong?" she asked them. They both shook their heads at the same time, and Kate thought they were starting to look alike, like people who had lived together for a long time.

"Nothing's wrong." Tammy was quick to reassure her and lowered her voice to a whisper. "We're pregnant, Mom. It worked!" She danced around and Kate hugged her.

"Oh, darling, I'm so happy for you," she turned to Stacey then, "I'm so happy for both of you. It's going to be a gorgeous baby!" she said to Tammy, since she knew she was the one carrying it.

"Not one baby, Mom. TWO!" Tammy said, as Stacey looked sheepish.

"You're having twins?" Kate looked ecstatic.

"Not exactly twins," Stacey corrected. "We decided to both do the insemination. I'm not sure who decided that but it seemed like a good idea. It was a spur of the moment decision."

"We both decided," Tammy reminded her. "We had the idea at the same time, and we had enough sperm for two syringes, so we did it together. And it worked! We're *both* pregnant!"

"Oh my God." Kate turned to Stacey. "You too?" She nodded. "How do you feel about that?"

"Scared to death. Tammy is much braver than I am," she said. "I never thought I'd have to go through a delivery. It was always going to be Tammy. I've seen some real horrors during my residency, but I love her so much and we wanted to do it together. It was our wedding day, so here I am, knocked up and terrified, but excited. Will you come with us, and be at the delivery?" she asked. "We might deliver on the same day. Maybe they'll let us be in the same delivery room, if we do. I'd really like that. I want to be with Tammy, and I want her there with me. Will you come too?" She looked so vulnerable as she asked, Kate was touched.

"Of course I'll be there," Kate said, still bowled over by their news. "I'd love to be," and she had promised to be at Claire's delivery too. Claire still hadn't gone to Lamaze classes and Kate thought she should.

"We're not going to tell anyone until we're twelve weeks," Stacey said sensibly, "but we wanted to tell you. You've been so supportive ever since Tammy told you about me."

"I'll be there with bells on," Kate promised. "Now we'd better get the ice cream into the dining room before it turns to soup. Congratulations to both of you!" They walked back into the dining room together and took their seats, and the rest of the evening was about Anthony and Alicia. But Kate kept thinking about their news and smiling at them.

Everyone left at midnight, and Anthony promised to stop by and give her a hug before he left two days from now. When she said good night to everyone Kate gave Tammy and Stacey an extra warm hug and a meaningful look they both understood. It was going to be a very busy year for the family, with three babies being born within six months. She thought about it with a smile after they left. Poor Stacey looked so anxious about it. She had gotten carried away by the romance of the moment on their wedding day, and now she had to face childbirth and was scared to death. Tammy was much more emotionally and psychologically ready for it than Stacey, who never thought of herself as a woman in a physical sense. She was psychologically much more male in her instincts, and now she had to face the ultimate female act, giving birth. As a doctor, she knew everything that could go wrong. But hopefully, it would all go smoothly.

Kate texted Scott after everyone had left, and told him it had been a very nice party. She didn't tell him about Tammy and Stacey's big news. She wasn't sure he was up to it, not having met them yet.

She was tidying the kitchen, when she heard him come in. He had his own key now, and he walked into the kitchen with a hangdog look.

"I'm addicted to you. I used to like my apartment. Now it's so lonely there without you." She smiled at him and held out her arms, and he came to her and put his arms around her, and kissed her.

"I thought you might show up after they left."

"Do you mind?"

"Of course not. I was missing you too."

"How were they? Was Claire difficult?"

"No, everyone was well behaved, and Claire is so terrified of the delivery, she's actually being nice again."

"Good. I hope she stays that way. A little terror might do her good," he said, and Kate didn't disagree with him, although she felt sorry for Claire. First babies were scary, as Stacey was already finding out.

They went to bed a few minutes later, and Scott settled into her arms with a sigh of pleasure. He felt like he had come home again. He wanted to be wherever Kate was now, in her bed, in her arms, in her life, in her world. And as they started to make love, it was all Kate wanted too.

Chapter 19

Kate and Scott were ready for a quiet weekend after the party for Anthony and Alicia on Friday night. They'd both had a busy few weeks at work, and their relationship was still new and exciting. They stayed up late making love every night.

Kate was washing some of the extra dishes from the night before, and Scott was reading the paper in his pajamas at noon the next day, when the doorman called from downstairs to say that Anthony was on his way up. Kate looked at Scott in a panic.

"Oh shit, Anthony is coming to say goodbye to me. Can you put your jeans on fast?" Scott made a wild dash for the bedroom, as Kate went to open the door, after a quick stop in the bathroom to put a robe on. She didn't know what to say to Anthony to explain Scott, since she hadn't told any of them about him yet, and didn't want to. She didn't want to hear their comments, or answer questions. It was all much too new. And what if it didn't work out? That didn't seem likely at the moment. They were getting along beautifully. But they were living in a cocoon, without her children as part of it, which wasn't entirely realistic given how close she was to them. She and Scott wanted time to themselves before they let the world in.

Kate opened the door and Anthony gave her an enormous hug. "I'm going to miss you, Mom. We'll talk on FaceTime. And I'll be home in six months for a nice long visit. Grandma says you'll come over on a trip. That was a great party last night. We loved it." As he said it, Scott wandered into the room, looking impeccably put together, in jeans and a long sleeved blue shirt, his hair neatly combed, and loafers without socks.

"You have a guest?" Anthony looked startled, and Scott smiled and extended a hand, as smooth as silk, with a broad smile.

"Scott White. You must be Anthony. Your mother and I have been working on a case together for the past few months, I dropped by to get some papers from her. I hear you're going to India. That's very exciting."

"I'm opening an office there for my company. I came to say goodbye to my mom. We're leaving tomorrow." He turned his attention to Kate then, and didn't seem the least put out by Scott being there. Scott was an easy person to have around anyway. He went out to the kitchen to leave them alone. "New man in your life?" he whispered to his mother, with a faintly mischievous look, and she shook her head.

"Old work friend," she whispered back. She was lying, but not ready to tell him. "We just finished a case. We're wrapping it up." He had never seen his mother entertain anyone in her bathrobe, even an old friend, but he didn't have time to discuss it with her. He looked like a nice guy anyway.

"I'm going to miss you," she said, as they sat down for a few minutes. "Take care of yourself, sweetheart."

"I love you, Mom. And don't let that little beast with the big belly push you around. She seems better these days." Kate nodded, drinking in her last glimpse of the son she loved so much. He stood up then. "I've got to go. I'll call you when we get there."

"Let me know how Alicia's auditions go," she reminded him, and they hugged for a last time in the doorway. She held him tight and he did the same. "I'm so proud of you. I love you," she said again, as he got on the elevator and then he was gone, and tears rolled down her cheeks as she walked back into the apartment and found Scott in the kitchen. He looked up when she walked in and saw that she was crying. He got up and put his arms around her and held her close.

"He's a sweet kid. You can see it in his eyes. He's a nice boy." He looked like a boy to Scott, not a man, and he was obviously devoted to his mother.

"Thank you for getting dressed," she said with a smile.

"Did he say anything about me?"

"He asked who you were. I said you were a work friend. He wasn't worried about it, and he's all wrapped up in leaving tomorrow. He asked if you were a new man in my life, and I said no. I hate lying to him, but I think you're right. It's too soon to tell them, and he's leaving now anyway. I'll tell him on FaceTime when we tell the others. I can always say it just got started whenever it is." Scott nodded and smiled at her.

"I'm going to enjoy getting to know him. He looks like a big kid. The girls scare me a little more, especially Claire."

"She's not great at the moment, but Tammy is a sweetheart. They're both pregnant, by the way."

"Who? Both?" He looked puzzled.

"Tammy and Stacey. Stacey did the insemination with her, and now they're both pregnant. They're turning into a baby factory." She smiled and sat down at the kitchen table across from him. "Are you going to be able to put up with us?" she asked him and he nodded.

"As long as I get my share of you, I'll be fine. I don't care how many babies they have. You're my baby, Kate, and the only one I want."

"Then that should work just fine." She finished washing the glasses, and they went back to her bedroom to lie on her bed, and the usual thing happened. They wound up making love again. She forgot about Stacey and Tammy being pregnant, and Anthony leaving and how long he would be gone, and Claire's delivery. All she thought about for that moment in time was Scott and how much she loved him. He was part of it now too. And when they made love, they only belonged to each other. She was his woman, and he belonged to her.

Anthony called Tammy on his way back to the hotel where he and Alicia were staying, at his company's expense, for their last few nights in New York. He had given up his apartment, and Alicia had given hers up too. They would get a new one when they moved back in two years. They were planning to stay with Kate when they came back in June.

Tammy picked up and Anthony laughed as soon as she answered. "I think Mom has a new boyfriend. I just went to say goodbye to her, and there was a guy there."

"There was? Who is he?"

"She says he's a friend from work, but I don't believe her. She was in her nightgown and bathrobe, and he was wearing a shirt and jeans, but he looked like he'd just climbed out of bed. He seems like a nice guy though. He looks a little younger than Mom, but not much, a couple of years maybe."

"Are you sure? I don't think she has anyone new. She's been with us a lot lately. She doesn't have time for a guy the way she works." Tammy sounded dubious.

"We thought that about you," he teased her. "She can make time if she wants to." He was smiling. He didn't mind, as long as Scott was good to their mother. He didn't like the idea of her being lonely and alone. "Just keep an eye out to make sure that Claire doesn't beat the shit out of Mom. She can be such a bitch to her."

"I think she's getting better. She needs Mom right now."

"I'm going to miss you guys," he said, sounding emotional himself.

"I was thinking last night, it's a good thing you broke it off with Amanda. You could never have taken this job if you were married to her."

"I thought about that too. Alicia is much more adventurous, even more than I am. She can hardly wait to get there."

"Let's FaceTime a lot while you are away," Tammy suggested.

"I will," he promised. "And see what happens with the new guy. I bet he's a new boyfriend. I just got that feeling about him. And if he is, good for her. He looks like a good guy. Talk to you soon, Sis. I love you."

"I love you too," she said and they hung up. She told Stacey about the man Anthony had seen in the apartment. "I wonder if she does have a new man. She hasn't said anything to me about it."

"Maybe she's keeping it to herself for a while. There's no harm in that. This is a big group, and we talk a lot. Maybe they're not ready for that," Stacey said thoughtfully.

"I doubt it," Tammy said. But Stacey was older and wiser and she thought Anthony was probably right. If he was, more power to her, and she was glad for Kate. She deserved it.

Anthony called his mother again from the airport the next day before he left, so she had another chance to say goodbye to him. He didn't ask her about Scott, and she didn't mention him.

She and Scott were having a quiet Sunday at the apartment, reading the paper in their pajamas.

They had a busy week ahead. They both had new cases, and old ones to wrap up. Kate knew the next few months would be hectic again. There was a constant flow of work for Kate, and Scott had a big trial scheduled in May.

By early February, Scott and Kate were both swamped.

Stacey was having violent morning sickness by then. She was six weeks pregnant and felt awful every day, and threw up six or eight times a day. Tammy felt fine, and sorry for Stacey, watching her throw up all the time. A few times, she was too sick to go to work and had to call relief doctors to replace her.

"Why do I feel so horrible, and you feel fine?" Stacey asked from the bathroom floor one morning.

"My mom never had morning sickness either," Tammy said as Stacey vomited again. She was on her knees with her head in the toilet bowl when Tammy handed her a wet cloth and stroked her hair. They called the obstetrician who said it was just the luck of the draw and they couldn't do much about it. There were medicines for it, but Stacey didn't want to take them. She didn't want to risk hurting the baby. The doctor told her that it should be better in another six weeks, at the end of the first trimester, but she said that with some women it persisted, even to the end of the pregnancy. Stacey knew that and cried when she thought about it. Morning sickness was much harder than she'd expected.

"This is miserable," she said, as Tammy led her back to bed, and put a damp cloth on her forehead. But even the faint smell of the laundry soap that had been used to launder the cloth made her throw up again. Everything did, and it persisted throughout the day. It was the worst thing Stacey had ever lived through. She talked to her patients' mothers about it, trying to find something that would help. She found that a lot of them had taken medication. Others just lived with it.

"I think I'm dying," she said to Tammy in the middle of the night on the bathroom floor, when she woke out of a sound sleep to throw up again.

"You're not dying, you're pregnant. And we're going to have two beautiful babies," Tammy said gently and then helped her back to bed. She felt guilty for how well she felt while Stacey was so sick. She was having to get other doctors to cover for her on the days she just couldn't work, and felt guilty toward her patients.

By the beginning of March, it was slightly better, but not much. She was only throwing up three or four times a day, instead of six or eight. Claire was two weeks away from delivery by then, and miserably uncomfortable. The baby was enormous. She could hardly breathe now, and she couldn't sleep at night. Tammy was feeling great. She had never had more energy. She loved seeing every sonogram, and she couldn't wait to learn what sex the baby was in a few more weeks.

Kate called to check on them almost every day, and felt desperately sorry for Stacey. She was having a terrible pregnancy so far, but the baby was healthy.

Scott and Kate had been together for almost three months by then, and everything was going smoothly. They met for lunch almost every day, since their offices were close together. And they spent their nights curled up together, reading, watching TV, talking, or working on their cases.

"You're not tired of me yet?" he asked her, worried about it one night.

"No way," Kate said, smiling at him. She'd never been happier in her life. He hadn't met the girls yet, but all of them were in various stages of pregnancy, and it didn't seem like the right time. She had told them she was seeing someone, but she was vague about it, and said it was very new.

Anthony was happy in New Delhi, and facetimed with Kate a lot. Alicia had gotten a couple of minor parts in small movies, but she had more auditions coming up, and the movie industry in India was booming. Directors and producers loved her look, and how exotic she was.

Kate had just come back from lunch with Scott in mid-March, when Claire called her sounding panicked. "It's happening, Mom, I'm at the hospital. It's early. My due date is still two days away." She'd been hoping to be late. She didn't feel ready to face childbirth yet and wanted to be overdue. "Can you come now?" Kate smiled when she heard her. Two days before her due date was not "early." It was fine. The baby was full term, and ready. Claire wasn't and had never gone to Lamaze in the end, nor read any of the books her mother sent her.

"I'll be right there, sweetheart. Everything's fine. This is great. You're going to have a baby today," or possibly by the next morning. Claire burst into tears.

"I don't want to have a baby, I'm too scared. It already hurts a lot, and they said it'll get worse. I'm sorry I've been such a bitch to you. Are you mad at me?"

"Not at all, just relax."

"Why can't they just put me out and give me a C-section?" She'd asked her doctor for that and he said there was no reason to. The baby was in the right position and everything was fine.

"You'd feel a lot worse afterward. Vaginally is better. As soon as the baby is out, it's all over, and you'll recover faster. And once they give you an epidural, you won't feel anything. I'll be there in a few minutes." She hung up, called Scott and told him what was happening, and she wouldn't be home that night until after the baby was born, which could take a long time for a first baby, maybe not until morning. Scott felt sorry for Claire even though he hadn't met her. The process of childbirth had always sounded terrifying to him.

Kate took a cab to the hospital and arrived twenty minutes later. Reed was already there when Kate walked into the room, and he looked as terrified as Claire did. Claire was sobbing hysterically. A nurse was trying to calm her down, and then left the room when Kate arrived.

"She wants an epidural and they won't give her one," Reed said, concerned. "They said it's too soon, and it will stop labor if they do."

"She'll have to wait awhile," Kate said calmly, and went to sit next to Claire. She was crying uncontrollably, and seemed totally unprepared for what was happening to her. They had put a fetal monitor on her belly and she said it was too tight and had torn it off. Kate spoke to her in a strong, motherly tone.

"Claire, you need to calm down, baby, you're just going to make it worse being so upset. They'll give you the epidural in a little while. Just try to hang in till then." Kate stroked her hair gently, and Claire pushed her away. She was only two centimeters dilated and the contractions were mild compared to what they were going to be. She wasn't ready for the ardors of labor, and she fought like a cat when they examined her. Claire was distraught and Reed was at the nursing desk begging for something for the pain his wife was in.

"If we give her anything now, it's going to slow down her labor," the nurse explained to him. "The pains have to get stronger so her cervix dilates and the baby can come out." He understood, but Claire didn't. She was screaming with every pain. He looked at Kate in despair when he got back to the room. He felt helpless.

"What can we do for her?" he said to Kate in a whisper when Claire went to the bathroom.

"Nothing much yet," she answered him honestly. "The labor has to get stronger so it can do its job. It's very early labor." She hated to see her in pain too, but she had to tough it out for a while. Claire wanted easy answers, and there weren't any yet.

Claire screamed and sobbed relentlessly for three more hours, fighting what was happening to her, as Reed looked more and more desperate. The labor was going slowly, but everything was normal.

An hour later, they started the epidural and Claire screamed through that too, as Reed stood by in tears. It was so much worse than he'd expected. He left the room for a few minutes and Kate stayed with her, while Claire fought the nurses every time they examined her.

Claire battled them for another two hours, refusing to cooperate or push when they told her to. And at midnight the doctor told Reed and Kate in the hall that they were going to deliver the baby by Caesarean section. She had been in labor for ten hours by then, which was not unusual for a first baby, and it could easily take longer.

The doctor said that there was no real medical reason for the C-section but Claire simply couldn't cope with what was happening to her, and it was becoming potentially psychologically dangerous for her, and could be too stressful for the baby.

"We usually see this in very young girls, in their teens, who aren't prepared for labor, not in women Claire's age at twenty-seven," the doctor said quietly.

They gave her a shot of morphine and she got drowsy immediately. They wheeled her away a few minutes later, and Reed and Kate waited in the waiting room. He looked utterly exhausted, and Kate felt sorry for both of them. She hoped Claire would be better prepared for motherhood than she was for her labor.

A nurse came to find them half an hour later. The baby was fine, a seven pound two ounce boy that Kate knew Claire could have delivered easily if she'd tried. Reed looked elated that it was over, and his son had arrived.

They went to see him at the nursery window. He was wrapped tightly in a blanket with a little blue cap on. He was awake and looking around, and Reed stood staring at his son in wonder as tears ran down his cheeks, and Kate looked at her first grandchild and hoped that Claire would be equal to the task of what lay ahead.

She was in the recovery room and they said she would be for several hours before they brought her down to a room. Kate hugged Reed and said she'd be back in the morning. They had said Claire would sleep until then. Kate felt sorry for them. The baby's mother was a child.

Kate took a cab home and slipped into bed next to Scott, relieved to be there, and sad for Claire. She had so much growing up to do. Reed had been wonderful to her.

Scott stirred for a minute and looked at her. It was two A.M. "Everything go okay?"

"The baby's fine and so is Claire." She could tell him the rest in the morning. She sank into his arms with a sigh.

A new life had begun, and she hoped it would be a good one. And however he had arrived, whether his parents were married or not, the baby had her blessing.

Chapter 20

Stacey and Tammy came to visit Claire the next day in the hospital. She had makeup on, and her hair had been done, and she looked exhausted, and was in pain from the C-section. The nurses and Reed had put the baby to her breast several times, and Claire said it was too painful. She didn't want to nurse him, or hold him. Her milk wasn't in yet anyway, but the baby sucking at her breast made her uterus contract, which was excruciating with the surgery, despite the pain medication she was on.

They were medicating her for the discomfort and she was groggy. She told Stacey and Tammy how awful it had been, worse than anything she could have imagined. It was like having her body sawed in half, as she described it, and Stacey looked pale as she listened. Claire said they told her she could have a C-section next time, but she didn't want any more babies.

They told her then that they were both pregnant, and she said she felt sorry for them. And then she asked for a shot of morphine and they left and told her they'd be back when she felt better. She was planning to stay in the hospital for four or five days.

Stacey looked deathly pale when they left, and when they got far enough down the hallway, Tammy stopped and grabbed her arm.

"Listen to me, don't listen to my sister. She's a spoiled brat, and she wants everything the easy way. She had a small baby, and my mom said she could have delivered it, but she wouldn't cooperate with them. She wanted them to put her out and give her a C-section. That's not going to happen to you. You're going to stop throwing up, and we're going to stay in shape, and we're going to deliver healthy normal babies, and it's going to be wonderful. We wanted this, and it's going to be great. So don't listen to all that whiney neurotic immature bullshit. She isn't grown up enough to have a baby, but we are. So are we straight on this?"

"Yes, Sergeant," Stacey said, grinning at her, and put an arm around her as they walked down the hall. "We're going to have healthy babies and easy deliveries." She repeated it like a mantra, and Tammy gave her a shove.

"And don't you forget it!"

"Yes, sir." Her step was lighter after Tammy set her straight. Stacey had seen deliveries like Claire's during her residency, usually with ignorant women who were too terrified to cooperate, or understand what was happening. And Tammy was right. Claire was spoiled and wanted everything to be easy, and some things just weren't. But with Tammy, Stacey knew she could do anything.

And two weeks later, as though by magic, she stopped throwing up. The first trimester was over, and within a week she felt better and like herself again. They went out to dinner to celebrate. Stacey felt like she'd gotten her life back.

Margaret went to see her first great-grandchild, and cried when she saw him. They let her hold him. Claire was feeling better by then, and had decided not to nurse the baby. They had a baby nurse to take care of him so Claire didn't have to. She told her grandmother how awful the birth had been. She said that next time, if there was one, she would have a scheduled C-section and wouldn't have to go through labor. But she didn't think she wanted any more babies, and Reed said he'd be satisfied with one if that was what she wanted. He gave her a big sapphire ring to thank her for his son. He was in love with their baby and with Claire. More than ever. She had given him the greatest gift of his life. And Claire kept reminding him of how awful it had been and how she had suffered. It had been the worst experience of her life.

A week later, Kate invited Tammy and Stacey to meet Scott, and they had a fun evening. He liked both of them. The only one he still hadn't met was Claire and she was in no condition to meet him at the moment. But dinner with Tammy and Stacey had gone well. Kate was delighted.

Tammy facetimed her brother in New Delhi as soon as she got home.

"You were right about the new guy. We just met him. He's cool, really smart, and he's crazy about Mom."

"What's his name?" Anthony asked her.

"Scott White. He's a lawyer."

"That's the one."

"Mom says they've been dating for about three months."

The big news from India, after Tammy reported to Anthony about Scott, was that Alicia had gotten a real part in a real movie. It was a small part, but the producer was well known. She was going to start shooting in April, and they'd be finished by June, when they were coming home.

"And how are you two?" Anthony asked her, and they both waved at him on the screen.

"We're pregnant," Tammy said, laughing.

"Both of you?"

"Both of us," Tammy said proudly. "Stacey was sick in the beginning but she's fine now. So we'll have two babies in September."

"That sounds scary. Like twins, but with two moms."

"That's the idea." Tammy beamed at him from the screen.

"How's Claire? I haven't talked to her since she had the baby."

"She's whining a lot, about how awful it was. Now that she has a kid, she may actually have to grow up and stop blaming Mom for everything. It's a painful process."

"She's spoiled rotten," Anthony said in disgust.

"Yes, she is," Tammy agreed with him. "And Reed is making it worse. He caters to her every whim. The baby's cute though. Not as cute as ours will be." She grinned at her brother.

They talked for a few more minutes and hung up. It was nice to be able to see him on FaceTime. Tammy missed him a lot, and so did Kate.

In April, Tammy and Stacey found out the sex of their babies. One of each. Stacey was having a boy, and Tammy was having a girl. It seemed just right to them somehow. Claire's baby was a month old by then. They had named him Gregory, for Reed's father. Gregory Bailey Morgan.

Claire was spending all her time at the gym to lose the weight she'd gained. She had two nannies for the baby, a day and a night nurse, and two relief nannies on the weekend. Reed was willing to give her whatever she wanted. Claire complained that he cried all the time, maybe because she hadn't nursed him or because he never saw his mother. She was taking three months off from work, and wanted to have fun before she went back, not take care of a newborn, which she didn't enjoy.

But Reed was in love with him, which was nice. Stacey and Tammy hadn't been to visit him since the hospital, but they planned to. They were busy turning their guest room into a nursery, which was more fun than they'd expected. Tammy had her grandmother paint a mural on one wall. She painted pink and blue teddy bears and ballons under a blue sky with puffy white clouds.

Two months later in June, Anthony and Alicia came home to get married. They loved India, living and working there. Alicia brought each of the girls a sari, and another one for Kate. She had finished the movie, and gotten a bigger part in another film that would start shooting in September. She had to learn lines this time and was taking acting lessons. And Anthony thought she had real talent.

Kate reintroduced Anthony to Scott, as soon as he got home, and as she'd hoped, they were crazy about each other. Tammy, Stacey, and Claire had met him by then. Claire was neutral about him, and Stacey and Tammy loved him. Anthony and Alicia got married the week after they got home, in a small wedding with only the family present. Alicia's mother was there, but her father didn't come from Puerto Rico. All of Anthony's family was there. Reed and Claire even brought the baby. He was three months old, and Reed carried him everywhere in a harness. He was a happy, smiley baby, and it was obvious that Reed adored him, and Claire. Claire acted as though he was someone else's child, which distressed Kate to see. She had just gone back to work.

Tammy and Stacey were six months pregnant by then, and both of them looked healthy and happy. Stacey was working and felt great now. And Tammy was planning to work at Chanel until the last day of her pregnancy, and then take two months off after the babies were born.

The wedding was noisy and friendly and warm. Kate had it at her apartment, with white flowers everywhere. Alicia wore a white and gold sari with a fabulous red sash and a red bindi on her forehead. She looked like an Indian princess. And she wore gold sandals with little bells on them. Anthony looked ecstatic. There was an Indian feast, and Indian music, all carefully researched by Kate and Tammy.

The young people stayed until three o'clock in the morning, and at two, Scott and Kate excused themselves, went to bed, and talked about the wedding. They could still hear Indian music drifting in from the living room.

"It's funny," Kate said to him, as they lay in bed talking, "a year ago, I was ready to kill all of them. Now Anthony is happy with Alicia. They're married and she's the best thing that ever happened to him. And Tammy and Stacey are married and expecting two babies. Claire has a lot of growing up to do, which was true a year ago too, but she has a sweet little boy. I just hope she can adjust to being a mother. It nearly broke my heart when she told me she was pregnant. Reed has the patience of a saint with her. I'm not sure he'll ever let her grow up, and she certainly doesn't want to. He makes everything easy for her. Too easy. She'll never mature that way." She was still telling everyone how horrendous Greg's birth had been, and how much she had hated it. And she seemed to resent the baby for it. She loved scaring Tammy and Stacey with the details, and she was urging them to have C-sections too. "At least I'm not on her hate list anymore," although Kate was sure she would be again at some point, whenever she didn't agree with her about something. Then Claire would punish her, as she had before, but it all seemed easier and better with Scott in her life.

He fit right in to the group, as Kate knew he would. Her children all liked him except for Claire. The changes and decisions they had made for themselves in the last year had freed Kate too. If the children could do whatever they wanted, there was no reason why she couldn't, especially with all of them grown up and gone. She had carved out a life with Scott, which included time for them. She was still attentive to her children, but he was a priority for her now too, and they all knew it. He was her strong ally, which she had never had before, and her staunch defender. Claire was the only one who took exception to it. She wanted her mother available to her whenever she wanted her, whether convenient for Kate or not. She had to behave better now with Scott around. And Reed kept her in check too.

Kate spent most of her free time with Scott now. The children had their own lives, their partners and careers, and were having children of their own. It was important for Kate to have a life too, and Scott was an essential part of it. It had been startling to her children at first that he and Kate were living together, but they had gotten used to it, and so had Scott and Kate. Everyone had their place, and there was room for all of them in Kate's life, her children, *and* her man.

As the sounds of the wedding revelers in the rest of the house began to diminish, Scott turned to Kate in bed with a question.

"Your mother says you're going to India with her, to visit Anthony." Kate hadn't told him yet, and he seemed surprised.

"I might. I haven't decided. It's a big trip. She's desperate to go, and I don't think she should travel alone, but I'd like to stick around here until Tammy and Stacey have their babies. Maybe we could go after that, later in the year." She had a thought then. "Would you want to come with us?"

"I'd love it, if I don't have any big cases then, scheduled for trial. Actually, I'd like to go with *you*," he said cautiously, not wanting to offend Margaret. He loved her but wanted time alone with Kate to travel. He'd never been to India. "Maybe we could go with your mom and leave her with Anthony for a while, and go off on our own for a week or two. I hear parts of India are incredibly romantic." He hesitated, and she could see that he had something else on his mind. "It would make an incredible honeymoon," he said softly, afraid of what she'd say, and she turned to smile at him.

"Would you ever want to make it legal with us? I'm kind of a traditional guy." It was something he had discovered about himself recently, that marriage was important to him. More than he had thought it would be. But with Kate in his life now, it mattered a great deal, and seemed like the right thing to do.

"I never thought about it. I didn't think it was an option," Kate answered. "Do we need it?" she asked with a startled look.

"Need it? No. I don't need a green card," he said and she laughed. "You told me a while ago, when we talked about Claire, that you believe in marriage profoundly. I do too. I think it's a statement of how much you love someone and how much they mean to you. It's a way of showing the world that you believe in that person and the life you share with them, which was why it seemed wrong to me for Claire to have Reed's baby and not marry him. That's like saying I believe in you enough to have your child, but not to stand beside you or tell the world that I love you. It's why what Tammy and Stacey did was so meaningful, because that's exactly what they were saying, whatever their sexual preference."

"Do you believe in me enough to do that?" Kate asked him, looking deeply touched and a little amazed.

"Yes, I do," he said seriously. "It's how I feel about you, Kate, and I'd like the world to know it. I'm proud to be with you. We belong to each other. Do you believe in *me* enough to marry me?" he asked her. "Maybe that's the more important question."

"Yes, I do," she said quietly. "I haven't believed in marriage for myself in a long time, ever since Tom. But I love you and I'm proud to be a part of your life." She hadn't thought they needed to be married but now she realized that maybe he was right. And the seven year age difference between them had proved to be insignificant.

"Then let's get married and go to India for our honeymoon," he said, smiling at her.

"Just like that? That easy?" she asked him.

"It's always been easy with us. We were meant to be together." He kissed her. "I knew it when I met you, and when you fell in the street."

"Does this mean we're engaged?" She smiled at him.

"If you want to be." He was smiling broadly. "Maybe we should make love to seal the deal," he said as he pulled her closer and she laughed.

"That seems like a very good idea," she said and then he took off her nightgown and proved it to her.

After they made love, she was half asleep and remembered what he'd said before. "When do you want to get married?" she asked him simply.

"Yesterday," he said, and fell asleep.

They told the children when Anthony and Alicia came back from their honeymoon in Mexico. Kate and Scott got married before Anthony and Alicia went back to India in July. They rented a house in Connecticut for the weekend and had the wedding there. The whole family stayed with them and they were married in a small church nearby. It was simple and pretty and just what they wanted. They exchanged vows and wedding rings and had agreed to postpone their honeymoon until October, after Tammy and Stacey's babies were born. And then they would go to India, with Margaret.

The time until September passed quickly, after their wedding. They both had a lot of work in August and September, but all of their cases had settled, and by the end of September, it was still warm, but fall was in the air. It was a beautiful late September afternoon the day after their due date, when Tammy's daughter and Stacey's son decided to be born, and arrive on the same day. Kate felt that they had consulted with each other and said "Okay, jump," and they both did. Tammy and Stacey went into labor within an hour of each other.

Tammy was arranging things in the nursery again when her water broke. She was startled and went to tell Stacey, and by the time she found her, she had slashing pains that felt as though she were being cut in half.

"Are you all right? What happened?" Stacey could see she was already in labor.

"I don't know. I came to tell you my water broke, and suddenly I started to feel like a knife was cutting through me." As she said it, she had another pain so sharp she couldn't speak.

"Let's go to the hospital now," Stacey was calm and in full control, since so far nothing had started for her. She was feeling fine. She had been carrying boxes of medical supplies for her office that had come to their home that morning by mistake.

Stacey kept track of Tammy's contractions in the cab on the way to the hospital. They were increasing in strength and were two minutes apart when they got there. Stacey was smiling and holding Tammy's hand as they wheeled her into a labor room, and Stacey took Tammy's clothes off and put a hospital gown on her as a nurse waited to examine her. She was already eight centimeters dilated when she did, and with the next pain she was at nine. The nurse said she was going to call the doctor and left the room in a hurry. It was moving very quickly for a first baby.

"It's going so fast," Tammy said to Stacey. "I didn't expect it to be this way." She was out of breath, the contractions were coming fast and hard. They'd taken Lamaze classes but the labor was moving with lightning speed. There was no time to call Kate so she could be there.

"Labor usually doesn't go this rapidly for a first baby," the nurse said when she got back. Tammy had only been in labor by then for about forty minutes, but the contractions were so powerful, she felt as though the baby would come any minute, and Stacey thought she might. She was holding Tammy's hand through another contraction, when Stacey's water broke, and she looked surprised. She was standing in a pool of water next to Tammy's bed, and suddenly the race was on. Her labor pains started immediately, and she sank into a chair next to Tammy.

"This is crazy," Stacey said, as Tammy started to push before they said she could. The nurse looked panicked and went to call the doctor again. It was too late for an epidural for Tammy, and Stacey's pains were so powerful and so rapid that within minutes, she couldn't speak. The two women held hands, as the nurse rushed back into the room with a gurney for Stacey and helped her onto it. They wanted to take her to another labor room and Stacey refused. She wasn't going to leave Tammy before the baby came. They needed each other.

Tammy's face was red and she was pushing with every pain, as the nurse undressed Stacey and put a hospital gown on her too. She smiled at Tammy through their pains to encourage her, and as soon as Stacey was undressed there was a wail in the room. Their daughter had arrived. Tammy lay looking stunned as she smiled at Stacey.

"I love you," she said to Tammy, as an express train suddenly sped through her. Stacey could no longer speak, and Tammy told her she could do it with a firm grip on her hand.

"I can't," Stacey whispered to Tammy between pains, as a doctor sped into the room, and cut their daughter's cord, while Stacey pushed with all her might. Tammy kept her hand in hers, and everyone told Stacey to push.

She felt everything within her force through her and a second angry wail filled the room, as Tammy and Stacey watched their son come into the world. They were laughing and crying as Stacey lay back, shaking. Their babies had been born within four minutes of each other.

Two nurses cleaned the babies, and weighed them, as two other nurses tended to Tammy and Stacey, still holding hands and smiling, shaken but victorious.

"That was easy," Stacey said as a second doctor arrived to help, and a pediatrician came to check the babies.

Their daughter weighed eight pounds nine ounces, and their son ten pounds two ounces. Both labors had taken less than an hour. The nurse placed each baby in its mother's arms. Their daughter went immediately to Tammy's breast, and Stacey found herself nursing their son without effort, and she had none of the resistance she thought she would. Everything about the deliveries had been easy and natural, as the room full of doctors and nurses stared at them in amazement. The two new moms said they were calling the babies Annabelle and John.

Tammy called Kate then and she arrived at the hospital twenty minutes later, and tears ran down her cheeks, as she saw Tammy and Stacey peacefully holding their babies, looking like twin Madonnas.

"What are you two doing?" she said smiling at them. "The nurse said you both delivered in less than an hour," and they were both big babies. They were the talk of the hospital and the nurses said they were lucky the babies hadn't been born at home. The girls had been wheeled into a room by then, with the babies in their separate bassinets in the room with them. They were a family now.

Kate gazed at each of them as both of their mothers looked on proudly. They were beautiful babies. Stacey and Tammy were talking and laughing as though nothing had happened. They were on a high like no other.

"I think you've set some kind of a world record." Kate beamed at them as nurses came and went to check on both mothers. Tammy wanted to leave the hospital that night since the babies were perfect, healthy, and had checked out with no problems. But Stacey convinced her to spend the night, and leave in the morning. Kate promised to bring a car to drive them home. She had to pick up their car seats to be allowed to leave the hospital.

Their return to their apartment the next day was chaotic and triumphant. It was going to take a little time to make the adjustment and a baby nurse Stacey knew had come to help them for a month. The two mothers were walking around their home, and looked radiant while the babies slept in the bassinets Kate had bought them, with pink and blue ribbons.

Tammy and Stacey looked like the poster children for motherhood. Stacey still couldn't believe how easy it had been, and neither could Claire when Tammy told her. Claire sheepishly admitted she was pregnant again. Gregory was only six months old, and it had been an accident. Claire said she really didn't want to be pregnant again, but Reed was over the moon about it. The baby was due in April by planned C-section this time. Claire made a point of telling her mother that they were not getting married. Kate just laughed when she said it. It no longer mattered. It was her decision. Claire seemed disappointed by the lack of reaction from her mother. Kate accepted whatever choice her daughter made. There was nothing to argue about this time. Kate had made her peace with Claire not wanting to be married. Reed was a wonderful father, and adored Claire and their son.

By the time Scott and Kate and Margaret were ready to leave for India three weeks later, Stacey and Tammy were on their feet and doing well, and the baby nurse had Annabelle and John on a schedule. Both mothers were nursing. They nursed whichever baby needed to be fed at the moment.

Scott and Kate left with Margaret to fly to New Delhi on a Saturday morning. They took an SUV with a driver to get them to the airport. Margaret was going to stay with Anthony while Kate and Scott spent two weeks exploring the country for their delayed honeymoon. They had planned the trip carefully to include all the temples and monuments that they wanted to see, including the Taj Mahal.

The trip was everything they had hoped for, and as they lay under a full moon on the verandah of their suite at The Raj Palace in Jaipur, Kate looked at Scott and knew they had done the right thing getting married. Events of the past ten months had proven to them they belonged together. Cast together by fate, their life was a celebration. It was their turn now, without children or babies taking up every moment of Kate's time.

Kate was wearing a sari that Alicia had given her, and as Scott slowly undid it, they looked at each other and smiled.

"Thank you," Kate whispered, "for everything," she said as he kissed her. It was a prayer and a wish and I love you, all rolled into one for the man she loved. Marrying him was the best thing she'd ever done and he felt that way about her too.

It was exactly what they had both wanted and thought they'd never find, and miraculously they had. Kate's children had grown wings in the last year, and so had Scott and Kate. Their wingspan was the broadest of all. The future awaited them and all the adventures they would share. It was their time now, as they walked back into the bedroom of their suite on a magical night. And whatever decisions and choices her children would make would be up to them, and hopefully, would turn out well. Kate and Scott had their lives to lead, and their time together with all its gifts and wonders, had only just begun.

About the Author

DANIELLE STEEL has been hailed as one of the world's most popular authors, with over 650 million copies of her novels sold. Her many international bestsellers include *The Dark Side, Blessing in Disguise, Silent Night, Turning Point, Beauchamp Hall, In His Father's Footsteps, The Good Fight, The Cast, Accidental Heroes,* and other highly acclaimed novels. She is also the author of *His Bright Light,* the story of her son Nick Traina's life and death; *A Gift of Hope,* a memoir of her work with the homeless; *Pure Joy,* about the dogs she and her family have loved; and the children's books *Pretty Minnie in Paris* and *Pretty Minnie in Hollywood.*

daniellesteel.com
Facebook.com/DanielleSteelOfficial
Twitter: @daniellesteel

About the Type

This book was set in Charter, a typeface designed in 1987 by Matthew Carter (b. 1937) for Bitstream, Inc., a digital type-foundry that he cofounded in 1981. One of the most influential typographers of our time, Carter designed this versatile font to feature a compact width, squared serifs, and open letterforms. These features give the typeface a fresh, highly legible, and unencumbered appearance.